教育部人文社科研究青年基金项目“美国记忆的后世俗化:唐·德里罗小说新究”(18YJC752029)阶段性成果
上海理工大学外语学院博士科研启动基金项目阶段性成果

唐·德里罗小说的后世俗主义研究

A Postsecular Reading of Don DeLillo's Novels

沈谢天　著

苏州大学出版社

图书在版编目(CIP)数据

唐·德里罗小说的后世俗主义研究 = A Postsecular Reading of Don DeLillo's Novels : 英文 / 沈谢天著. —苏州: 苏州大学出版社, 2022.5
ISBN 978-7-5672-3929-6

Ⅰ.①唐… Ⅱ.①沈… Ⅲ.①唐·德里罗—小说研究—英文 Ⅳ.①I712.074

中国版本图书馆 CIP 数据核字(2022)第 066303 号

Tang·Deliluo Xiaoshuo de Houshisu Zhuyi Yanjiu
书　　名: 唐·德里罗小说的后世俗主义研究
A Postsecular Reading of Don DeLillo's Novels

著　　者: 沈谢天
责任编辑: 沈　琴
装帧设计: 吴　钰

出版发行: 苏州大学出版社(Soochow University Press)
社　　址: 苏州市十梓街1号　邮编: 215006
印　　装: 镇江文苑制版印刷有限责任公司
网　　址: www.sudapress.com
邮　　箱: sdcbs@suda.edu.cn
邮购热线: 0512-67480030
销售热线: 0512-67481020

开　　本: 700 mm×1 000 mm　1/16　印张: 13　字数: 208 千
版　　次: 2022 年 5 月第 1 版
印　　次: 2022 年 5 月第 1 次印刷
书　　号: ISBN 978-7-5672-3929-6
定　　价: 58.00 元

TABLE OF CONTENTS

Introduction

Don DeLillo (1936—), a contemporary American writer of great distinction in such genres as novel, short story, play and essay, has won himself wide acclaim that is proved by numerous awards he has been receiving ever since the 1980s. For the 18 novels, 20-odd short stories, 5 full-length plays and a few essays he has published over half a century, DeLillo has been granted the National Book Award, the PEN/Faulkner Award, PEN/Saul Bellow Award, and the Commonwealth Award of Distinguished Service for Achievements in Literature, etc. DeLillo's literary fame culminates in three of his major novels, *White Noise* (1985), *Libra* (1988) and *Underworld* (1997), which, in a survey organized by *The New York Times Book Review*, were voted by 125 preeminent writers, critics, and editors into the shortlist of "the best American novels of the past 25 years". John N. Duvall, a DeLillo expert and professor of English at Purdue University who has been committed to an extensive study on American postmodern fiction, even positions him on an equal footing with most distinguished American novelists like "Thomas Pynchon, Toni Morrison, Philip Roth, and John Updike" (Duvall, 2008: 1).

Though he is recommended by Ted Gioia as "a strong candidate for the Nobel Prize in Literature" (Gioia, 2012), DeLillo has his bidding for "the Nobel candidacy" hampered by a harsh fact that a stable rise of fame in the circle of literary professionals and critics does not too well warm up the relatively cold reception of his works in the reading public. Some critics would attribute DeLillo's fall into the general readership's disfavor to his writing style. Bruce Bawer, for example, claims that "DeLillo is a novelist of ideas who delivers sententious, shallow philosophizing rather than a good plot and credible characters" (Schneck, Schweighauser, 2010: 9). Whereas Dianne Johnson suggests that the reason why readers are not comfortable with DeLillo is that he writes "deeply shocking things about America that people would rather not face" (Johnson, 1997: 13), or in Leo Robson's regard, "the 'secret history' of observable phenomena and recorded facts" (Robson, 2010: 50). DeLillo's disturbing representation of a "secret" and "shocking" underside of American reality and his equally displeasing but regular practice of philosophizing on it scared away his fellow Americans within a rather long period after his career started, over which, DeLillo has never seemed to feel regretted. In his opinion, "the writer is working against the age and so he feels some satisfaction at not being widely read. He is diminished by an audience." (LeClair, McCaffery, 1983: 87) An incompatibility, in both subject matter and writing technique, between DeLillo's works and what was acceptable to the American book market at the time when he began his writing as a profession brought about a gloomy start of his career and avoided him any chance of coming to the forefront of public recognition until his first great hit *Libra* won him such a wide audience that DeLillo himself might feel much reluctant to see.

DeLillo's purposeful distancing himself from the American reading crowd and his choice of media as a dominant theme for all his creative writings result, to a large extent, from his college study and brief engagement in a non-creative writing business. In the year after he got a bachelor's degree in "something called communication arts" (Passaro, 1991: 38), DeLillo commenced his bread-winning life by working for Ogilvie & Mather, an ad agency, as a copywriter. Much bored with this "uninteresting advertising career" (Goldstein, 1988: 56), DeLillo was in his spare time committed to creative writing whose charm he found so irresistible, which led him to the publication of his first fictional work in 1960, a short story titled "The River Jordan" in *Epoch*—a literary magazine Cornell University ran to help tap some great literary potential in Thomas Pynchon, Philip Roth and Joyce Carol Oates, all of whom were still as young as DeLillo was in the 1960s. In the 1960s that sees no publication of his full-length novels, *Epoch*, *Kenyon Review*, and *Carolina Quarterly* brought to light more of DeLillo's short stories and it is this moderate success of his first literary endeavor that hardened his determination to quit the job at the ad agency to "embark on my life, my real life" (Passaro, 1991: 38). However, at the start of his "real life", DeLillo had to support himself as a full-time writer by hiring himself out in other odd writing jobs. These "constant interruptions to earn money" (Champlin, 1983: 7) put off DeLillo's publication of his first full-length novel—*Americana* until 1971, 5 years after he gave the novel a start in 1966.

Americana is indeed the first reward to all the hardships he had ever endured in the process of learning "how tough to be a serious writer" (Champlin, 1984: 7). The meager income of 2,000 dollars a year and the confining space of a small apartment in Manhattan exacerbated the difficulties he had to overcome in sorting out the entangled narrative structure of *Americana*, which benefits him a lot by obtaining him a novelist's confidence, as he once recalled: "About halfway through *Americana*, ... it occurred to me almost in a flash that I was a writer." (LeClair, McCaffery, 1983: 81) The shaping influence of his earlier experience of working as an ad copywriter upon his novel-writing career could be first seen in his plot designs and character portrayals in *Americana*. Modeled after the author himself who once worked as a copywriter, David Bell, a TV network executive, travels with his close pals to the American West in the hope that he could tear apart the image-dominated surface of American mass culture to find a real America and the wholeness of a genuine American self. The disintegrating effect of TV commercial images on the self and David's persistent but futile effort to counteract it sharpens the ironic edge of DeLillo's well-chosen title, *Americana*, which refers to all the objects that come from or relate to America, especially when they are in a collection.

Through the title, DeLillo sends a clear message to his readership that the novel might have in it all that need to be known about America—a culture where the images prevail and the formation of an integrated self is no more than an illusion. DeLillo's ambitious writing scheme to develop a panorama of America through a literary lens has been going on with no stop for half a century, during which the novelist has been trying his hands on a great variety of American themes and their corresponding aesthetic representations.

The 4 years from 1972 to 1976 witnesses the first outburst of DeLillo's artistic ingenuity as he published *End Zone* (1972), *Great Jones Street* (1973) and *Ratner's Star* (1976) in quick succession. Michael Oriad reads these first 4 novels as a thematically connected quartet in which all the main characters are found obsessed with discovering "the source of life's meaning" (Oriad, 1978: 6), and he concludes that though DeLillo refrains from providing any clear-cut answer to this biggest question of life, the quartet does "establish DeLillo as an important original voice in contemporary fiction" (Oriad, 1978: 23). A close reading of the latter 3 novels of these first four, especially, *End Zone* and *Great Jones Street* can reveal that DeLillo's "original voice" is issued out on the subtle relationship between one's pursuit of his "source of life's meaning" and such human-made media as language and music. DeLillo finds for his long-standing concern with media a new voice in Gary Harkness, the protagonist of *End Zone*. DeLillo's portrayal of Gary as a star player of American college football league who cannot free himself from his fascination with language illumines on the intricate connection between words and violence. In the novel, language, as a medium applied to both the American football and the nuclear war, is a sign for "how logocentrism structures contemporary American culture" (LeClair, 1987a: 111), and DeLillo, through examining Gary's use of the English language, exhibits "the conditions, tropisms, and consequences of the logocentric ideal" (LeClair, 1987a: 111) that has been plaguing America, a nation so secularized[①] and commercialized. DeLillo's deep interest in media shifts from language to music in *Great Jones Street*, a novel as short as *End Zone* is, which came to print just one year after the latter was published. Bucky Wunderlick, a rock star, like DeLillo before *Americana*, withdraws from his rising stardom to a small apartment in Great Jones Street of New York City, harboring an illusion that he could thus preserve the authenticity of his music, a medium that he takes to be under his full control, from being contaminated by the commercial exploitation of the industrial world. The novel is a "clinical probing into the almost seamless meshing of 1960s counterculture with the commercialism it had formerly opposed" (Johnston, 1989: 262). DeLillo's conscientious study on the history of mathematics for one entire year brought to print in 1976 *Ratner's Star*, which crystallizes the profoundest thoughts contemporary American novels have ever cast upon reason and science. A child prodigy of math is invited to work in a mysterious facility on cracking a code-like message that seems to come from outer space, only to find at last that it is no more than an ancient human-made prophesy about a soon-to-come eclipse. In a "Menippean satire"-like tone, DeLillo launches an attack on "maddened pedantry" or narrow-mindedness of modern science (Frye, 1990: 309), which, as he sees, works no better than mysticism in alleviating mankind's inborn existentialist anxiety and therefore offers no respite from man's fear of death. DeLillo's fifth novel *Players* (1977) foreshadows what is to come in DeLillo's oeuvre about its setting, subject and plot development. With New

---

① To "secularize", first of all, is to rationalize one's cognizant scheme so that all the visible in the world, to him, can be understood or explained in reason's terms, either scientific or technological, and as a result, religion is swept off into one's margin of consciousness and loses all its significance as a mode of perceiving the world, once validated and respected in some historical periods before the advent of "a secular age" (Charles Taylor's term, to be discussed in detail later in the book). In the second place, the aforementioned philosophical sense of the word can be concretized if it is applied on the social level. To "secularize", when talked of in sociological studies, is to rid social institutions, either governmental or non-governmental, of all their religious heritages or taints, with ideals and beliefs initiated and consolidated by reason, whose strength has been enhanced to a great extent since the Enlightenment and growing, in certain scholars' eyes, more and more unfriendly towards religion.

York Stock Exchange and World Trade Center as its two main settings, the novel features a self-made and failed conspiracy in which Lyle Wynant, a stock broker, works with a gang of terrorists to explode the Stock Exchange. Drawing a ludicrous portrait of Lyle as the main "player" who volunteers to entangle himself in the terrorist plot to kill off the boredom of his unchanging life, DeLillo illustrates how an American commoner's understanding of the conspiratorial nature of American politics shapes his everyday life, or as Le Carre argues, *Players*, together with other American spy novels whose development gained its momentum after the Watergate scandal, "encapsulate the public wariness about political behaviour and about the set-up, the fix of society" (Lewis, 1985: 11). In *Running Dog* (1978), DeLillo's plot design, which revolves around "conspiracy", a dominant motif of nearly all his works, escalates as CIA, the greatest conspiracy-making body in America, turns its blade edge against one of its own agents, Glen Selvy, who is ordered to run like a dog for a hypothetical pornographic film purported to be made in Hitler's bunker before his self-immolation. The ruthless decapitation of Glen upon the completion of his mission throws much light upon the devastating effect of both the political conspiracy and the cinematic imagery—two necessary constituents of contemporary American culture, upon American individuals. Mark Osteen even discerns in the novel a horrible probability of the fascism colluding with the cinematic art in shaping the human subjectivity② and recording their history as he suggests: "DeLillo mounts a complex contradiction ... of the convergence of fascism and film in pornographic representation." (Osteen, 2000b: 135)

Throughout the 1970s, DeLillo's 6 novels were published in installments in America's main periodical publications like *Sports Illustrated*, *New Yorker*, *Atlantic*, and *Esquire*. Though the 6 books did earn him money to cover his living expenses, they did not win DeLillo wide recognition from the American book purchasers. A turning point of his writing career, which is marked by his publication of three novels that obtained him warm applause from both the literary critics and the common readers, came in the 1980s, In 1982, DeLillo's past 3 years of Guggenheim-fellowship-sponsored travel through and research in Greece, the Middle East and India ended with his publication of *The Names*, which he wrote in an Athens apartment near Mount Lykabettos. James Axton, a risk analyst working with an American insurance company, finds himself entangled in and fascinated with a "language cult" while going on a business tour in Greece. The cult performs a ritual of slaughtering a chosen human victim whose name initials must match those of the place in which he is found. James is narrowly saved from his downfall into the cult's membership by reading his 9-year-old son Tap's self-composed short story, in which a multitude of misspellings afford James a chance to re-approach the enchanting mystery of

---

② The subjectivity of a subject or individual, in the context of the book, is understood as a concept that cannot be defined without reference to its opposite end—objectivity. Subjectivity consists in the manners in which a subject chooses to interact with or wields his power upon the objective—other human subjects, animals and inanimate objects, including perceptions, experiences, expectations, personal or cultural understandings and beliefs. However, it could be seen that subjectivity, a subject matter of central importance to Western philosophy, is in effect a dynamic concept of degree because the interaction between a subject and all the objects other than himself is an ever-going two-way process in the sense that one's cognizance of the objective, on a specific occasion and at a specific moment, is to a certain extent decided or even shaped by the objective too. So, as the "subject" and the "object" exerts mutual influence upon each other, to what extent subjectivity can be clarified or asserted comes as a riddle that might never be resolved with accuracy or exactitude, in any philosophical framework, either ready-made or yet-to-come.

language that he used to see only in the cultic practices. As Bosworth remarks, what DeLillo tries to do in *The Names* is to "impress upon us his view that what matters about language is its 'pattern', the design behind the signs rather than what they signify" (Bosworth, 1983: 30). More importantly, DeLillo cautions his readers against the probability of a language's morphological charm transforming itself to either a saving grace or a random use of violence. *The Names* can be labeled as a sign of DeLillo's meditation on "language", profounder than what he had done in *End Zone*, and it is a work that opens the 1980s as the first stage of recommendable success in the author's entire career. In the 1980s, DeLillo's quick rise of fame should be attributed to *White Noise* (1985). Often taught and recommended as an example of American postmodern literature, *White Noise* won DeLillo a National Book Award for Fiction in 1986, and therefore is regarded by almost all his readers and critics as a "breakout" work. Recommended by *Times* as one of "the Best English-language Novels from 1923 to 2005", the novel practices a more in-depth exploration upon the profound impact of public media on the perceptive mode and even the life quality of American individuals. The disintegration of an American self, which is caused by the unstoppable permeation of media into every tiny aspect of American life implants a deep fear of death in Jack Gladney, a college professor in Hitler studies, and his wife Babette. Their fear is aggravated by a chemical spill called "Airborne Toxic Event". Babette chooses to offer Mink a sexual bribery in exchange for his Dylar, a magic pill that is alleged to be able to cure one of her fear of death. Having known what is going on between Babette and Mink, Jack tries to shoot the latter to death but desists from doing so at the last moment and takes wounded Mink to a hospital. Leonard Wilcox attributes Prof. Gladney's life predicament to the fact that he is "a modernist displaced in a postmodern world" (Wilcox, 1991: 348), in which arrives "a new form of subjectivity colonized by the media and decentered by its polyglot discourses and electronic networks" (Wilcox, 1991: 353). Unaccustomed to such "a new form of subjectivity", Jack feels ill at ease in this postmodern landscape where "heroic striving for meaning has been radically thrown into question" (Wilcox,

1991: 356). DeLillo casts his thought again on the construction of American subjectivity in *Libra* by narrating the hell-bound struggles of Lee Harvey Oswald, the accused assassin of John F. Kennedy, against an American cultural milieu, in which the conspiracy and the media reign hand in hand. Under the direction of a team of conspiratorial ex-CIA agents and delicate influence of American public media, Oswald positions himself at Dealey Plaza, Dallas, ready for his fatal mission of shooting the President, for which he would be held solely responsible by the government. Born a Libran, Oswald tends to waver a lot between two opposing sources of influence, which is part of the reason why DeLillo should select him as a living sample of the Americans who would exert themselves in vain in patching up their disintegrated subjectivity. As for Frank Lentricchia, one of DeLillo's most quoted critics, media as a DeLilloesque theme outweighs conspiracy in *Libra*, as he comments as follows:

> The novel portrays the charismatic environment of the image, a new phase in American literature and culture—a new arena of action and a power of determination whose major effect is to realign radically all social agents (from top to bottom) as first-person agents of desire seeking self-annihilation and fulfillment in the magical third. (Lentricchia, 1991a: 198)

The image-saturated media present a uniform and "the magical third"③ for all American subjects, which amounts to the "annihilation" of an American self, and so, *Libra* is in this sense more an exemplar of cultural criticism than a political thriller. Mostly read as a classic specimen of the latter, *Libra* gained an instant and high popularity in the reading public who had since long got bored

---

③ Lentricchia's use of the term results from his slight adaptation of "universal third person", a phrase Don DeLillo works out and employs in his *Americana*. For a detailed explanation of "universal third person", see Note 28.

with "The Warren Report"④. Since the book hit the American best seller list for a row of weeks in the summer of 1988, DeLillo was invited to do interviews on National Public Radio and NBC's Today Show. It also won DeLillo much critical acclaim, which is evidenced by his being awarded the Irish Times-Aer Lingus International Fiction Prize and nominated for the American Book Award of the year.

Unlike the rest of his oeuvre, *Underworld* (1997) is DeLillo's first literary endeavor to chronicle the American history in an unofficial and epic-like manner. A 833-page novel, *Underworld* helps disclose what is not in the official edition of the Cold War history, and therefore, "under-" is the key to understand the thematic significance of the novel warmly recommended by Remnick as DeLillo's "longest, most ambitious, and most complicated novel—and his best" (Remnick, 2005: 132). Having admitted that the title *Underworld* draws its inspiration from a rediscovered film *Unterwelt* by Sergei Eisenstein, DeLillo explained the prefix "under-" in an interview as follows:

> In this book "under" can apply to suppressed or repressed memories or even consciousness ... I kept finding myself treating subterranean realities of one kind or another ... The underhistory of the Cold War, a curious history of waste which forms an underground stream in this book, waste and weapons, and then they merge toward the end. There's a curious kind of cultural history, mostly informal, of drugs, garbage, condoms. The baseball forms a kind of underhistory as it bounces from character to character. (qtd. in Echlin, 2005: 146)

"The baseball" is indeed the starting point of DeLillo's multilayered delineation of the American life during the Cold War, which covers a temporal

---

④ The Warren Commission was established upon President Lyndon B. Johnson's request on November 29, 1963 to investigate the assassination of John F. Kennedy. The Commission, on September 24, 1964, presented its 888-page report to President Johnson, which concluded that President Kennedy was assassinated by Lee Harvey Oswald and he acted entirely alone.

span of nearly 4 decades from the early 1950s to the early 1990s. In the prologue titled "The Triumph of Death", the baseball "bounces" to its first owner Cotter Martin, a 14-year-old boy from Harlem, after George Thomson hits a home-run that helps New York Giants secure its victory over Brooklyn Dodgers in that well-known baseball game held on October 3, 1951. In the middle of the game, J. Edgar Hoover hears from his inferior agent that the Soviet Union has just succeeded in its second atomic test. The odd mixture between the excitement of a great sporting event and the horror of the Cold War's unpredictable course of development sets the basic tone for the post-prologue narration which DeLillo does in 6 parts. It begins with and ends in telling the tales of Nick Shay, the novel's central character, in a reverse chronological order. Set in the 1990s, as its title suggests, "Epilogue: Das Kapital", tells how capitalism rules all in the age by narrating Sister Edgar's mysterious or perhaps makeshift re-engagement in a spiritual life after she "witnesses" the spirit of a raped and murdered Esmeralda incarnates itself as a blurry image on a billboard advertising Minute Maid.

After *Underworld*, before whose length most of his readers should flinch, Don DeLillo decided not to test the readers' patience as he published *The Body Artist* in 2001, a 128-page novella. Having finished writing the book long before 9/11, DeLillo meant it to embody his thought-provoking reflection upon how an individual, especially an artist, should regain his lost balance in life after it is traumatized by, for example, a sudden bereavement. In this sense, *The Body Artist* is highly prescient of what is to come in his 3 post-9/11 novels. Lauren Hartke, the titular heroine, is in deep mourning over the death of her husband, Rey Robles, a film director, who shoots himself to death in his ex-wife's apartment at Manhattan. In order not to drown herself in sorrows, Lauren keeps training herself of the aerobic and stretching techniques required of a body-performance artist like her, and besides, she seeks great comfort in a ghost-like figure from nowhere, whom she calls Mr. Tuttle since he can conduct a certain feat of performing some fragments of the past conversations between Lauren and her late husband with a verisimilar simulation of their gestures and intonations. Figuring in the novella as another body artist, Mr. Tuttle offers Lauren a miraculous performance, which, though baseless and unreasonable, could well complement Lauren's body performance in curing her of a trauma that could otherwise go beyond the reach of any medical treatment's remedial power. DeLillo's artful characterization of the two body artists align him with Wallace Stevens in believing that "after one has abandoned a belief in god, poetry is that essence which takes its place as life's redemption" (Taylor, 2013: vignette page). In *The Body Artist*, Lauren's own and Mr. Tuttle's body performances both count as Lauren's effort to poeticize her life, which DeLillo describes as a trauma-relief project. However, DeLillo is ambiguous about its effect as he designs an ending, in which Laura throws open a window to "feel the sea tang on her face and the flow of time in her body, to tell her who she was" (126)⑤. DeLillo carries on his exploration upon the trauma-motif in his thirteenth novel, *Cosmopolis* (2003), as he extends his range of subject matter from the trauma in an individual life and its treatment to certain potent factors in contemporary America that might traumatize Americans. By the novel, DeLillo prophesies that the "dotcom bubble" of an increasingly digitalized and globalized economy, if remaining uncontrolled, will lead to a catastrophic end, which is all crystallized in a one-single-day episode of the protagonist's life. Eric Packer, a 28-year-old multi-billionaire asset manager, is crossing in his luxurious, spacious and technically sophisticated white stretch limo a traffic-clogged mid-town Manhattan to get his hair cut. On this one-day and one-way trip, DeLillo plots for Eric a few encounters with, for example, a presidential motorcade, the funeral procession of a rap star and above all, a blood-spilt anti-globalism demonstration which foreshadows the quick downfall of Eric's investment empire and his premature demise. At the blink of an eye, Eric loses all of his gigantic fortune by betting against the rise of yen. With his entire world turned upside down, Eric kills his bodyguard for no good reason and gets shot to death by Benno

---

⑤ In this book, all the textual details extracted from Don DeLillo's novels will be marked off in parentheses only by their page numbers as concrete versions of these novels have been all listed in the book's Bibliography.

Levin, the antagonist, who bears Eric deep grudge for being once sacked from his company. Reminding DeLillo's readers and critics of James Joyce's *Ulysses* by a similarity in both plot and character, *Cosmopolis* represents Eric Packer's one-day odyssey as a metaphor for a risky journey in which a digit-flooded global economy is leading the human race. As for DeLillo, the journey, whose final destination cannot be prophesied at all, should be held responsible for the coming of an apocalypse-like terrorist attack upon American homeland in September, 2001. In the sense, *Cosmopolis* can be read as a prologue to *Falling Man* (2007), Don DeLillo's 9/11-centered novel that is published 6 years after this greatest traumatizing event in the American history befell the country. DeLillo accounted for his 6-year pause simply by saying, "I just didn't want to work for a while." (Barron, 2003: 1) It is more than understandable that a catastrophe of such a magnitude should cast DeLillo, a native New Yorker, into a bottomless pit of despair and silence, from which he tries to free himself by giving the 9/11 trauma an artistic treatment in *Falling Man*. The novel's portrayal of Falling Man, a performance artist named David Janiak, helps "once again underscore DeLillo's longstanding concern with the role of artist" (Duvall, 2008: 9) in the trauma-curing process. Dangling upside down with a harness, David, clothed in suit and tie, suspends himself from the architectural structures in New York to remind New Yorkers of how 9/11 victims fell headlong to the ground in total despair. Lianne is among the spectators of David's eye-catching performance, whose estranged husband Keith, a lawyer working in World Trade Center on that hellish morning of 9/11, returns, bloodied and dazed with certain minor injuries, to her and their son after he walks out of the soon-to-collapse North Tower. Keith works hard to heal his physical and psychological wounds by having an affair with a black woman Florence, his fellow survivor from the Towers, and quitting his job to become a professional poker player, but all his self-treatments end in a pathetic failure as the horrible scenes of the 9/11 morning haunts him just as before. Lianne recovers at least a bit from her despondency into which both her father's suicide and 9/11 throws her by hosting for some Alzheimer's patients a writing group in which Lianne and her "students" hold warm and frank talks on the subjects of religion and terrorism. In the texture of the novel is embedded DeLillo's idea that Keith's escapism will take the traumatized Americans nowhere in the pain-killing process, while Lianne's witness of Falling Man's performance, which is so vividly reminiscent, could help Americans fulfill a brave confrontation with their traumatic past—the first step to the full recovery which could be at last achieved by a talk therapy as one that is practiced in Lianne's writing group. Intrigued by his painful meditation on the 9/11 trauma in *Falling Man*, DeLillo continues his philosophizing on death and time in his fifteenth novel *Point Omega* (2010). DeLillo's titling of the novel is largely inspired by a phrase "Omega Point" that Father Teilhard de Chardin contributes to mean a consummate stage of perfection that the universe will reach at last. The final arrival at "Omega Point", though, takes a very slow even eternal flow of time, as DeLillo suggests in the central plot design of the novel. In the first part titled "Anonymity 1", two of the novel's three main characters make their debut in New York's Museum of Modern Art on September 3, watching *24 Hour Psycho*, a Douglas Gordon adaptation of an Alfred Hitchcock classic *Psycho* that has been slowed down to two frames a second to last 24 hours instead of one hour and a half. Among the two spectators is Richard Elster, a 73-year-old scholar and government war planner, and his interviewer Jim Finley, a much younger movie director who is making a documentary on Elster. Though interrupted by the 4 chapters in between, the last part titled "Anonymity 2" continues the narration of Jim Finley alone watching *24 Hour Psycho*, with no explanation about Richard Elster's whereabouts. For most of the in-between chapters, the two characters sit on Richard's porch, drinking and talking, when Richard's daughter Jessie comes to visit and after a short while vanishes into thin air. Richard and Jim also trudge in the Arizona desert, where his fatherly tenderness plunges Richard into great despair in mourning his daughter's sudden and inexplicable disappearance. Richard expresses his gnawing grief by saying, "The omega point has narrowed, here and now, to the point of a knife as it enters a body." (98) For Richard Elster, who has plotted for thousands of deaths in his war-planning job and suffered to experience the probable death of his own daughter, and for DeLillo too, "Omega Point" means nothing but death, the point of perfection which, as the finish line for all courses of life to reach, causes an existential angst⑥ that cannot even be appeased by a new perceptive mode of time as one that has been jointly developed by Richard Elster, Jim Finley and DeLillo himself through watching *24 Hour Psycho.*

Amazons, a novel whose authorship has never been acknowledged by DeLillo himself, was published in 1980 under the pseudonym Cleo Birdwell which is believed to be shared by DeLillo and his partner in writing the book. With *An Intimate Memoir by the First Woman to Play in the National Hockey League* as its subtitle, the novel is an autobiographical narration by a fictitious Ms. Birdwell of what she experiences in the games of National Hockey League as its first woman player in history. Though widely recognized as a commercial effort of little literary value, the book could be read as DeLillo's re-assertion of his confidence in treating sports as one of his recurring motifs, which had been represented in *End Zone* and would be represented soon again in *Underworld.*

DeLillo's widely acclaimed story-telling talent is also well epitomized in his writing of short stories, the best of which are gathered into a collection titled *The Angel Esmeralda: Nine Stories* (2011). Written between 1979 and 2011, the nine stories help Americans record and foresee three decades of their life. The advanced skill involved in narrating these American stories and their great cultural significance won DeLillo 2012's The Story Prize Finalist (Runner-up) and 2013's inaugural Library of Congress Prize for American Fiction. Of all the

---

⑥ The canonical explanation of the term that is common to most existentialist thinkers is that it refers to a negative feeling arising from one's personal experiencing of his freedom—freedom that thrills him with profoundest dread when, for example, he is standing on a cliff and feeling that "nothing is holding me back". It is inferred, in the context of this book, that "angst", as has been caused by "nothing"—a great sense of meaninglessness or absurdity that mortality attaches to life, is in fact one's fear of insignificance of his physical existence and in the meantime deep craving for ultimate meaning of life. To relieve such an "angst" that involves both "fear" and "craving", as Paul Tillich has argued, religion is born. See Paul Tillich's "What is Basic in Human Nature". *Pastoral Psychology*, 1963,14(1): 13–20.

nine stories in the collection, the title story *The Angel Esmeralda* (1994) is in every sense the greatest because it marks off DeLillo's signature cast of thought which would come to blossom in his gigantic work *Underworld* (1997). An image that looks like the visage of Esmeralda, a raped and murdered girl, is projected upon an ad billboard by the light of a passing train, which re-ignites in all the spectators an ardent and redemptive belief in the spiritual hemisphere of their life. The alleged incarnation of Esmeralda's spirit on the billboard manifests DeLillo's persistent concern with certain form of spirituality lurking in some material and phenomenal aspects of the world, which has been attested to by one of his main critics, Joseph Dewey, who labels him as "a profoundly spiritual writer, perhaps the most important religious writer in American literature since Flannery O'Connor" (Dewey, 2006: 13).

DeLillo dabbles in theater too. He has written five stage plays and one screenplay. *The Engineer of Moonlight* (1979) is his first theatrical effort, which, though, has not been produced till now. Four more plays ensue and they have all been produced, including *The Day Room* (first produced in 1986), *Valparaiso* (first produced in 1999), *Love-Lies-Bleeding* (first produced in 2005) and *The Word for Snow* (first produced in 2007). 2005 saw the first production of DeLillo's only screenplay *Game 6*. When asked what gets him interested in theater, DeLillo answers, "Being a New Yorker, I always, even as a kid, was aware of theater." Besides, for him, "each form, play and novel, is an antidote to the other" (McAuliffe, 2005: 173-174).

Obviously, as for Don DeLillo, play is not the only antidote to novel since he sharpens his competitive edge in struggling for the shaping power of public consciousness also by writing essays. In *Rolling Stone* of December 8, 1983, he published "American Blood: A Journey through the Labyrinth of Dallas and JFK", in which he admitted to the American reading public how JFK's assassination unfolded a roadmap for the development of his historical consciousness that would soon culminate in his great success—*Libra* in 1988. On *Underworld*, DeLillo published "The Power of History" in the September 7, 1997 issue of *The New York Times Magazine* and gave an acceptance speech titled "A History of the Writer Alone in a Room" in 1999 on the occasion of being awarded the Jerusalem Prize for the novel. Through these two essays DeLillo put forward his peculiar understanding of the American history, especially the Cold War history and explained how he had managed to interweave the historical facts with his designed plots in *Underworld*. In December 2001, three months after 9/11, DeLillo published in *Harper's* an essay of greatest importance to his career, "In the Ruins of the Future: Reflections on Terror and Loss in the Shadow of September". It is a written response a native New Yorker should have made to 9/11, a terrorist attack that takes the greatest toll ever on the American people, both physically and psychologically. The essay would make his *Cosmopolis* and *Falling Man* better understood and reveals a lot about his perception of the Age of Terror. Conte argues that the essay "not only offers a penetrating reading of the relationship of globalization and terrorism but also provides a personal reflection on the tragedy" (Conte, 2008: 191).

The fame DeLillo established in the 1980s by winning the significant literary prizes for his *White Noise* and *Libra* laid a solid foundation for his reception of more awards in the 1990s and the new millennium. For *Underworld*, the American critics and book reviewers presented to him a bounteous supply of honors, including the National Book Award finalist in 1997, *The New York Times'* Best Book of the Year nominee in 1997, a Pulitzer Prize for Fiction nomination in 1998, the American Book Award in 1998, the Jerusalem Prize in 1999, William Dean Howells Medal in 2000, and *The New York Times's* "The Best Work of American Fiction of the Last 25 Years (Runner-up)" in 2006. In the new century, DeLillo won for his novels significant literary prizcs, including James Tait Black Memorial Prize shortlist for *The Body Artist* in 2001 and *The New York Times'* Notable Book of the Year for *Falling Man* in 2007, and some other awards that celebrate his general contribution to American fiction, for example, Common Wealth Award of Distinguished Service for Achievements in Literature in 2009, PEN/Saul Bellow Award for Achievement in American Fiction and St. Luis Literary Award in 2010.

Don DeLillo's quick rise of fame in the past three decades is a strong impetus to an exponential growth of a scholarship on his works in America. Up till now, more than 25 publications have been exclusively engaged in the DeLillo studies and other published works on contemporary American novels have at least one chapter contributed to their discussion on one or two motifs of DeLillo's novels. The most recommendable research accomplishments on a wide range of the DeLillo motifs could be better presented after DeLillo's literary identity is first settled, about which his critics have made substantial efforts. In an essay issued in September, 1977 when DeLillo had not made any breakthrough in career, J. D. O'Hara ascribes DeLillo's lack of fame to his apparent obstinacy in keeping all the questions asked in his works open and proffering no answers, either clear-cut or ambivalent. (O'Hara, 1977: 250 - 252) O'Hara's hint at DeLillo being a questioner rather than a solver is echoed in Christopher Douglas's judgment that "his work can only marginally be considered in terms of a formal, literary postmodernism" (Douglas, 2002: 104). Douglas allows DeLillo's art a label of postmodernism though he expressly states out his reservation about the postmodernist formalistic features of his novels. John N. Duvall, one of DeLillo's canonical critics, in *Don DeLillo's Underworld: A Reader's Guide*, partly agrees with Douglas by claiming that DeLillo should be identified as a postmodern, if not postmodernist, writer because his subject matter has always been postmodernity. (Duvall, 2002: 21 - 22) Scott Rettberg expands on Duvall's assessment as he insists that "(DeLillo) is distinctly postmodern, in that it presents the stories of characters who face life in a postmodern, postindustrial, televisual culture" (Rettberg, 1999: 1). In his *Appreciating Don DeLillo: The Moral Force of a Writer's Work*, Paul Giaimo argues against other critics who tend to call DeLillo as either modernist or postmodernist since DeLillo, in his regard, is a realist who follows the line charted out by Dickens, Mark Twain, and Dreiser. The dispute could be resolved with certain ease since Giaimo and most of other critics agree upon DeLillo's realistic concern with postmodern American culture, which can well justify an approximate unanimity in labeling DeLillo a postmodern novelist.

Consumerism, which fuels the engine of a postmodern culture, is DeLillo's foremost thematic concern that no critic could afford to leave unexplored. Marc Schuster's *Don DeLillo, Jean Baudrillard, and the Consumer Conundrum* (2008) deals at length with DeLillo's inquiry into and improvement of Baudrillard's theorization on consumer culture by comparing, in an all-round way, DeLillo's novels and Baudrillard's theoretical works. Schuster argues that though their writing careers run on two different routes, DeLillo and Baudrillard could work hand in hand in exposing the alienating effect of consumerism. Alienation is, to a large extent, fulfilled by the technology-driven media whose high development is spurred by consumerism's request for its self-expansion. Critics are mostly inclined to take *White Noise* as an exemplary text when commenting on DeLillo's artistic treatment with media representation or mediatization. Douglas Keesey, in his *Don DeLillo*, the second book-length monograph in DeLillo criticism, presents his incisive assessment of the leading characters in *White Noise*, whose "contact with the real world is being interrupted by media representations of that world" (Keesey, 1993: 135). John Frow, in an essay edited by Frank Lentricchia into *Introducing Don DeLillo*, reiterates the representational nature of media and draws a conclusion similar to Keesey's on *White Noise*'s main characters that they cannot "distinguish meaningfully between a generality embedded in life and a generality embedded in representations of life" (Frow, 1991: 178). A relatively concentrated exploitation upon the subject of mediatization in *White Noise* cannot obscure the fact that DeLillo's fictional treatment with this subject matter persists throughout his entire career, of which, his critics are well aware. In his *Rewriting the Real: In Conversation with William Gaddis, Richard Powers, Mark Danielewski, and Don DeLillo* (2013), Mark C. Taylor suggests that DeLillo holds on to a belief that media not only represents the real world but also reshapes, or even blurs it.

DeLillo's consistent engagement in representing media as a dominant theme in his works is not confined to disclosing the mechanisms by which American media works. He, instead, moves on to probe into the effects that mediatization could yield upon the subjects of contemporary American society. For Leonard Wilcox, Jack Gladney, the protagonist of *White Noise*, is the best specimen of a disintegrated subjectivity, which is one of the most direful consequences mediatization has ever brought about. Wilcox claims that "colonized by the media and decentered by its polyglot discourses and electronic networks", Gladney's subjectivity has "thrown into question" his "heroic striving for meaning" (Wilcox, 1991: 356). Frank Lentricchia believes that Lee Harvey Oswald, the accused assassin of JFK in *Libra*, is another pathetic victim of the media-shaped subjectivity, of whose disastrous effect DeLillo had developed a keener perception. Lentricchia identifies Oswald, like other social agents in "the charismatic environment of the image", as a "first-person agent of desire seeking self-annihilation and fulfillment in the magical third" (Lentricchia, 1991a: 198). Lentricchia even goes as far as to suggest that it is "the magical third", fabricated under the influence of mediatization, that plants in Oswald an understanding of his self as a man who would win his consummate glory because of his violence. Arnold Weinstein's critical stance is one seldom seen with respect to DeLillo's understanding of how media works on subjectivity. To conclude his reading of *White Noise*, Weinstein argues that DeLillo still believes in authentic subjectivity being asserted as long as the subjects pay sincere attention to or take a look again at the dignity of "surfaces", or in other words, what has just been visually consumed in the mass-mediatized imagistic landscape. In this sense, Weinstein continues to argue, neither despair nor violence is a response DeLillo intends his audience to make after they read *White Noise*. (Weinstein, 1993: 144)

Though Arnold Weinstein cannot see any harm media could cause to subjectivity, he does perceive in DeLillo's works a warning that media has a horrible potential of "making it possible for us to savor erupting disasters, to watch, with relative impunity and vicarious thrills" (Weinstein, 1993: 133). The thrilling pleasure with which the audience watch the gory massacres or the overwhelming natural calamities covered in TV amounts to a new category of aesthetic enjoyment that they find so irresistible.

Don DeLillo's postmodern worldview determines his unfailing concern with and deliberation on the media-dominated postmodern conditions and furthermore, often raises him to a metaphysical sphere where he philosophizes, in a postmodern fashion, on the subjects that interest him. "System" is a term of central significance to Tom LeClair when he, in his book on Don DeLillo's works, tries to comprehend what is most essential to the author's philosophical musings. Tom LeClair, in his *In the Loop: Don DeLillo and the Systems Novel*, the first critical monograph on DeLillo, claims that *End Zone* and *Underworld* best execute DeLillo's self-imposed mission of cutting open any closed system, at whose center logos[7] resides. In the book, LeClair's Derridean analysis of *End Zone* throws into relief the destructive power that a logocentric thought could exercise, while in *Underworld*, DeLillo, who sets the basic tone for the novel with a slogan "Everything is connected" (825), does more in propagating an anti-logos perspective on "system" by showing "how a new perception of what is now natural—systems among systems, communications, inherent uncertainty, mysteriousness—can accommodate man to his condition as knower and even squeeze a modicum of hope" (LeClair, 1987b: 229 - 230). In *In the Loop*, LeClair succeeds in tapping the great potential of a system-theory reading, asserting that DeLillo's belief in the connection of all things could afford contemporary individuals a chance to take their initiatives in fulfilling their responsibilities and regaining their long lost subjectivities.

Paul Civello also sees in *Libra* a DeLillo who exerts himself to demonstrate how a tightly closed system like "conspiracy" can be cut loose. Civello argues

---

⑦ What the word "logos" refers to, in the context of this book, is restricted to an original, irreducible and external truth or reality about the material world, whose access, as mankind has assumed, can never be denied to them if they can give full play to their reason in applying their invented scientific or technological means. Accordingly, their belief in and devotion to logos, in the book, is a logocentrism that means their unconditional trust of reason's ability to find the ultimate truth about a world, which is purely material or god-free in their very eyes. The making of logos' contextual meaning in the book has been inspired by two entries posted in www. wikepedia. org-logos and logocentrism.

that by a structural design of great ingenuity, DeLillo implies that Oswald starts to work hand in glove with those ex-CIA agents-turned conspirators by sheer chance, and by so doing, he deconstructs the conspiracy-theory that a paranoid American public is so pleased to believe. Civello takes it as *Libra*'s highest accomplishment that its reader might recognize the necessity of "trying to locate himself in and reconcile himself to a new world of nonlinear causality and uncertainty ... control or 'mastery' over the external world is no longer available to him" (Civello, 1994: 141). Civello's recognition of DeLillo's deconstructive predisposition in *Libra* is echoed in Lentricchia's identification of the novel as a "double narrative" in which "an amorphous existence haphazardly stumbling into the future where a plot awaits to confer upon it the identity of a role fraught with form and purpose" (Lentricchia, 1991a: 202).

As a novelist, Don DeLillo would never fail to have his deconstructing endeavor spearheaded at language, a system he cannot do without and also means to crack. Paula Bryant propounds a reading of *The Names* that the cult's practice of choosing its victims by matching their name initials to those of the locations where they are found is designed by DeLillo to enlighten his audience on the fact that the arbitrary strictures of language turn it to a closed system where a killing instinct could lurk. Meanwhile, as Bryant argues, DeLillo's audience could still see in the novel a glimmer of success in dispelling the looming instinct towards destruction as 9-year-old Tap Axton accomplishes "the deliberate disordering and recreation of language" (Bryant, 1987: 23) in his ungrammatical, fragmentary and misspelled short narrative, which, in Paul A. Harris's regard, is an exemplary text DeLillo sets in ridding language of its artificial closedness or tapping the liberating potential of a "reshaped" language—"new forms that reveal something unseen within their makeup" (Harris, 2010: 6).

While standing at the forefront of the cause of combating any logocentric or closed system, DeLillo does not forget to caution his readers against a crisis, even global in scale, that an absolute open-endedness could give rise to. In the concluding chapter he wrote for John N. Duvall-edited *The Cambridge*

Companion to Don DeLillo, Joseph M. Conte argues that in *Cosmopolis*, DeLillo tells how Eric Packer's investment empire collapses within one single day as a metaphor for the excruciating truth that though the world capital market, so profoundly affected by the US capital market, enjoys a boundless freedom of capital flow that has been greatly facilitated by cyberspace technology, it could entail some damaging fluctuations the much weaker economies like those in the Islamic world cannot withstand, which could at least partly explain why the terrorists should pay almost undivided attention to plotting against the US, a country that in their eyes is the actual manipulator of the capital market and therefore must be held responsible for all the catastrophes that befall the world's capital market. (Conte, 2008: 180 – 181) Reflecting, in a spirit of cool-minded self-criticism, on America's own accountability in making such a man-made catastrophe as 9/11 possible, DeLillo works hard on giving a clearer shape to the role a contemporary American novelist should perform in winning the escalating war against the global terrorism.

While trying to work out certain means to weaponize it to launch a battle against terrorism, DeLillo does recognize in contemporary American narrative a great healing power that could help the badly traumatized Americans gain a quick recovery. Annie Longmuir expounds her reading of *The Body Artist* in *Modern Fiction Studies* as a text that could afford all a chance to introspect on how a trauma works on an individual's mental health, which counts as the first step to de-traumatize oneself. Longmuir suggests that DeLillo characterizes Mr. Tuttle as a hallucination-like figure to substantiate the incursion of an untouchable trauma from one's past into Lauren's once sound state of mind, and DeLillo delineates the weird interaction between the two in the hope that his readers could see the way in which one gets along in a traumatized life. (Longmuir, 2007: 541) Two books deserve to be recommended as enlightening works on DeLillo, 9/11 and trauma. Peter Boxall in his *Don DeLillo: The Possibility of Fiction* (2006) reads all of DeLillo's works that come to print after *Cosmopolis* as an epitome of all the best thoughts the American novelists could cast on how the American fiction should engage itself in combating the global terrorism and healing the 9/11-caused traumas. For Boxall, all these efforts must be concentrated on a task of figuring out the possibilities of fiction, one that DeLillo's been performing since September, 2001. Peter Schneck-edited *Terrorism, Media, and the Ethics of Fiction: Transatlantic Perspective on Don DeLillo* is a collection of essays contributed by DeLillo's critics from across the Atlantic. Both American and German researchers treat the 9/11-caused traumas as a starting point for their discussion on redefining the fiction writing in an age of terror and ascribing to these traumas a "positive" role in reconfiguring the 9/11 survivors' concept of life. What distinguishes it from other critical books on DeLillo is that the book employs a cross-Atlantic perspective in DeLillo criticism, which is a clear indicator of the great significance of an international horizon for the studies on contemporary American fiction.

The successive translation into Chinese of DeLillo's signature works like *The Names*, *White Noise*, *Libra*, *Cosmopolis* and *Falling Man* has given the Chinese literary academe a good start in their DeLillo studies whereas in the meantime, it cannot conceal the fact that it has not yet gone beyond a preliminary stage of its development, which could be verified by the two shortcomings China's DeLillo studies should try hard to overcome. In the first place, the research papers of all sorts on DeLillo's novels are still small in number. Less than 20 papers have been published in China's top-notch journals of literary criticism—for example, *Foreign Literature*, *Contemporary Foreign Literature*, and *Foreign Literature Research*—and no more than 5 Ph. D. books have been finished off, though a considerable number of MA theses have been available online. Besides, the Chinese scholars' vision on DeLillo studies is confined to the 5 translated works of his with *White Noise* being paid too focused an attention. Having still a lot to do to catch up with the development pace of foreign DeLillo scholarship, the Chinese literary critics and scholars have done much pioneering work that blazes the trail for all the soon-to-come research accomplishments that are expected to win them greater international recognition.

Dr. Fan Xiaomei in her Ph. D. book *A New Historicist Study on DeLillo's*

Fiction complicates foreign critics' identification of DeLillo as a postmodern novelist by claiming that DeLillo's fiction is not only postmodern in subject matter but also embodies his postmodern views of history and culture and exemplifies certain postmodernist narrative strategies, all of which Dr. Fan well attests to by her close New-Historicist readings of her selected DeLillo texts. In all of DeLillo's thematic concerns, media and an American culture shaped under its determining influence are also the most talked-of ones in China, upon which Dr. Zhang Ruihong commits herself to an in-depth exploration in her Ph. D. book *Pleasure and Anxiety: A Study on the Media Culture in Don DeLillo's Novels*. Having chosen from DeLillo's oeuvre *White Noise*, *Underworld*, *Cosmopolis* and *Falling Man* for detailed textual analysis, Dr. Zhang anatomizes American media culture that is depicted in these novels, hoping to throw more light on the relationship between media images and violence, terror and trauma.

DeLillo's fictitious rendering of the problematized or disintegrated subjectivity in a highly mediatized American society draws much critical endeavor from Chinese literary scholars, among whom, *White Noise* remains the most popular text. Zhang Yaping defines "the quandaries of the postmodern characters in *White Noise*" as a deplorable loss of "their individual subjectivity and dimensions of spiritual independence", which, she argues, should be largely attributed to media technology and other realms of technological advancement that delimits one's "field of expertise" and thus deprives him of a "humanistic spirit". (Zhang, 2009: 167) By comparison, Fang Cheng looks into DeLillo's worrisome concern with a mediatized subjectivity in *White Noise* by following the vein of naturalistic thoughts in American fictional tradition. Fang suggests that loss of subjectivity has since long been dealt with as a major thematic concern in American naturalistic novels, and so what DeLillo achieves in *White Noise* is no more than applying American naturalism's ideas of predetermination, existentialism and frequent resort to violence to reshaping in his characters a fake subjectivity against a postmodern cultural milieu. (Fang, 2003: 93) Zhou Min traces DeLillo's almost obsessive focus on media and resulting loss of subjectivity to his literary effort as early as *Americana*, the very first novel DeLillo ever wrote in his career. Inspired a lot by Guy Debord's theory of the Spectacle Society, Zhou Min sees "the third person", the meaning-laden and recurring phrase in the novel, as DeLillo's artful design that could to a large extent, if not a full one, explain how a subject should integrate certain media images into his selfhood and forfeit his original identity, or in other terms, how he reduces his self to "an image of the likeness of image" or "the third person". (Zhou, 2010: 112) Ma Qunying tries to diagnose such a self-reduction in *White Noise* and describes an outburst of Thanatophobia in both the protagonist and his wife while attributing their strong fear of death to the loss of subjectivity that is caused by not only mediatization but also an uncurbed development of high technology. (Ma, 2009: 92)

Mediatization, as a force that propels the move-on of a consumerist society, is fueled and refueled by a never-ending upgrading of American technology, which DeLillo characterizes as a diabolical power that fails one's pursuit of an integrated subjectivity and thus devastates their humanity. On the latter, Li Nan explores in an enlightening way through her detailed textual analysis of *Cosmopolis*, whose hero, the billionaire investor Eric Packer, according to Li, is sent off by DeLillo on a mission of guiding his readers around Manhattan and so helping them feel "the chilly and merciless atmosphere in a city controlled by machine" that devalues the humanity by enforcing both "spiritual and physical oppression and containment". (Li, 2014: 159) Other Chinese critics seem to agree that the "physical oppression" that technology enforces on DeLillo's characters could be most manifestly seen in the health-degrading influence of technology-incurred ecological crises, and thus, *White Noise* again comes to the forefront of critical attention. Mustering his expertise on ecocriticism, Zhu Xinfu daringly labels *White Noise* as "an ecocide novel" and claims that DeLillo fulfills in the novel a truthful and macabre delineation of the conflicts between a growingly technologized civilization and the environment, which, as DeLillo prophesies, could result in retributive ecological crises and also a bleak prospect of mankind's "spiritual ecology" (Zhu, 2005: 174). Zhang Yaping endows the environmental crisis on which DeLillo places a handsome part of his thematic focus in *White Noise* with a new signification because she sees in the novel its creator's careful avoidance of describing the natural sceneries, which Zhang reads as a hint DeLillo drops on "the marginality of nature" or man's pathetic loss of straight access to nature that has been to a considerable extent "constructed" by a postmodern culture in which technology prevails. (Zhang, 2009: 167) Zhu Mei recognizes in *Underworld* DeLillo's attempt to sublimate the eco-motif in *White Noise* by tying it tight with the postwar American politics. Zhu reads the novel as DeLillo's scathing criticism of American social policies after World War Ⅱ as DeLillo works to convince his readership by his intricate design of plots and characters that the escalation of the country's ecological crisis and its citizen's fear of death should be by and large blamed on the Cold War Mentality that permeated into the foundation of America's national strategies for its ecological safety. (Zhu, 2010: 165)

The Cold War and a black-or-white Mentality that inheres in the era are the motifs no Chinese critics could afford to skirt while reading *Underworld*. Zhou Min reads *Underworld* as DeLillo's long-standing and ambitious scheme to dissect the "Us versus Them" logic that serves as the very basis of the Cold War Mentality by studying "selectively the illusiveness of an American identity, which is the premise of the logic" (Zhou, 2009: 126). The "illusiveness" of "American identity" is rooted in its "constructedness", which refers to the fact that "American identity" grows much less essential and stable as it has been constructed by the multiple operating forces of an American society that is so highly postmodernized. The American history, as a constituent of America's national identity, is no less constructed. On DeLillo's keen awareness of the constructed nature of the American history, Chinese critics have been contributing a great body of insightful arguments, among which Chen Junsong's and Fan Xiaomei's stand out as the most incisive and pungent. Inspired by Linda Hutcheon's "poetics of postmodernism", Chen Junsong, in his Ph. D. book *Political Engagement in Contemporary American Historiographic Metafiction*, goes at one chapter's length to read *Libra* as "an exemplary text of historiographic metafiction" (Chen, 2010: 99). Chen believes that "self-referentiality" as characteristic of a historiographic metafiction is an aesthetic tool DeLillo so adroitly employs in *Libra* to disclose the constructedness of a fictitious text, which, furthermore, helps DeLillo deconstruct the "official truth" that is as constructed as a novel is in DeLillo's regard. When estimating the effect of DeLillo's deconstructional effort in *Libra*, Chen concludes that an "alternative truth" is born to complete the novelist's mission of "political engagement", which he explains as an attack upon "the pervasive dishonesty and manipulation of power of the Reagan Administration" (Chen, 2010: 26). Not restricting her textual analysis to *Libra*, Fan Xiaomei in her Ph. D. book *A New Historicist Study on DeLillo's Fiction* draws a more panoramic picture of the interactions between fiction and history in DeLillo's texts. Under the guidance of certain theoretical principles of New Historicism, Fan argues for a full assertion of DeLillo's literary identity as "the chronicler of contemporary history of America" since *White Noise*, *Libra*, *Underworld* and *Falling Man* could all be treated as historical records that might well "pass for a history of postmodern America". (Fan, 2014: Abstract Ⅲ) Though her use of "counternarrative" in summing up the New Historicist feature of DeLillo's fictional texts does not depart too much away in meaning from Chen Junsong's "alternative truth", Fan Xiaomei makes her book a work of distinction by exhibiting a variety of narrative strategies DeLillo resorts to in representing "the chaos, fragmentation, randomness, absurdity, and indeterminacy" (Fan, 2014: Abstract Ⅲ) of the ways in which the American history has been recorded and passed on to the country's younger generations.

The fragmented and thus unreliable pass-on of American "historical truths" epitomizes the "randomness, absurdity, and indeterminacy" of a postmodern culture DeLillo's characters find themselves entrapped in. Having been divested of the initiatives they could have taken to construct a stable identity and standardize a code of conducts and morals, these characters are harassed a lot by a strong sense of imminent danger and so convert themselves to a company of pitiable paranoids. In an article on *The Angel Esmeralda: Nine Stories*, a collection of DeLillo's short stories, Chen Junsong inventively terms DeLillo's persistent concern with and representation of terror in the collection as "the poetics of terror". Chen argues that DeLillo's idiosyncratic poetics consists in his keen perception that his characters' "isolation and alienation from society" is a possible source of terror, or in other words, terror might come from within the hearts of "men in small rooms". (Chen, 2014: 157) Li Gongzhao laments over the adoption of such a paranoid mindset of "men in small rooms" by the American decision-making body while conducting a political reading of *The Names*. Li claims that DeLillo presents in the novel the cult's blood-soaked obsession with and fanatic worship of the arbitrariness of language as a metaphor for the American ruling class's outrageous enforcement of their political power in instilling in the public subconscious a much simplified logic of "Us versus Them" and so, disguising or justifying their dirty practices of "political violence, cultural hegemonism and state terrorism" (Li, 2003: 100). Through a thoroughgoing investigation into DeLillo's exploitation on the subject of terrorism in *Falling Man* and *Point Omega*, Li Xiaolong (2012) proposes in his Ph. D. book *The Pathogenic Mechanism of Terrorism in Don DeLillo's Novels* that the arbitrarily decided and simplistic logic of "Us versus Them" followed in both American politics and mass culture counts as "the pathogenic mechanism" that gives rise to the international terrorism, "highly religious" in nature. Li's close and systemic reading of DeLillo's terrorism-centered novels helps him glean the sporadic clues DeLillo drops throughout his texts regarding the role America itself plays in causing the rise of terrorism as a global pestilence—a simplistic logic of binary opposition that America follows in tackling its relations with "others" might backfire in a cataclysmic manner.

The worst backfiring effect has been so unfortunately exerted upon the vulnerable psychology of the common Americans. 9/11, a terrorist attack of unprecedented magnitude, has left the entire nation remarkably traumatized. Piao Yu and Zhang Jiasheng deal with DeLillo's reaction against and treatment of the 9/11-caused trauma in his *Falling Man*. Piao commends *Falling Man* as a representative work by contemporary American novelists who are endeavoring to "bear witness to traumatic histories and raise ethical concerns about trauma healing" (Piao, 2011: 59) in a literary way. Zhang Jiasheng's critical edge is spearheaded at the aftermath of America being traumatized by 9/11 by his reading of DeLillo's *Falling Man* as a text typical of American 9/11 fiction. Zhang holds it as true that the trauma that the American society suffers after 9/11 is growing worse day by day, which results in an American social value, much more conservative than before. (Zhang, 2012)

It goes without saying that all criticisms and commentaries of strong instructional significance in the expanding DeLillo scholarship cannot be exhaustively presented hereby in this book, which, though, up till now has enumerated the most recommendable arguments from the monographs, journal articles and Ph. D. books in both English and Chinese on the key thematic concerns of DeLillo's novels that interest the world's literary academe the most. It could be foreseen that with DeLillo's fictional works gaining more and more worldwide recognition, a growingly large body of critical works in the DeLillo studies will come to print, both in China and abroad, which is sure to deepen the reading public's insight into and perception of Don DeLillo, a novelist of distinction in both fictional art and philosophical thinking.

As Jesse Kavadlo, a critic whose fame in the field of the DeLillo studies has been on a steady rise since his 2004 publication of *Don DeLillo: Balance at the Edge of Belief*, once commented: "We live in DeLilloesque times ... One gets the distinct impression, as DeLillo himself might put it, that there are things Don DeLillo knows." (Kavadlo, 2004: 1) The reason why DeLillo deserves to be awarded the appellation of a "Mr. Know-all", in Kavadlo's regard, is that his works are "revealing what it means to be human, not just at the end of the twentieth century, but for all of modernity⑧" (Kavadlo, 2004: 5) DeLillo's thoroughgoing exploration on and revelation of humanity, as Kavadlo continues to argue, help his works "transcend" all the ready-made understandings obtained from such widely-adopted perspectives as "systems, language, culture, or the postmodernism" (Kavadlo, 2004: 5). As could be seen in the suggestive subtitle *Balance at the Edge of Belief*, Kavadlo tends to conclude that DeLillo's stock of knowledge on humanity is accomplished by his "balancing" himself on the border "belief", or in other words, DeLillo should take it as true that man's pursuit of a certain form of religious belief is an essential constituent of his humanity. Kavadlo's reading of DeLillo as a novelist who works in deep fascination with a quasi-religious belief finds itself warmly echoed by Joseph Dewey in his *Beyond Grief and Nothing: A Reading of Don DeLillo*, a book that has ranked itself as a canonical work in the field of DeLillo criticism. Dewey's writings can convince the DeLillo readers that the novelist is a profoundly spiritual writer, perhaps the most religious writer in American literature since Flannery O'Connor. (Dewey, 2006: 13) Having examined in sequence, "retreat", "failed engagement" and "recovery" as the motifs that are all of central importance to DeLillo's religious writings, Dewey comes to a judgment that all of these have been crystallized in his narratives of "redemption"—a goal DeLillo intends his readers to fulfill, whose contextual meaning in his works

---

⑧ Heidegger offered, in his essay "The Age of the World Picture", a most accepted definition of the term that it is a "post-traditional and post-medieval" (1977: 66 - 67) historical period, and his definition is related to the contextual meaning of the term in the book in the sense that it is hereby held as true that what helps mankind turn a new leaf in their history is their emancipation from religion, especially the dominating presence of Christianity, and the resulting secularization, which is accepted here as central to the sense of "modernity" contextualized in the book. Besides, this book also holds that reason, which, together with its offspring—science and democracy, works in the process of modernization or secularization as its engine, should, by a large degree, be held accountable for all that the word "modernity" can connote and denote. So, in some contexts of the book, modernity can be understood in the same way as reason or logos is. For Heidegger's "The Age of the World Picture", refer to *The Question Concerning Technology, and Other Essays*. Trans. William Lovitt. New York: Harper & Row, 1977.

consists in one's re-assertion of his meaning of life and rectification of his once deformed morality. (Dewey, 2006: 28)

Kavadlo and Dewey seem to have reached a tacit agreement on a truth, neglected for so long a time, about Don DeLillo's novels that the author perseveres in imparting to his readers his belief in "belief", which, as Paul Giaimo has argued in his *Appreciating Don DeLillo: The Moral Force of a Writer's Work*, has given shape to "the moral force" of his works. Giaimo's sagacity of a DeLillo critic could be furthermore evidenced in his attributing the "moral force" of Don DeLillo's novels to his Catholic Italian-American cultural background. Admittedly, Catholicism of a Bronx-based Italian-American community has been imprinted upon DeLillo as his cultural birthmark, which inspires in him a non-systematic system of belief that in turn forms a line of development stringing up all the segments of his writing career.

Don DeLillo was born and reared up in Bronx, a district in the north uptown of New York City. This is a neighborhood of Catholic immigrants from south Italy. As a high-school student, DeLillo enrolled in Hayes Cardinal School, which is situated in Bronx and gives admission to and only to the boys of the Catholic families within the district. Upon his graduation from high school, DeLillo was admitted into Fordham University, sponsored and run by the Jesuits, where he engaged himself in both media and theological studies. DeLillo spoke frankly of his indebtedness to the Bronx Catholicism by saying, "There's a sensibility, a sense of human, an approach, a sort of dark approach to things that's part New York, and maybe part growing up Catholic, and that, as far as I'm concerned, is what shapes my work far more than anything I read." (Hungerford, 2006: 343) The Bronx Catholicism that, in Amy Hungerford's terms, makes DeLillo's "important subject, eternal subject" takes on some prominent features not shared by any institutional system of religious beliefs. Robert Orsi, an expert in Catholic studies, was born in Bronx as DeLillo was. He, in one of his works published in 2010, presents his found truth that the Italian immigrants in Bronx have promulgated and practiced in their community "an incarnational faith"⑨, which teaches them to believe that heaven is right above their heads and never even try to "set the two worlds (their own and heaven) completely apart" (Orsi, 2010: 227). Orsi's definition of the Catholicism with the Bronxian characteristics suggests that the Italian-American residents' faith is more an idiosyncratic way of perceiving their life and the world than a set of beliefs in a doctrinal religion. Besides, to the Italian immigrants, what emanates from the heaven is something larger than the indoctrinated form of the Catholic divinity and meanwhile can be more easily accessed as it is "incarnated" in their quotidian life. So it follows that "spirituality"⑩ other than "God" should be more accurate a term to call the

---

⑨ Robert Orsi's presentation of "the incarnational faith" as the key phrasal term in his work suggests that his understanding of Catholicism in the Bronx-based Italian immigrants' community does accord with postsecularism's main standpoint, which is to be explained at great length in Chapter One of the book. A faith is incarnational in the sense that the faith-holder believes that a secular activity or phenomenon is an incarnation of the spiritual, which entails his decision not to worship or pay homage to anything spiritual or divine hanging above or hidden behind the secular. So, "the incarnational faith" is just another way of saying a postsecular spiritual pursuit, whose theoretical core—secular spirituality—is also what an "incarnational faith" is targeted at.

⑩ Spirituality, in the book, is defined in so ambitious a manner as to encapsulate all that can be abstracted from "the original shapes" of main organized religions of the world—"in Judaism the Torah, in Christianity there is Christ, for Buddhism, Buddha, and in Islam, Muhammad" (Waaijman, 2002: 315). It is hereby held as true that abstracted from these "shapes" is what transcends the material aspects of life or all its physical limits, and can be revered as holy in the sense that it is assumed to answer for the making and running of what is phenomenal in the world. Accordingly, spirituality should enjoy the same status with Christian God as a supreme being that is to endow ultimate meaning on human life. Besides, it can be seen that though not as "shape-ful" as "Torah, Christ, Buddha or Muhammad" is, "spirituality" is the result of a conceptualization of the supreme being that institutional religions are targeted at and so, deserves to be shared by all other forms of faith, especially those non-institutional in essence. Moreover, "spirituality", a term used on a regular basis in the book, is anti-traditionalist to a certain extent because it incorporates subjective experience of pursuing what is transcendental about the material world and gives birth to "the deepest values and meanings by which people as individuals live" (Sheldrake, 2007: 1 - 2). In this sense, "spirituality" is much more apt, than either God or gods, to be used as a regular term in the postsecular realm of studies, one that is postmodern in temperament.

sacred object that the Italian immigrants choose to believe and worship. Their adherence to the belief that "the two worlds are never set completely apart" could throw into relief a fact that as for them, the spirituality is immanetized[11] in their secular[12] life. Their rigid observance of the Catholic rituals like Eucharist and Transubstantiation helps them assert the immanent nature of the Italian immigrants' spiritual pursuit. The wine and bread in the Last Super transubstantiate into Jesus Christ's flesh and blood. This transubstantiation between material substances of bread and wine and the spiritual constituents—flesh and blood—of "the original shape"[13] makes it evident that the Catholic theology of the Italian immigrants stipulates that the divine should reside right inside all the material symbols, both seeable and tangible, to which, Amy Hungerford attests by saying, "Italian Catholics, who made up DeLillo's family and much of the Italian immigrant population in New York City in the early twentieth century, have historically favored popular mystical practices of Catholicism over regular attendance at Mass and reverence for the parish priest." (Hungerford, 2006: 346 – 347) The Italian immigrants' faithful practice of the

---

⑪ To immanetize is to incarnate, a word whose sense has, in this book, been contextualized in the theoretical text of postsecularism. A postsecular immanetizing job is to conjoin the secular and the spiritual in so seamless a manner that the incarnation of the latter in the former is perfected to the point, at which the spirituality incarnate or the secular, in its own right, is all that a worshipping believer's piety is directed at. So, to immanetize, in the postsecular sense of the verb, is to represent a more radical anti-secularization stance that institutional religions and even Pantheism cannot afford.

⑫ As one of the terms that lay down the theoretical foundation for both postsecularism and postsecular readings of American literature, "secular", in the book, will be assigned a sense that is formulated on two presumably separate levels—philosophical and social. On the philosophical level, "secular" is to work as an antonym to "religious" and so, refers to a particular mode of human perception that is governed and led by reason and thus, operates with no commitment to any form of belief in the transcendental or the spiritual. On the social level, "secular" is used to describe a society in which, as reason prevails and so, weakens religiosity and marginalizes established institutions of religious faiths, all other regular institutions can operate with no interference from the religious sector of social life, and most importantly, in religion's place, a new faith-like devotion to reason or logos is forged.

⑬ See Note 10 for details about the phrase.

Eucharist and other mystical rituals enables them to get on intimate terms with the spirituality and break free from the bondage of the Catholic dogmas. Robert Orsi therefore draws a conclusion that the mystical tradition of the Italian immigrants' unique mode of communion with God, specific to their own community, is at odds with the rules of the Catholic hierarchy and its established institutions. (Orsi, 2010: 23) Andrew M. Greeley, a Catholic sociologist, agrees with Orsi as he argues that the Italian immigrants accept their Catholic identity as something that means much more than whether they can agree to the church hierarchy or not, whereas to them, to live as a Catholic means far more a marker of their Italian nationality than a system of belief. (Hungerford, 2006: 348) Greeley's argument suggests a close tie between the Italian immigrants' version of Catholicism and traditional Catholicism since the former is made possible by communality, a property essential to Catholicism and the world's other institutional religions. Marginalized a lot as it is, the ethnicity of the Italian immigrants has strengthened the communality of their adamant pursuit of the spirituality with the Bronxian characteristics. DeLillo and his neighbors in the community are not Anglo-Saxons in ethnic terms, nor are they Protestants in religious terms, which doubles their marginalization from the mainstream WASP (White Anglo-Saxon Protestant) culture. The Italian immigrants' marginal cultural identity has for sure enhanced the communality of their united community that also works as a spirituality-hunting body. This communality of the marginalized Italian group of immigrants he grew up with has exerted profound impact on DeLillo as a novelist. He wishes to position himself and other contemporary novelists at the border of American mainstream culture since he admitted once in an interview that "I have gained a clear understanding of the people who live on the margin of society" (DePietro, 2005: 59). Immanence[14] and communality, the two components that are indispensable to the Bronx Catholicism, endow DeLillo with a strong religious consciousness[15] that has been pulsating throughout his writing career. His religious consciousness, as is solidly configured by the Bronx Catholicism, has significantly corroded the institutionality and hierarchy of Catholicism and in consequence become the reason why traditionalist Catholics should scold DeLillo and his fellow immigrants in the neighborhood as "unpracticing Catholics" (Hungerford, 2006: 345). At the threshold of his adulthood, DeLillo quit all the church services of Catholicism and settled himself down as a lapsed Catholic, and so the "unpracticality" of his belief is much more thoroughgoing than most of his Italian-American neighbors. Nevertheless, however "unpractical" DeLillo as an observer of religious rituals is, he has got the Bronx Catholicism deeply ingrained in the texture of all his fictional writings as a cultural heritage he

---

⑭ Immanence is the foremost character of secular spirituality. Secular spirituality is immanent in the sense that the spirituality, with none of its sacredness reserved, right incarnated in a secular object, activity or phenomenon, elevating its accessibility to the highest possible level with the irreducible "shapeful-ness" of the secular. More importantly, it is well worth arguing here for the difference between the immanent character of secular spirituality and that of Pantheistic gods. A follower of Pantheism does assent to the idea that all of reality is identical with divinity, however, the divinity or the god he pays homage to is still hanging high above the real, or to put it another way, the real is not incarnation of the divine in the strictest sense of the word and the assigned role of the real in Pantheism is no greater than a reminder of or passage to the spiritual. The immanence of secular spirituality refers to a complete fusion between the secular and the spiritual in the sense that as an incarnation of the spiritual, the secular is the spiritual itself and it is also true the other way round, so that spirituality incarnate is by itself the very object of all worshipping efforts. So, a conclusion can be drawn that the immanent character of secular spirituality distinguishes postsecularism, of which secular spirituality is a theoretical core, from Pantheism because it is an indicator of how seamless a joint postsecularism has wrought between the secular and the spiritual, which Pantheism has not yet fulfilled.

⑮ Religious consciousness, in the context of the book, is what stimulates one's conscious or deliberate act of coming to understand and explain his life and the world with a heavy dependence upon his religious belief, especially one that is non-institutional in essence, for example, a postsecular belief.

inherits from his Italian forebears. As Brian Conniff claims, DeLillo has since long been a practitioner of "Cultural Catholicism" (Conniff, 2013: 69), a name given to his peculiar religious consciousness, which affords him a chance to "skirt doctrine while maintaining a Catholic understanding of immanent transcendence" (Hungerford, 2006: 343). Capable of "skirting doctrine" and "maintaining a Catholic understanding of immanent transcendence", DeLillo's signature mode of faith is deconstructive of both secularism and doctrinal religion, which could be accepted as an exemplar of postsecularism—a new development of Western theological thought that inherits its poststructuralist gene from the postmodern philosophy and has been gaining its momentum in both American sociological and literary studies. Postsecularism in turn will operate as a brand-new theoretical framework, against which more implied meanings of DeLillo's novels can be excavated, his quasi-religious consciousness shaped and its working mechanism demystified.

Postsecularism is a school of thought that branches off from the Western realm of sociology as its reflection on and criticism of reason. It is Jurgen Habermas (1929—) who first invents and proposes "postsecularism" as a term in the field of Western sociology. On the one hand, Habermas approves of an active role religion can play in counteracting reason's almost irreversible dissolution of values and meanings of human life and meanwhile, refutes the point of departure Mark Horkheimer (1895—1973) takes for his set of arguments on religion, which read, "Without God, one will try in vain to preserve absolute meaning." (qtd. in Habermas, 2002: 6) Having replaced "absolute" with his own "unconditional", Habermas, instead, insists that he can see in the secular life a great potentiality of "recovering the meaning of the unconditional without recourse to God" or seeking for "transcendence from within". (Habermas, 2002: 108) The phrase "without recourse to God" betrays Habermas's purposeful downgrading of the role God plays in the religions as he comes to recognize that He and other named deities are all but an institutional veneer of the religions whereas the spirituality lies behind at the core of all the world's major religions since it is the spirituality that gives birth to the "unconditional meaning" or value of life. Additionally, "from within" is a phrasal indicator of the source of the spirituality, which is precisely the secular life itself. Habermas claims that one should grope for the spirituality and thus regain his faith by seeking it out in or through all material aspects of life in which, as he believes, the spirituality must have been immanetized. Habermas also argues against a simplistic binary opposition between the secular and the spiritual, established as a ritualized practice unjustifiable though carried on by most of the institutional religions. Habermas allows mutual permeation between the secularity[16] and the spirituality, by which he calls an end to the absolute reign of "secularism"[17] and so, to the word, he adds the prefix—"post-"—so as to label the set of thoughts on the innovated return of the religious faiths as "postsecularism". His proposal to secularize the spiritual pursuit complies well with his fame of a secularist philosopher, and as a result, is warmly approved of by William Connolly (1938—), an American sociologist, who ascertains the high feasibility of relocating the spiritual in the secular by arguing that "secularism needs refashioning, not elimination" (Connolly, 1999: 19). Connolly assigns to the returned spirituality a role of ameliorating secularism by

---

⑯ Defined in line with what has been explained in this book about a related term—"secular", "secularity" is the attribute of a quotidian activity, thought or institution that dissociates it in all possible manners from religious beliefs. So, it follows that "secularity" is a product yielded after reason is allowed to purge the world of its sacredness that religion once endowed it with. Or, in other words, "secularity" comes into being as a result of reason's desacralization or demystification of the human world, whose effect has been more strongly felt since the Enlightenment.

⑰ A derivative that draws its lexical root from "secular", "secularism" is given, in the book, a contextual meaning as general as to entail all that "secular" is intended to mean when applied on philosophical and social levels. On the philosophical level, "secularism" is to denote a religion-free epistemology that is framed under a singular principle of reason and therefore works to explain all phenomena from an unmixed perspective, scientific or technological in nature. On the social level, "secularism" is meant to refer to enthusiastic advocacy of sheer separation between all other established social institutions and religious ones, which is to, further on, debilitate and at last abolish a role religion used to play in social life and so, help foster in the minds of its members an unchallengeable embrace of reason as the only underlying mechanism that can keep a society moving on well.

"refashioning" it. Habermas bestows a clearer shape upon "refashioning" as he suggests that to refashion is to "counteract the insidious entropy of the scarce resource of meaning" (Habermas, 2003: 114) within the secular. Moreover, Habermas sees the postsecular "refashioning" of the secular as a change, not in social or political spheres but more in public consciousness. To cause a "change in consciousness" (Habermas, 2003: 116) is to loosen reason's boundless control over human being's epistemology, or their perception of the cosmos and the human life. The loosening device will be secular spirituality, or a secular incarnation of the transcendental. Wikipedia offers "secular spirituality" an independent entry that reads: "Secular spirituality refers to the adherence to a spiritual ideology without the advocation of a religious framework. It covers all aspects of life and human experience which go beyond a purely materialistic view of the world and does not require belief in a supernatural reality or divine being. Secular spirituality emphasizes humanistic qualities such as love, compassion, patience, forgiveness, responsibility, harmony and a concern for others." To what extent "secular spirituality"[18] will be accepted as a new

---

[18] Inferred from Wiki's entry—explanation, what is most significant to the sense of the term can be summarized as follows: secular spirituality is an amalgam made of both the secular and the spiritual. A secular object, activity or phenomenon, whose grandness in size or magnitude defies all human efforts to reach or cognize and so, inspires profound awe and respect, can, in the first place, function as a reminder to those non-believers, who has since long lost their faith in institutional religions, of the truth that the spirituality never abandons human beings and still permeates the Earth, and its presence cannot miss any eyes keen enough to discern. In the second place, the secular is in its own right an incarnation of the spiritual and so, deserves to be worshipped as "the original shape"—the highest divine title that used to be conferred only upon those "original shapes" of institutional religions, such as Christ, Buddha, and Muhammad, etc. So, secular spirituality, as a result of organic and harmonious coalescence between the secular and the spiritual, is, at the same time, deconstructive of both the secular and the spiritual because though no less spiritual than Christ, Buddha or Muhammad is, secular spirituality is much less "shape-ful" than those "original shapes" are, as it can metamorphose with its secular incarnation varying from time to time and its worshipping subject changing from this individual to that. In this sense, secular spirituality is to trigger off a unique paradigm of spiritual pursuit that is not in the least congruous with beliefs in organized or doctrinal religions, whereas it can fulfill all purposes that institutional religions are created to fulfill.

starting point off which a mode of faith can be framed up will determine whether Habermasian "change in consciousness" is to be fulfilled or not. American postmodern fiction has been playing an active role in introducing to and disseminating among its readers the concept of "secular spirituality", establishing itself as an ideal interface through which postsecularism advances into the realm of contemporary literary criticism.

Several of the best novelists in contemporary America, for example, Don DeLillo, Thomas Pynchon (1937—), Toni Morrison (1931—), Navarre Scott Momaday (1937—), Leslie Marmon Silko (1948—) and Louise Erdrich (1954—), have been re-assessed from a postsecular perspective. The postsecular critics have been striving towards the construction of a unified theoretical framework against which the American novels, labeled as "postmodern" works, can be criticized in a new light. As could be revealed by the unified theoretical framework, the postmodern American novels have been functioning a lot in advancing the "post-secular project of resacralization" (McClure, 1995: 144). These novelists make a tactful use of the devices and techniques of the postmodern aesthetics in demolishing traditional realism and revolutionizing the readers' epistemological mode and in their own manner help complete the "project of resacralization". As John McClure has revealed, the readers, while reading these postmodern novels, will develop in themselves "a mode of being and seeing that is at once critical of secular constructions of reality and of dogmatic religiosity" (McClure, 2007: ix). The "mode of being and seeing" can help the readers improve their old secular mode of perception, which would set them ready to accept the secular spirituality. To offer sufficient guidance to the readers in so revolutionary a process, the novelists should crystallize an eminent postsecularity[19] in the artistry of their works, about which McClure sums as "focusing the reader's attention on events that remain mysterious or even 'miraculous', and by making all sorts of room for religious or spiritual discourses and styles of seeing" (McClure, 1995: 143). John McClure also indicates that the "mysterious" or even "miraculous" event most typical of a postsecular narrative is its leading character's "turning" or "spiritual reorientation" (McClure, 1995: 143). The abruptness of the "turning" taunts institutional religion's rituality and tears down "secular constructions of reality" as well, and so, the "turning" is indeed the motif of a narrative, in which postsecularity can be epitomized. Magdalena Maczynska calls the narratives in which she can catch a glimpse of postsecularity "the postsecular text" that she defines as "narratives that openly question or destabilize the religious/secular dichotomy on the mimetic, formal, or metafictional levels by juxtaposing religious and secular discourses within the economy of the fictional construct" (Maczynska, 2009: 76). The "mimetic-level" texts simulate the probable scenes in life with their recourse to a tactic of careful delineation. The "formal-level" texts work with much assiduity on framing up their distinct narrative structures. "The metafictional-level" texts reflect upon themselves for a self-inspecting survey on both their language and writing techniques. Maczynska's stratification theory should be better understood as an effort to present the different textual features of various postsecular texts, which is not so decided as it seems to be since one postsecular text might stand itself astride two or even three levels. Don DeLillo, as a highly acclaimed representative of American postmodern novelists, has been cruising on and across the three levels for almost half a century, during which he commits himself to a multi-dimensional

---

⑲ In line with John McClure's postsecular reading of those American postmodern writings, postsecularity can be defined as the postsecular quality of a literary work that would advocate the idea that the secular and the spiritual should not be separated and so, endeavor to represent, often with postmodern writing techniques, certain scenarios that reason, on its own, fails to explicate, in the hope that the cognitive schemata of the reading public can be revolutionized in a way that the spiritual is re-ushered in as a probable starting point of understanding their world and seeking their meaning of life.

exploration on the postsecular subject matters.

The layout of the book is designed on the basis of an analogy drawn between DeLillo's novelistic pursuit of the postsecular faith and the commonest structure of an argumentative essay, which is, in general, divided into three separate parts—the proposal of the problem, the analysis over the problem and the solutions to the problem. Accordingly, the book tends to assign one chapter of its main body to deal with each of the three structural elements, essential to not only an argumentative essay in general but also DeLillo's postsecular writing in particular. To be more exact, the book will be composed by three main parts, each of which is going to deal with one of the three missions of Don DeLillo's postsecular endeavor—"problematization", "analysis on possible solutions" and "conclusion". In the "problematization" part, the book will present a world DeLillo builds in his fiction where his characters endure all the pains of a life from which the spirituality is not accessed and argue that DeLillo sees their existential angst as rooted in their total loss of subjectivity resulting from a highly secularized and spiritually arid life. In the "analysis" part, the book will suggest that DeLillo takes his second step forward after his proposal of the problem by analyzing the probability of reframing a new type of spirituality—secular spirituality—to reduce or even dispel the existential angst. In this part, the book will try to enumerate all the efforts DeLillo has ever spent on seeking out the possible incarnations of secular spirituality. In "analysis on possible solutions" part, the book will exhibit DeLillo's profound thoughts on "to-dos" and "not-to-dos" in the seek-after process of secular spirituality as DeLillo, who is as liberal-minded as all other postmodern theoreticians and novelists are, is keenly aware of the fact that if not controlled by a certain set of rules, secular spirituality, like all other spiritualities of institutional religions, could run a high risk of being reduced to something no better than fundamentalism that could breed fanaticism and terrorism. The "conclusion" part, together with the former two, will bring forward the book's basic understanding of DeLillo's fiction that Don DeLillo, when seen in line with postsecularism, has his moral concern run through the veins of all his significant works and so the postsecular criticism of DeLillo's works is a sub-type of the ethical criticism. These three parts of discussion will be conducted in Chapters Two, Three and Four respectively in the book since Chapter One will go at length to present an all-round introduction of postsecularism as a sociological thought, which lays down the theoretical basis for all the postsecular criticisms on Don DeLillo that are to be unfolded in the following chapters.

The book's framing of its theoretical groundwork in Chapter One will start with its revelation of the sociological origin of postsecularism. Postsecularism is the restructuring of the religious discourse that Western sociology commits to review and criticize reason and the secularization of the Western society. The restructuring is poststructuralist in nature, which is evidenced in the joint efforts Jacques Derrida (1930—2004) and his American disciple John D. Caputo (1940—) have made in the field of religious philosophy. The next section of Chapter One will place its sole focus on secular spirituality, whose characteristics will be displayed in detail one after another and importance as a central idea of postsecularism argued for. The last section of the chapter comes down to a conclusion on the ethics that postsecularism could come up with to better the human life and the world. The section will state that postsecularism could accomplish its ethicizing mission on two levels—the individual level and the social level. As for the individuals, postsecularism could help embed in their mindset most cherished merits of character like justice, commitment, forgiveness, enthusiasm and love, whereas for the society as a whole, postsecularism can settle down pluralism and tolerance as its basic values, which can remove the breeding ground for extremism and terrorism and enhance the probability of the world achieving a long-term peace in a foreseeable future. More importantly, the section will argue that the ethicization of the society is predicated on the ethicization of the individual.

Chapter Two is committed to an anatomical survey of the DeLilloesque fashion in which the novelist proposes his understanding of the existential predicament that contemporary Americans find themselves mired in. The chapter will select from the DeLillo oeuvre the first three novels—*Americana*, *End Zone* and *Great Jones Street*—and his first National Book Award winner *White Noise* for close reading as they are the most reflective of DeLillo's artistic effort in revealing the three aspects of his characters' existential crisis. DeLillo first describes the symptoms in his characters that their existential crisis has given rise to. As DeLillo has depicted in these four novels, the primary symptom is their voluntary withdrawal or self-banishment, which is most vividly seen in his characterization of David Bell in *Americana* and Bucky Wunderlick in *Great Jones Street* and culminates in his portrayal of Gary Harkness, the protagonist of *End Zone*, who develops a strong proclivity for the monastic asceticism. The secondary symptom, as DeLillo has ascribed to his two well-known characters in *White Noise* Jack and Babette Gladney, is a pathological fear of death. The verisimilar delineation of the symptoms ushers in DeLillo's diagnosis of their pathogenic mechanism—a complete loss of subjectivity and its resulting dissolution of their meaning of life. DeLillo further on accuses American media industry that prevails in its postmodern conditions of initiating such a pathogenic mechanism, which becomes a recurring subject that DeLillo has so skillfully covered in *Americana*, *Great Jones Street* and *White Noise*. Last but not least, DeLillo is so sharp-witted as to see the wrongful welcome-back of a specious faith than can never work as an antidote to the existential angst but instead is part of "the problem" too, of which he tries to convince his readers by his characterization of Gary Harkness in *End Zone*, an inexperienced college football player who fails to redeem himself from his existential predicament by practicing certain ascetic rituals, quasi-religious in nature. DeLillo's careful analysis of the existential crisis that his American peers confront themselves with works as a prerequisite for his postsecular path-finding efforts that would soon to be spent on his later novels.

Written in accordance with the aforementioned "analysis" part of DeLillo's postsecular writing plan, Chapter Three will deliberate on the novelist's seemingly unsystematic detection of the diverse modalities in which secular spirituality is incarnated. The chapter tends to argue that immanence or secularity is a property that is essential to all these incarnations. As a novelist in masterly command of the English language, DeLillo in his *The Names* strips language of its arbitrariness—the compulsory exertion of man-made linguistic conventions—so as to enlighten his readers on a hidden truth that spellings and sounds, the two material features of language, are a probable source from which the spirituality can emanate. In *Libra*, his first commercial success in history, DeLillo first implies that the spirituality's power can be seen in the shaping effect that Libra—an astrological sign Lee Harvey Oswald is born with—exercises on Oswald's development of an irresolute personality that is so susceptible to multiple sources of influence. More importantly, through his design of two narrative lines that run parallel and at last converge at a point near to the ending, DeLillo tries to suggest to his readers that the historical development, whose randomness or contingency could be strongly evidenced in *Libra* by Oswald's accidental collusion with the conspiratorial group of ex-CIA agents in assassinating John F. Kennedy, can be another embodiment of the spirituality. *Underworld* and *Cosmopolis*, though diametrically different in length, both help Don DeLillo demonstrate that the grandeur of a postindustrial American society, unprecedented in magnitude, well complies with the qualifications Immanuel Kant and Edmund Burke set for the sublime and therefore, is also a probable dwelling place for the secular spirituality. This chapter will come to its close with a conclusive argument that DeLillo's seemingly unsystematic effort to locate different incarnations of the spirituality in the secular life is a hint he drops on the truth that the spirituality is not hanging over the mortals' heads in heaven but could be ferreted out in every nook and cranny of this visible world.

Chapter Four is meant to bring DeLillo's postsecular writing to its most critical stage in which the novelist attempts to propound his list of possible means to pinpoint the spirituality in the secular life. The list is DeLillo's "solution" to the existentialist problem, which is of certain redemptive value no matter how tentative. By and large, DeLillo's list is composed of "to-dos" and "not-to-dos". *Falling Man*, *White Noise*, *Underworld* will be chosen for close readings to present the "to-dos" that DeLillo tries to remind his readers of. Gravity, most often taken for granted when *Falling Man* is being read, is a motif replete with allegorical meaning. Gravity is an irresistible natural force that makes Falling Man's performance possible and thus symbolic of a lesson DeLillo teaches his readers that the spirituality cannot be accessed without mankind, in the first place, humbling down himself before a natural force as vivid an embodiment of the spiritual as gravity is and correspondingly, coming to an understanding of the cosmos's boundlessness in comparison with his own pettiness. *White Noise* and *Underworld* have at least one scenario in common, in which the spectators involuntarily gather as a loosely-structured congregation and as a result, they not only gain access to the secular spirituality but also considerably intensify its redeeming or at least comforting strength. These two non-institutional and makeshift congregations erect for DeLillo a teaching platform on which he imparts another lesson that communality, a ritualistic property of all main doctrinal religions, can be conducive to shortening the distance between the secular spirituality and its pursuers, if stripped of religious institutionality and delimited in scope. *The Names* is a fable that hints at the "not-to-dos" that DeLillo sees as the impediments to the "pilgrim's progress" to the secular spirituality. The worship of linguistic arbitrariness in *The Names* is nothing but a manifest symptom of the cultists' fundamentalist obsession with a concretized object, which can work no better than a breeding ground for fanaticism and terrorism and so is just a spirituality-pursuing mechanism in name but still a logocentrism-caused craziness in substance.

All the foregone argumentation will be brought into a natural conclusion in which certain ethicizing purports of DeLillo's postsecular writing will be expounded on the basis of postsecularism's ethicizing functions that have been dealt with in the last segment of Chapter One. DeLillo has fulfilled his ethical commitments on two planes—individual and social, which will be fully elaborated on with relevant textual evidences in the Conclusion.

CHAPTER ONE

Postsecularism

—A New Faith That Originates from Postmodern Philosophy

As a new paradigm Western sociology frames to make itself more reflective on and critical of modernity, postsecularism tends to regard the modernization of the Western society as a process of rationalization or secularization that accomplishes itself by separating the secular from the religious, and meanwhile, it claims that to a large extent, a multitude of rationality-caused tricky problems should be attributed to the spiritual void left after the religious is compelled to retire by secular reason. To make the void full again, postsecularism distills from the theoretical essentials of both philosophy of postmodernism and philosophy of religion a high-quality filler, which is also a spiritual antidote born out of deconstructionism and placed right in between the secular and the religious. It is an antidote that could redeem the ills and vices of not only the secularized West but also the Westernized world.

The birth of postsecularism as a new variety of discourse has its starting point in the Western academe's reflection on the secularization process of the Western society. The postsecular thinkers in the first place concentrate their theorizing endeavor on enumerating all the possible denotations and connotations of "the secular" so as to give the term a clearer shape. Talal Asad holds on to a rigorous distinction between "the secular" and "secularism" as he argues that "'the secular' is conceptually prior to the political doctrine of 'secularism' that over time a variety of concepts, practices, and sensibilities have come together to form 'the secular'" (Asad, 2003: 16). The reflection postsecularism commits itself to is ultimately directed upon "the secular" but not "secularism" that functions mostly as a political discourse. Jose Casanova delineates "the secular" as a social landscape the West advances into after "the marginalization of religion to a privatized sphere" (Casanova, 1994: 211). Charles Taylor replies to Casanova's personal understanding of "the secular" in his 2007 tour de force—*A Secular Age* by saying that the shift to the secular is "a move from a society in which belief in God is unchallenged and indeed unproblematic, to one in which it is understood to be one option among others, and frequently not the easiest to embrace" (Taylor, 2007: 3). Taylor is hereby suggesting that secularization is a process in which religion has been reduced from a default category to an optional one in Westerners' cognitive scheme. In consequence, the holistic system of belief is torn asunder, and what take its place are multiple values, among which, no single one can be given a default or unchallengeable legitimacy. Besides, Taylor argues in his book that the change in attitude towards God is part of a grander scheme the Western society undertakes in disenchanting and immanetizing its world view. The immanetized world view helps develop a "buffered self", a phrase Taylor coins in his terminology of the book, which refers to a self, rational, arrogant and impervious to any impact of transcendent beings. Taylor sees the formulation of this "new self" as a sign for "an anthropocentric turn" in the human epistemology or the advent of "an exclusive humanism". (Taylor, 2007: 301) Through this set of terms, Taylor intends to make it crystalline clear how fierce the Westerners' will is to establish their selves as the dominant class of beings who both cognize and control the world with no recourse to any form of transcendent being. "A secular age", as Charles Taylor has put it, has therefore come to birth.

Forcefully spurred by reason, the secularizing process has been aggravating the existential angst of the Westerners as it goes on and on into depth. Paul Tillich, a German American who is widely recognized as one of the most influential theologians of the 20th century, ends one of his essays by concluding that human beings are plagued by the angst because of their "awareness of that element of non-being which is identical with finitude, the coming from nothing and the going toward nothing" (Tillich, 1963: 19). It follows from Tillich's conclusive statement that human life is what lingers between "nothing" and "nothing", and so its inborn "finitude" confers upon itself an indispensable ridiculousness, which further on causes the angst in the depth of every living soul. To quell the angst, as Tillich argues, human beings are craving with their heart and soul certain means to transcend the limitedness of their puny selves, and religion is thus born as a probable response to the human desire for transcendence. Pitiably, secularization demolishes the platform religion once proffered to human beings, where they could erect and bathe themselves in the divine grace of transcendent beings, and so Martin Heidegger defines this transcendence-free scenario of human society as "default of God", or an age "for which the ground fails to come, hangs in the abyss" (Heidegger, 1971: 91-92). Much in resonance with Heidegger's standpoint in understanding the secular age, David Tracy adopts a Freudian term "uncanny" to encapsulate, with much vividness, "not-at-homeness" and "overwhelming absence of all meaning" that mankind has been suffering ever since secularization starts and especially when it reaches its peak in the 20th century. (Tracy, 1981: 357-363) In religion's absence, reason undergoes a rampant development. The scientific and technological revolution, which escalates itself one stage after another, has been elevating the general living standard of mankind but meanwhile left more than a dozen disastrous records in the chronicle of human civilization. The two world wars in the last century, intermittent outbreaks of regional skirmishes and terrorist attacks and seemingly unstoppable occurrence of ecological crises work conceitedly in issuing a verdict for reason that has been wreaking havoc with both the value and meaning of a human life. John McClure comes to realize that mankind, much enlightened by their collective memory of the most eventful 20th century, has bore in their bosom a growing awareness that "secular modernity's promises of peace, prosperity, and progress fail to materialize" (McClure, 2007: 10). In face of a world of disorder and commotion, human beings lose their confidence in the brilliant prospect reason alone once convinced them of, and more importantly, they are divorced from a stable breeding ground of the meaning and value of their life. Holding on to no footing in the spiritual sphere of life, mankind cannot acquire any sense of safety and satisfaction in their material life, so in total, as McClure states, "worldly life becomes intolerable" (McClure, 2007: 10).

To correct the wrongs that the secularization has done to the Western society, more and more theoreticians especially those from the realm of Western sociological studies broach the subject of the return of religion. They have reached a consensus that since it has never truly left the human civilization, religion could return in all probability. In what is aforementioned, Charles Taylor still considers religion as an option available to mankind in modern times, while Jose Casanova never believes that religion has died and what he concedes to is that religion is indeed marginalized. It is more than obvious that Taylor and Casanova both agree that religion just retreats to the recess of human consciousness but never gets itself killed off. Graham Ward also claims that "the Western imaginary has been shaped profoundly in the past by its Judeo-Christian institutions and shaped equally by the gradual secularization of, or secular replacements for, those institutions. No author can distill from the cultural imaginary a purely religious or a nonreligious view of the world" (Ward, 2010: 82). It could be inferred from what Taylor, Casanova and Ward speak of religion's return that religion in their common regard denotes the religious consciousness hidden deep in the secularized human mind but not any specific institutional religion, and so it follows that religion should return in the form of consciousness rather than established institution. Religion that returns in the form of consciousness is exactly what postsecularism is purported to achieve. Jurgen Habermas defines its purpose as a change not in social and political hemispheres of human life but in "consciousness" (Habermas, 2008: 20).

It is the deconstructing tool of poststructuralism that helps traditional religion despoil itself of an institutional husk and return to the secularized modern civilization as an influential cultural awareness. The systemized research on religion Jacques Derrida commits himself to in the later years of his career inspires many of his followers to extract the spirituality from institutional religions by deinstitutionalizing them, which is done so as to reveal that spirituality, in its own right, is something that transfigures institutional religions to a consciousness ingrained in a human mind. The deconstructionist restructuring of traditional religion earns itself a proper naming "postmodern theology", which philosophically predisposes postsecularism towards poststructuralism and also theoretically prepares the spirituality for being re-implanted in the nourishing soil of secular life.

Having selected Christianity as an exemplary traditional religion in question, postmodern philosophy succeeds in de-legitimatizing the institutional object of faith by its deconstructionist reexamination of Christian God. Derrida's revolutionary re-interpretation of a non-academic word "impossible" fulfills his deconstruction of God. "'Impossible' is the most impossible possible, more impossible than the impossible if the impossible is the simple negative modality of the possible." (Derrida, 1982: 43) John D. Caputo, Derrida's American follower and colleague, tries to explain Derrida's esoteric theorization with this most commonly used word by saying: "For Derrida, the 'possible' means the programmable and formalizable, the routinizable and the rule bound, the predictable and foreseeable, so the impossible means an interruption of this horizon of possibility and deconstruction concerns itself with the unprogrammable possibility of the impossible." (Caputo, 2002a: 6) Derrida's proposal of the new term and Caputo's deliberation on it can well illustrate that "the possible" is an invented way to refer to the secular that has been programmed, formalized and routinized, while "the impossible" is an epithet for "the imperceptible", which is so reflective of poststructuralism's ultimate goal to loosen the stringent bondage of logocentrism and its longing for the non-rational. In this sense, a natural alliance could be established between poststructuralism and religion, on which Caputo comments, "Religious passion is religious precisely when the tensions of the impossible are raised to their highest pitch, when the easy routine of the possible is shattered by the impossible, which evokes or provokes a genuinely religious passion." (Caputo, 2002a: 4) Caputo even goes as far as to believe that there is certain similitude in structure between deconstructionism and religion as he argues, "Deconstruction is structured like a religion—even as I never tire of taunting the faithful with the notion that religious faith is a deeply deconstructive undertaking that cannot be contained within the borders of institutional religion." (Caputo, 2002a: 5) What Caputo means to say and help Derrida say is that God is nothing but a verbal device that Christianity institutes itself by, and "the impossible" or "the imperceptible" hidden behind is what "the faithful" are truly worshipping. Besides, both Derrida and Caputo imply that the structural similitude between religious faith and deconstructionism lies in a tacit agreement that they both should yearn for the shapeless and ever-changing "unknown". Caputo's deconstructionist effort directed at the Christian concept of God carries itself on in Catherine Keller's theory. Keller sums her theorization on religion up with a phrasal term "a theology of becoming", in which she believes that faith should target itself at "a world of becoming", a world where "the divine invites the becoming of the other, by feeling the becoming of the other, the divine itself becomes" (Keller, 2003: 98). Keller's "becoming" shares a lot in common with Derrida's "impossible" in that changeability and indeterminacy, which constitute the worldview that a religious faith should have entailed, are characteristic of them both. William Connolly agrees to and re-examines the world with Catherine Keller's "becoming" theory, who thus pictures the world he sees as one "consisting of multiple interacting force fields that is open to an uncertain degree" (Connolly, 2009: 1126). To both Keller and Connolly, the divine is no more than one of those "force fields" that far exceed what delimits the range of human reason. Keller and Connolly are both engaged in a deconstructionist restructuring of classic theology, and what's more, they hold a pessimistic outlook at the possible effects the deconstructionist theology could bring upon "the faithful". Though they two both admit the academic legitimacy of "the world of becoming", they assume that it could lead mankind into a "human predicament" since the ever-present indeterminacy innate in "becoming" "breaks up hopes for an afterlife and/or consummate human agency (for example, Christian God) in this life" (Connolly, 2009: 1132). The two scholars' gloomy view most vividly reflects their positioning of deconstructionism as one subgenre of nihilism, which keeps them at a great distance from the constructionist significance of the Derridean theory. Deconstructionism's constructionist significance looms large in Derrida's research accomplishments in the field of religious studies.

John Caputo writes a lot to affirm that deconstructionism is to a great extent constructionist. He first of all stresses that "according to Jacques Derrida, the least bad definition of 'deconstruction'—which is his life's work—is that deconstruction is the 'experience of the impossible'" (Caputo, 2002a: 2). By his empathic quotation of Derrida, Caputo sends off an implicature that Derrida's acceptance of a tentative definition of "deconstruction" is indicative of the actual involvement of certain "undeconstructible element in deconstruction". Caputo furthers his argumentation by giving a clearer shape to the "undeconstructible element": "Deconstruction is structured by a movement 'beyond', which is itself the precisely undeconstructible element in deconstruction, what it always affirms." (Caputo, 2002a: 3) What Caputo is saying is that the undeconstructibility of deconstruction, or its solid determination to move beyond "the possible" or the secular, is constructionist in the truest sense of the word because the prefix "im-" does not work as an absolute negation of the possibilities at all. On the contrary, it encourages the construction of multitudinous modules of possibility and allows the constructional work to proceed on and on. No traditional religious beliefs, as are exemplified by Christianity, can be born without their prenatal craving for "the impossible", about which, Caputo reiterates, "Not only Christendom, but Christianity itself is deconstructible for Christianity is driven by a passion for the impossible that is not deconstructible and that cannot be contained within the boundaries of Christianity." (Caputo, 2002a: 23) At least two deductions could be drawn from the dialectic alternation between "deconstructible" and "not deconstructible" in Caputo's reiteration. Firstly, in the movement towards "the impossible", faiths or beliefs of diverse structures could be constructed in an endless or unstoppable manner. Secondly, the deconstruction of God or the generalization of God to "the impossible" is the very first step a faithful or believing agency should take in constructing his faith, which confers upon him more freedom, greater responsibility and as a result tremendous sense of accomplishment gained upon the completion of his faith construction, instead of, as is foreseen by both Keller and Connolly, a feeling that he is entrapped in "the human predicament" where no light of redemptive hope glitters.

To concretize the way in which traditional religion is deconstructed so as to construct an anti-traditionalist and spirituality-oriented mode of faith, John Caputo spares no effort in probing as deep as possible to the function the Derridean concept of differance could perform. Caputo first explains in what sense differance, one of the greatest philosophical innovations that have ever come out in the 20th century, is related to Derrida's outlook on religion. "In the approach I make to Derrida, the odd way he spells *differance* does not spell the death of God or the destruction of religion, but a certain repetition of religion, a reinvention of a certain religion." (Caputo, 2006: 92) Derrida and Caputo co-name "a certain religion" "religion without religion", which is a "non-dogmatic double of dogma", one that "'repeats' the possibility of religion without religion" (Caputo, 2002a: 8). Conspicuously deconstructionist in nature, "religion without religion" should be the product yielded by "the undeconstructible" manifested after institutional religion is deconstructed—"the impossible". Besides, "repetition" is how differance is called when Derridean deconstructionism is applied to the religious studies. Just like differance, repetition could lead to a constructed mode of faith, in the boundless terrain of "the impossible", with a non-stop or infinite movement towards the next wait-to-be-constructed mode and the next. To better explain repetition—the deconstructionist faith-yielding mechanism, Caputo works out an analogy between it and "recollection" as he points out: "Where recollection repeats backwards, trying to reproduce what was once present, repetition recollects forward: that is, it remembers the vow, the promise made, the commitment given, the first 'yes', and keeps in mind, in its heart, and is faithful to it all the days of one's life." (Caputo, 2002a: 13) The analogy is with no doubt peculiar to the Derridean research on religion and rich in implications. It tells all that intend to convert themselves to "the faithful" that to construct a new mode of faith is predicated on saying "the first 'yes'" to "the impossible", keeping this simple affirmation as a "vow" in mind, and most importantly, consistently pushing forward the renovation of the faith in "the impossible". The analogy also teaches "the faithful" a lesson that the mode of faith could forever change like shapeless flow of water but their adherence to the legitimacy of "the impossible" should be as solid as a rock. In this sense, Caputo's analogy most enlighteningly displays the constructivity[20] of a deconstructionist theology and illustrates how the deconstructionist construction works.

However, a challenging voice comes from Danielle Sands who propounds a problem for John Caputo to consider and resolve. Through his careful reading of all classic Derridean arguments, Sands judges: "Derrida is alert to the possibility of such terms being interpreted as evidence that differance is transcendent or divine." (Sands, 2008: 537) Sands poses a question mark against whether "repetition", as a specific application of differance to the theological studies, can work as a faith-construction mechanism. Caputo reaffirms repetition's capability of constructing faith as he continues to elaborate that "repetition must, on the one hand, remain *constant* in the face of the flux, and on the other hand, produce something *new* by the repetition" (Caputo, 2002a:

---

[20] The deconstructive theology, which John Caputo tries to develop from his understanding of Jacques Derrida's arguments on religion, is constructive in the sense that "the impossible", a concept Derrida propounds, is, according to Caputo, the most deconstructive of logos and all its derivative grand narratives and thus, can not be further on deconstructed. In other words, "the impossible" should be the non-essential essence of poststructuralist thoughts on religion and is constructive in outlining a spiritual destination, which is not a fixed and ultimate end as institutional religions have claimed, and therefore, cannot be reached but only approached nearer and nearer in an ever-going process of "repetition". It can also be inferred from John Caputo's elucidation on Derrida's ideas on religion that "the impossible" derives itself from what is most "essential" about poststructuralism—to be deconstructive of logos, whereas "repetition" is analogous in structure to "differance" and can be even called a "differance" in the realm of poststructural theology.

13). In his further explanation of "repetition", Caputo adds to the clarity of the concept as he suggests that repetition, by nature, is a tool, one that is not deconstructible, whose task is to construct, with no stop, an ever-changeable mode of faith, namely, "something *new*", and "something *new*" is something transcendent or divine that structures itself in a certain way in the course of repetition. Nevertheless, repetition works only as a passage to the transcendent or the divine and so, the passage itself is not endowed with any form of divinity. Having explained "repetition" further on in reply to Sands' question about it, Caputo asserts with much confidence that "Driven to spiritual exhaustion and emptiness, crushed by the vanity of every human effort, the way is made clear for repetition" (Caputo, 2002a: 17). Repetition, as long as it gets under way, will turn itself to a prelude to a grander chapter of postmodern theology, which is a new spirituality conceived in it and to be rooted in the secular life. Given therefore a seemingly paradoxical name "secular spirituality", the new spirituality lies at the theoretical core of postsecularism and its central significance is not disputable.

In the Derridean poststructuralist theory on religion, "repetition" is conducted to construct or give certain shape to "the impossible", or the divine being once represented by Christian God and other objects of faith in the world's leading traditional religions. "The impossible" can deconstruct the institutionality of traditional religions and also epitomize the general character they all share while volunteering to ignore. Stimulated by the Derridean theology, Western researchers who are committed to religious studies tend to contextualize "the impossible" by "spirituality" in their particular realm of discourse, a concept that has been of fundamental importance to Western studies on religion since ancient times. Among all the endeavors to define "spirituality", P. C. Hill's stands out as both brief and relevant to the definition that is accepted herein[21]. According to him, spirituality is the term that "refers to a divine being, divine object, *Ultimate Reality*, or *Ultimate Truth* as

[21] See Note 10.

perceived by the individual" (Hill, 2000: 66). It could be seen from Hill's definition that spirituality is a transcendental being more "Ultimate" than Christian God or any other "original shapes"[22] of doctrinal religions and a sort of "divinity" abstracted from these "shapes" but untainted with their shared institutionality. In this sense, spirituality can work just well as the very guarantee of mankind's realization of their value and significance of life, or in other words, it can give birth to "Ultimate Reality" or "Ultimate Truth" human beings so badly yearn for. Judged from this perspective, "spirituality" agrees well with the religious connotation of Derrida's "the impossible", which has been explained in detail by John Caputo, and so, is, in its own right, an embodiment of the constructivity of deconstructionist theology. In the meantime, "spirituality" does not abandon its pluralist characteristic that originates from deconstructionist philosophy. Paul Tillich once made such an assessment as "the Spirit is not bound to the Christian churches or any one of them" (Tillich, 1962: 28). Tillich's extraction of Spirit from the commonality of institutional religions is a prerequisite upon which spirituality could be pluralized. The central argument of Charles Taylor's colossal work *A Secular Age* makes the similar point that there are indeed a great variety of passageways that might lead one to God as "he admonishes us to remain open toward the varieties of religious transcendence" (qtd. in Gordon, 2008: 648). However, Taylor's budding pluralism cannot come at last into full blossom because he later in the book insists that the diversity of "religious transcendence" he seems to advocate must be achieved within Christianity, or put it another way, only Christian God awaits after "transcendence" is fulfilled. The book is thus addressed only to the Christians rather than the rest of "the faithful". To Taylor, none of such secular enterprises as going to concerts, operas or reading great literature can help people gain access to real spirituality, which, in his regard, can only refer to God. There is no wonder Taylor's reader and critic Peter E. Gordon should interpret his view on God as "for Taylor, the sacred is

---

[22] See Note 10.

historically invariant, *always and only* God. Other experiences do not count in his view as *actual* transcendence since they are ultimately reducible to an exclusive humanism" (Gordon, 2008: 670). On Taylor's compromised pluralism, Gordon continues to comment: "This is to pre-decide which are to be valid candidates for sacred experience. What I am trying to suggest is that Taylor's richly-textured history of the background should also have awakened him to the (possibly distressing) thought that there are many modes of the sacred and many kinds of wonder, and that the Christian religion is merely *one* historical deposit of sacred experience amongst many." (Gordon, 2008: 670) Based on his mild criticism of Taylor's pluralism in religious belief being compromised a bit by his single-minded contextualization of "spirituality" by "God" in "the Christian religion", Gordon convincingly "ranks Taylor within a tradition of religiously and politically progressive Catholic philosophy" (Gordon, 2008: 670).

A German scholar, at his most daring, makes a breakthrough from Charles Taylor's discounted pluralism and carries on an uncompromised pluralism in his construction of spirituality. He is Jurgen Habermas, who brings postsecularism to the forefront of religious studies. He is so determined as to announce that spirituality will become rootless and inaccessible without secularity mixed in it, and so, he is adamant in harmonizing, in an organic way, the secular and the divine, the two opposite sides of an antinomy, into his constructed spirituality. He, further on, calls his seemingly paradoxical standpoint on the spirituality construction by his new coinage—"postsecularism". It is also under Habermas's guidance and encouragement that postsecularism is first accepted as a settled term by Western sociology. Jurgen Habermas, in his journal article *Transcendence from Within, Transcendence in This World*, disproves his Frankfurt School predecessor Max Horkheimer's argument on "absolute meaning" that reads "without God, one will try in vain to preserve absolute meaning" (qtd. in Habermas, 2002: 6) by claiming that people should seek after "transcendence from within" and "recover the meaning of the unconditional without recourse to God" (Habermas, 2002: 108). "Without recourse to God" is indicative of Habermas's approval of transcendence being poststructuralist in nature, while "from within" is to evidence his strong belief in the probability of groping for and at last locating spirituality in secular life. Transcendence inborn in the secular world is an idea Jurgen Habermas, a secularist philosopher, has come up with after he has exerted himself in figuring out an eclectic plan to reconcile the religious with the secular. He also states with much emphasis that postsecularism, with transcendence immanetized[23] in the secular life as its theoretical core, is not meant to fulfill a "hostile takeover" of the role traditional religion has since long assumed, but to "counteract the insidious entropy of the scarce resource of meaning" (Habermas, 2003: 114). William Connolly assents to the Habermasian proposal of secularizing spirituality and enriches the connotation of postsecularism's non-hostile-takeover tenet. In *Why I Am Not a Secularist* (1999), William Connolly maintains that though absolute secularism is being dismantled, the practice of settling a particular institutional religion as one the public is ordered to observe will do no more than to aggravate the on-going cultural conflicts. Therefore, "secularism needs refashioning, not elimination" (Connolly, 1999: 19). Connolly does not say no to the necessity of spirituality's return to the secular, whereas what he argues for is that stripped of institutionality it once had when embedded in doctrinal religions, spirituality should be ingrained in the secular and as a result, imbibe into itself "immanence"[24] as part of its nature. In other words, William Connolly comes to recognize that postsecularism should not be configured to replace secularism with hostility either. Immanence is a component of spirituality's character with which it could be incarnated in an object or an activity of the secular life, and therefore is highly reachable to ordinary people and exercises direct impact upon their lives. Spirituality, bred out of postmodern theology as a mixture between immanence and transcendence, is secular spirituality. As postsecularism's theoretical core and greatest invention, secular

---

㉓ See Note 11 for a detailed explanation of the term.

㉔ See Note 14 for a detailed explanation of the term.

spirituality[25] is also the reason why the theory is called as it is. The prefix "post-" is to declare the ending of an age when only secularism prevails and the spiritual, either institutional or non-institutional, is dismissed from the public consciousness. "Post-" also functions as an intimation of the fact that postsecularism cannot live without absorbing some theoretical nourishment from other "post-studies". John Thatamanil in his *The Immanent Divine* (2009) credits Adi Sankara and Paul Tillich with the theorization on "immanent divine", arguing that both the two prophesy "divine immanence" since "both characterize divinity not as an infinite being among other beings but rather as being itself, that which gives being to all beings but is not itself one of those beings" (Thatamanil, 2009: 10). The immanence Thatamanil goes in length to speak of in his book is a clear manifestation of the two great theologians, representative of both the Orient and the Occident, embracing hand in hand the cause of implanting the divine in the secular. From all the foregoing arguments, an understanding could be reached that secular spirituality, as a theological concept, has its validity rooted in a rather postmodern integration between immanence and transcendence, two opposites in a binary opposition that secularism holds tight to. The accepted integration legitimatizes secular spirituality and is conducive to settling it down as the conceptual core of a new theological discourse—postsecularism. Charles Winquist proposes his "secular theology" as a warm echo with postsecularism. On "secular theology", he stresses that "it is a demand that theology think of itself as a this-worldly and thus secular or be silent. I think it is eventually a demand that theology do something to the ordinariness of experience while speaking within the ordinariness of experience. Theology is unsettled but it must also be unsettling" (Winquist, 1994: 1028). His "ordinariness of experience" resonates with the immanence or secularity of spirituality that postsecularism advocates with no effort spared, and "unsettled" and "unsettling" are here to confirm another proposal of postsecularism's that spirituality must be pluralistic or multi-faceted.

---

[25] See Note 18 for a detailed explanation of the term.

Plurality and secularity of secular spirituality have determined that the ways to pursue it should be very much distinguishable from traditional religious rituals.

Simone Weil (1909—1943), a Jewish French philosopher, wrote a multitude of essays on her spiritual pursuit in her 34-year life. Editors compiled all what she wrote into one book and titled it *Waiting for God* (1951), in which Weil recorded with much religious ardency her first experiencing of the transcendent and all the sentiments she ever felt thereafter in her spiritual pursuit. Santa Maria degli-Angeli is a 12th-century Romanesque chapel in Assisi, to which St. Francis once paid very regular pilgrimages. It was in this saint-frequented chapel that young Weil for the first time in her life felt gently touched by a certain form of divinity as she later wrote: "Something stronger than I was compelled me for the first time in my life to go down on my knees." (Weil, 1951: 56) As was "compelled" by "something stronger", she from then on devoted much of her time to seeking after spirituality in ardent passion, which did not hamper her from sympathizing with the political stances of Leon Trotsky (1879—1940) who once resided with the Weils in their house. For all the remaining years of her 34-year life, Weil had framed her mindset with both allegiance to the leftist political thought and piety towards the transcendent. For this reason, she was known for both an ascetic leftism and a fervidly Catholic piety and therefore, dismissed by many with much scorn as "the Red Virgin". Even so, Weil never held in mind even a faintest idea of giving up her peculiar philosophy of life in exchange for public acceptance because she believed in the power of an individualized faith in bridging the gap between secular politics and spiritual pursuit. About her idiosyncratic structuring of her faith, Weil left in her *Waiting for God* a highly suggestive statement that reads: "Attentiveness without an object is prayer in its supreme form" (Weil, 1951:56). Prayer to no object of faith and leftist political concerns can work together to validate the secularity of the spirituality Weil had been aspiring to throughout her life, and more importantly, prove that her means of pursuit is objectless, unorthodox and therefore individualistic choice she made at her own will. Spirituality cannot be accessed in the secular life without an individualized means of pursuit, which also represents the way postsecularism shows its approval of and respect to the initiatives the believers should have taken. While performing a role in a certain activity, one comes to an epiphany, in which he fulfills an unobstructed communion with a transcendent being and by so doing, gains much spiritual comfort. The activity itself and the resulting structure of the transcendent being both come as a result of one's personal option. *Newsweek* issued in November 28, 1994 published a front page story titled *In Search of the Sacred*, in which two coauthors Barbara Kantrowitz and Patricia King illustrate through a plenty of well-chosen cases how Americans, at the turn of the 21st century, individualized their spiritual pursuit in a way so emblematic of their asserted self. The cases selected into the story feature quite a few American celebrities who have established their renown in the fields of literature, music, TV-program hosting and politics. Among them are, for example, Andre Agassi, David Mamet, and Winfrey Oprah. The highly individualistic hallmarks of their means of pursuit convince both the two writers that "cafeteria religion, a very American theology" (Kantrowitz, Patricia, 1994: 55) should be the best way to define these means and the spirituality thus gained. Amy Hungerford, a postsecular critic of DeLillo, also admits that high individualization of means of pursuit could function quite well in enriching the constitution of spirituality. She argues that means of pursuit, if individualized but not standardized, could greatly diversify and hybridize the composition of a spirituality, which could incorporate since long marginalized or even neglected spiritual elements like traditional European sorcery and magic and select components of African-, Indian-American and Oriental spiritual cultures. It goes without saying that diversity and hybridity are both the faithful embodiment of the pluralist nature of secular spirituality.

It could be inferred from the individuation of one's means of pursuit another inherent feature. The individuation must urge the believers to take full initiatives to experience the spiritual, or in other words, his means of pursuit is individualized and so, experiential too. Ignacio Gotz takes experiencing as a specific means by which the subject can fully play their potential in embracing the spiritual. He recommends that one could volunteer to participate in a secular activity and so, unexpectedly, somewhere and sometime, he can activate his senses to experience the spiritual's magnificent strength of offering a soul its craved-for consolation. He exemplifies what he recommends to be done by two cases featuring two professional sportsmen. One retired surfer called Michael Hynson talks of how he feels when surfing, "When you become united with a wave, you feel like you're in total harmony with the divine at every level." (Gotz, 2001: 10) Besides, John Brodie, an ex-quarterback of the San Francisco 49ers, comments on the magic feeling he could often gain in the games, "Sometimes in the heat of the game a player's perception and coordination improve dramatically. At times, I experience a kind of clarity that I've never seen described in any football story." (Gotz, 2001:10) The two well-known professional athletes describe their individual experiencing of the transcendent in a similar manner. The chosen verbs like "feel" and "experience" suggest that secular spirituality cannot be accessed if one fails to take his initiatives in experiencing the secular first and then, believing the spiritual. In addition, as Daniel Born sees, an idiosyncratic and experiential means of pursuit can enhance the consolatory strength of a secular spirituality if the believer should allow himself to join a believers' community. The traditional religious rituals, as Daniel Born observes, cannot be properly implemented without a believing community of certain scope, because in his regard, "the sacred is about community, the cementing of communal bonds" (Born, 1999: 214). "Cemented communal bonds" opens up a trail for secular spirituality, on which it can steadily strengthen itself by the power of faith gradually concentrated with the believing subjects congregating to form a community. What Daniel Born implies in his observation on communality is that secular spirituality's means of pursuit can not dispense with communality because secular spirituality, though born as a deconstruction of institutional religion, cannot completely shrug off traditional religion's impact upon its operating mechanism, which could be evidenced by the believers' predisposition to developing a group or even congregation with other believers who hold their faith in one common secular spirituality. The believers' community by itself is a kind of replica of traditional religion's organizational units like church or parish.

Having finished defining secular spirituality and the characteristics of its means of pursuit, the postsecular thinkers are so cool-minded as to orient the reading public's attention towards postsecularism's theoretical deficiencies—potential dangers that hide themselves deep in secular spirituality. Mark C. Taylor warns all believers of a crisis that immanence could incur by citing from Philippe Lacoue-Labarthe (1940—2007), a French philosopher, his commentary on Nazism, which reads, "Adolph Hitler ... who in no way represents any form of transcendence, but incarnates, in immanent fashion, the immanentism of a community. This will to immediacy is precisely what has been caesura-ed, for it was, ultimately, the crime—the boundless excess—of Nazism." (Taylor, 1999: 22 – 23) Lacoue-Labarthe attributes part of the reason why Nazism should rise in Germany to its people's false orientation of their spirituality-seeking efforts. During World War Ⅱ, the Germans, like their fellow human beings, were determined to quench their thirst for the transcendent by seeking out spirituality in "immanence" or secular life, which, however, resulted in a war devastatingly destructive of the world's peace and prosperity. They overemphasized "immanence" in their spiritual pursuit or faith construction by ossifying their belief in Hitler, too incarnate a being of flesh and blood, who was so skilled at abusing the German public's burning desire for religious faith. Nazism, in this sense, came into being as a result of Germans' misplaced desire for immanent or secular spirituality. What's more, "this will to immediacy" manifests a probability in which "immanence" could be misunderstood as a utilitarian end towards which one's pursuit of spirituality could deviate from its rightful course. By his reference to "community", Lacoue-Labarthe makes it clear that people with common interests in some immanent spirituality can congregate and unite, whose fervid enthusiasm, if not checked in a proper way, could escalate to a state of "ecstasy", and in consequence, the congregation could in all likelihood reduce itself to a violent gang of killers, typical of which is German Nazism, a form of national religious fanaticism. Antoon Braeckman partly agrees to what worries Lacoue-Labarthe in the communality of a secular spirituality's means of pursuit. He argues that affected by the institutionality it necessarily inherits from traditional religion, secular spirituality cannot avert all the risks caused by traditional religion's "community-instituting" function and the "community-instituting" capability of a religion is a precondition on which religious strife and intolerance is provoked. (Braeckman, 2009: 292) Rather than communality, the characteristic of secular spirituality's means of pursuit that worries Graham Ward is individualization. He holds that the individualized means of pursuit will lead to a type of spirituality that counts no more than "forms of hyper-individualism, self-help as self-grooming, custom-made eclecticism that proffer a pop transcendence" that could befuddle the pursuers and become "unable to tell the difference between orgasm, and adrenalin rush and an encounter with God". (Ward, 2006: 185) Ward's adamancy in still naming the spirituality God proves his incomplete postsecular stance. However, Ward's review on and criticism of the postsecular discourses are highly reflective of freedom of speech and openness that postsecularism has fought hard to defend. Starting off from these reviews and criticisms, the postsecular thinkers push forward the postsecular studies into depth and so with much confidence they proffer a package of strategies to overcome the thorny difficulties of the secular world, which all work well in revealing postsecularism's values, both theoretical and practical.

Postsecularism, through its deconstruction of both the religious and the secular, blazes a non-black-nor-white trail to redemption. "The double deconstruction" endows postsecularism with both religious and secular characters, which is of the greatest importance to the fulfillment of its promised "redemption". The postsecular researchers have reached a consensus that its value consists in a two-level ethicization—of an individual and a society. The ethicization of a society is predicated upon the ethicization of an individual, to which the religious character of postsecularism is an indisputable prerequisite. Gianni Vattimo realizes that the capability of the religious in offering an ultimate answer to the question on human life's meaning or value should be credited with its ethicizing effect on the believing individuals. Once in a dialogue, Vattimo asked a question most fundamental to the human life in his regard, "Why 'being' rather than nothingness?" (Vattimo, Zabala, 2002: 463) Further on, Vattimo argues that as one that cannot be answered, the question shall corner all theories, either scientific or humanistic, on to the brink of nihilism, and so religion is the only discourse that can possibly offer an answer as it can best of all meet the human request for the realization of life's meaning. Paul Tillich in his representative work *Systemic Theology* also confirms religion's role in affirming one's value of life by commenting: "The object of theology is what concerns us ultimately. Only those propositions are theological which deal with their object insofar as it can become a matter of ultimate concern for us." (Tillich, 1951: 12) Clearly seen in the foregoing statements, the two theologians of high fame have reached an agreement that religion's engagement in responding to the "ultimate concern" has laid a legitimate basis for the human existence, without which the value and meaning of a human life will become worse than unthinkable. Another celebrated theologian Charles Winquist tries to corroborate religion's ethicization of individuals by taking as an example Milan Kundera's yearning for the immortal. "The desire for theological thinking is a desire for a thinking that does not disappoint us. It is not unlike Milan Kundera's gesture of longing for immortality that is at the same time a longing for a relationship to the infinite that does not disappoint us." (Winquist, 1994: 1025) Having sung praises of "theological thinking's" inability to "disappoint us", Winquist mocks at science and other secular theories as Vattimo does by saying, "Desiring to think theologically is an unsettling of any scholarship that refuses to ask the question of meaning." (Winquist, 1994: 1025) Relatively speaking, John Caputo goes further in disclosing the ethicizing effects of religion's confirmation of life's value because he most daringly announces that Christianity is deconstructionist by itself and affirms that postsecularism can function just as well as traditional religion does in asserting the meaning of an individual life. Caputo takes Jesus Christ's declaration of the Kingdom of God to be an example of deconstruction, a prophetic indictment of the status quo conducted for the redemptive and affirmative purpose of keeping on mind a decent expectation of something new "to come", of a new truth that is ruled by justice, gift, forgiveness, hospitality and love. (Caputo, 2007: 63 – 80) It is crystal clear that John Caputo is encouraging all mankind to project all these moral traits to their ethic make-up so that they could bear in mind a genuine expectation of "the new truth". Besides, Caputo goes on to remind that only an ethicized "new truth" can have actual socio-political implications for responding to the widows and the orphans, the oppressed and the disenfranchised. (Caputo, 2007: 63 – 80)

The moral characters of an individual that could come to shape in "the new truth" can contribute to postsecularism's completion of its second-level ethicization—its ethicization of a society. For postsecularism, to ethicize a society is to multiply its values. The pluralization of social values is accomplished by secular spirituality's immanence or secularity because to secularize both postsecularism's spirituality and its means of pursuit can first of all ethicize the individuals and at the same time, its inborn deconstructivity can make pluralism a generally accepted value for the progress of a society. William Connolly works to help determine the nature of the value by saying, "Crafting an ethos of deep, multidimensional pluralism requires that we both weaken the power of the evangelical-neoliberal machine and rewrite some of the understandings and aspirations of secularism." (Connolly, 2011: 651) Connolly refers "the evangelical-neoliberal machine" to a collusive role that the Christian religion plays in working with capitalism's political system—neoliberal in nature—to deepen capitalism's exploitation on and deprivation of the weak, either economically or politically, by thrusting Christian values into the hands of those weaker "others". His advice to "weaken the machine" and "rewrite secularism" is the actual implementation of postsecularism's double deconstruction of both the religious and the secular. The non-deconstructionist religionization cannot complete its grand mission of ethicizing or pluralizing human society, and instead, will incur outrageous violence of religious fundamentalism or extremism, of which both Vattimo and Caputo have been sharply aware. When interviewed, Vattimo poses his challenge against an unconditional return of traditional religion to the secular as he says, "The return may cause us to have a feeling that I have reached bedrock, a foundation at which no questions can or need be asked—that state, in which questions are lacking, is not the end product of violence, but its origin." (Vattimo, Zabala, 2002: 455) Caputo agrees with Vattimo that without the deconstructivity or a question-asking ability, the returned religion could place a society in a scenario where "there is triumphalism, dogmatism, the illusion that we have been granted a secret access to the Secret. That is the illusion that makes religion so consummately dangerous and fires the fundamental religious hallucination" (Caputo, 2002b: 94). In breaking the hallucination and eliminating the violence, postsecularism still has a great potential to be fully tapped, because secular spirituality as its theoretical core and greatest experimentalist theological idea, has, in all sincerity, carried on postmodern philosophy's deconstructionist cause of supplying some inexhaustible motivating force to the realization of an intra-cultural and inter-cultural peace. To resolve the seemingly irreconcilable conflict between the two civilizations, Christian and Islam, Talal Asad appeals to both the two sides that dialogue or communication conducted under the guidancc of pluralism can be the only possible way out as he says, "The members of each tradition should be prepared to engage productively with members of others, challenging and enriching themselves through those encounters." (Asad, 1997: 195) Additionally, Vattimo does not comment without optimism that the two traditions in conflict, if engaged in a dialogue practiced through a "progressively wider application of the principle of consensus, reciprocity, consultation", can in all likelihood achieve "the reduction of violence and the resultant increase in justice". (Vattimo, Zabala, 2002: 457) Neither Asad nor Vattimo is so biased as to impose the notorious name of extremism on Islamism alone. Instead, both of them are so insightful and perceptive to realize that there is a proclivity in Christianity too to become fundamentalist or extremist. The demand for dialogue issued out of this introspective mode of thinking could lead the world to genuine pluralism, which could fulfill the promise of peace and prosperity that reason or rationality alone has failed to fulfill.

Postsecularism comes to being as a result of postmodern philosophy's restructuring and optimizing of traditional Western theology. The ineradicable poststructuralist character of postsecularism will nullify any effort to systemize or stylize it. So it follows that postsecularism can never elevate its status to a label that can integrate all related arguments and their makers to one uniform whole. Scattered in journal articles, theses, books and monographs written by poststructuralist philosophers and contemporary theologians, the non-systemized postsecular thought has exhibited to the academic world its promising capability of facilitating the cross-disciplinary researches. Having benefited a lot from postsecularism, the studies in the fields of literature, politics, sociology and culture have developed a much broader horizon for their later progress. To a world where the importance of religious belief is increasingly clear while religious extremism is still ravaging, to push the postsecular studies to both its depth and width is of great value, both academically and realistically.

CHAPTER TWO

Problematization

—The Human Predicament and Losing Battles to Fight

When he set off his half-century-long literary career in the 1960s by publishing *The Jordan River*, a short story, in *Epoch*, Don DeLillo, with or without his approval of the term, did witness the inevitable entry of contemporary American culture into the postmodern conditions, which, according to Fredric Jameson, are "purely and simply the effects of late capitalism on contemporary culture" (Nicol, 2009: 10). Daniel Bell (1919—2011) and Jean Francois Lyotard (1924—1998) also agree to each other that at the end of the 1950s, the American society stepped into "what is known as the post-industrial age" and its culture "entered what is known as the postmodern age". (Lyotard, 1979: 3) Immersed in a postmodern American culture that manifests its complexity and multiplicity day by day, Don DeLillo records and studies it by unfolding a long and artistically appealing scroll of literary portrayals, which, as Frank Lentricchia observes, has helped establish DeLillo as a critic of postmodern culture, who "takes for his critical object of aesthetic concern the postmodern condition" (Lentricchia, 1991b: 3). Nonetheless, though his fiction "can be read as a fictional history of the process of American postmodernity" (Fan, 2014: 54), Don DeLillo scowls or at least wears a worried look on his face while writing about it as he cannot concede to Lyotard's depiction of postmodern condition as "potentially more positive, even liberating" (Nicol, 2009: 11), while instead, he "sees more of the loss, more of the cultural vacuity in the postmodern age when there is no metaphysical court of appeals for humanity" (Rettberg, 1999: 1).

"The cultural vacuity" is a gaping and bottomless hole where humanity is badly lacking and what's worse, the postmodern condition never cares to present any means to replenish the "vacuity". William Connolly, an American sociologist, describes the harrowing situation as "the human predicament", "a situation lived and felt from the inside and it is something you seek to ameliorate or rise above" (Connolly, 2009: 1121). It could be inferred from William Connolly's definition of "the human predicament" that it is one's crisis of life in which he cannot help but subject himself to the irresistible pressure of contemporary cultural conditions. In the postmodern age or what William Connolly calls "the late-modern era", "the human predicament" becomes much worse than the early modern times when the humans are cut off from "providential transcendence", while in the postmodern era, besides that, their "secular notions", acquired in the early modern or secular era, of "linear, progressive time" are no longer well-grounded or valid. (Connolly, 2009: 1137) In other words, the malfunction of mankind's reason-instructed perception of timc's linearity and progressivity signifies their almost irredeemable loss of a stable and singular subjectivity, which was once part of the lesson they were taught by the secular too. This new subjectivity-disintegrating property of "the human predicament" is most stimulatingly represented in Don DeLillo's *Americana*, *Great Jones Street* and *White Noise*, which all with great verisimilitude delineates how the postmodern cultural engine works to advance the de-legitimatization[26] of human subjectivity and what the subjects could suffer as "the human predicament" is aggravated.

William Connolly goes on further with his explanation of the "human predicament" by asserting that the breakup of "secular notions of linear, progressive time" should be in a way dealt with by "either engagement or repression". (Connolly, 2009: 1137) Most of DeLillo's heroes, like the ones in *Great Jones Street*, *End Zone* and *Underworld*, try to "repress" what the postmodern conditions have done to their subjectivities by choosing to take no heed of all their sufferings thus caused, whereas David Bell, the hero of *Americana*, DeLillo's first novel, takes the initiatives to "engage" the postmodern culture in addressing his "human predicament" or subjectivity crisis. However, none of the means, either "engagement or repression", on which these DeLillo characters have tried their hands, bear fruit as expected, by which, the novelist should have suggested that none of the crisis-addressing mechanisms that have not broken free from the restriction of the reasonable can

---

[26] In the book, to "legitimatize" a subjectivity means to mould a subjectivity in a dynamic and two-way process of interaction between "subject" and "object", or in other words, a subject, thus constituted, to a certain extent and on a particular occasion, can feel his exertion of will in deciding how he is to cognize and transform the objective though meanwhile, he can also sense the shaping influence of the objective on his self-formation. With "legitimatization" of a subjectivity explained, "de-legitimatization" can be better understood in the postmodern conditions, in which, the alienating power of the objective is said to have reached its apex in the sense that the interaction between "subject" and "object" is cut short as "subject" is controlled by or trapped in "object". So, there is no wonder that, in the postmodern conditions, subjectivity has lost its legitimacy as it has become "shifting, fragmented, multiple and depthless" (Jameson, 1992: 166), and as a result, the subjects of the age should strive to re-legitimatizes their self. However, as for contemporary Americans that Don DeLillo has so vividly characterized, the "legitimatization" of a self is a concept that has been over-interpreted. To them, "legitimate self" is just another way of saying "authentic self" (see Note 29), a concept that Charles Taylor has explained and criticized in *A Secular Age*, because American minds, as DeLillo has depicted in his works, have been so much informed by reason that in their regard, if "subject" can not exercise absolute reign over "object", it cannot deserve to be called "subject" at all. As despairing failures in which those characters' pursuit of "authentic self" ends have suggested, "legitimacy" of such a self is illusory and not worth any one's personal effort at all.

be the very answer to the existential problem of the postmodern age, and this is the reason why the open-up of a passage to a mode of faith, postsecular in nature, is necessitated.

Contemporary American subjectivity is thrown into question all because it is both embedded in and formulated by American postmodern culture. So, a better understanding of Don DeLillo's novelistic rendering of the subjectivity problem cannot be accomplished without reference to the theories of Western philosophers who have gone far in theorizing on the postmodern conditions. Among them, Daniel Bell and the "Holy Trinity" of postmodern theorists—Lyotard, Baudrillard and Jameson should stand out as most preeminent contributors to the cannon of postmodern thoughts that can both describe and prescribe the subjectivity crisis in DeLillo's works. Though DeLillo once claimed in public that he did not read a lot of "the theoretical work being done in philosophy and literary criticism these days" (qtd. in Morley, 2009: 124), as Catherine Morley argues, if one decides to read DeLillo, he "is to encounter in his fiction many of the observations articulated by contemporary theorists of the postmodern, (because) his work lends itself to definition by way of example rather than formulation" (Morley, 2009: 124). *Americana*, DeLillo's very first full-length novel, is such an "example" that will exemplify the profundity of DeLillo's understanding about the problem of the postmodern age he and his characters live in.

The American society in *Americana* is one in which nothing but "late capitalism" rules. The society in this developmental stage of capitalism is the "post-industrial" one in Daniel Bell's terms, and also as Bell puts it, the post-industrial society cannot proceed with its high-speed growth without its adamant belief in "privileging of self-gratification and hedonism to keep the economy expanding" (qtd. in Faigley, 1992: 10). Having weakened the constraining forces of Puritanical moral codes, the post-industrial society, according to Bell, succeeds in "eventually undermining traditional authority" (qtd. in Faigley, 1992: 10) and allowing the supreme ideal of buying, consuming, using and then throwing away to infiltrate into its subjects' existential consciousness, so as to meet the high requests of its self-development. What facilitates the post-industrial society in hardening its subjects' will towards gratification, pleasure and individual fulfillment is its self-made tool—an image culture. Image can dominate the postmodern culture because, as Daniel Bell suggests, the post-industrial society is an information society whose main products are not any commercial goods but images created by its advanced electronic communication technology. (Bell, 1973: 221) It goes without saying that contemporary American media is the most influential specimen of "electronic communications technology" and it functions with high efficiency as a platform on which images exert their enchanting power on the potential buyers. Nevertheless, the postmodern philosophers, especially Jean Baudrillard, see in the media-empowered image more it can do—to wreak havoc with identities of the subjects in the postmodern age by constructing them in its own way. Baudrillard interprets this seeming paradox by saying "identities are constructed by the appropriation of images, and codes and models determine how individuals perceive themselves and relate to other people" (qtd. in Kellner, 2002: 52). It follows that the image-determined construction of subjectivity is exactly what deconstructs or de-legitimatizes it. Unfortunately, David Bell, *Americana*'s hero, is the subject of a postmodern America, who has been learning and practicing the trade of "appropriation of images" to construct his self since his early boyhood.

The 28-year-old David Bell is a young and promising TV network executive, a profession that DeLillo designs for David so that he can characterize David as a first-class image dealer. For his early success of making his way to the forefront of the image-making industry, David should feel much indebted to his farther, Clinton Bell, who worked and retired as a successful advertising executive at a New York ad agency. When David is a small boy, Clinton projects the commercials produced by his agency onto a basement screen to amuse David and his siblings. Watching TV commercials has, in the way, become a childhood entertainment for David. With a mock nostalgic feeling for his childhood, David Bell explains how the image-saturated commercials shape his young self-consciousness by recollecting that "all the impulses of the media were fed into the circuitry of my dreams" (130). "The impulses" sent off from the images are not only "fed into the circuitry" of David's subjectivity but also restructure it so as to distance it from David's real self, or even reduce his real self to a flimsy fake. The restructured self comes as a result of a constructedness that is so devastating to David's and his fellow Americans' subjectivity. A severe crisis is in the way caused, which is defined by Jean Baudrillard as one in which "Contemporary man is now only a pure screen, a switching center for all the networks of influence" (Baudrillard, 1983: 133). The original texture of the "screen" or the running mechanism of the "switching center" is negligible and it goes without saying that what trivializes "what's behind" or real self are "networks of influence", which, to a great extent, refer to the images broadcast one after another from the media. "Networks of influence" converge upon one subject and cause it to take on some postmodern characters, which Chris Barker describes as "shifting, fragmented and multiple" (Barker, 2002: 225). Paul Maltby complements Barker's brief but relevant description by arguing for a postmodern subjectivity's distant separation from "a depth model". (Maltby, 1996: 268) In sum, the "shifting, fragmented, multiple and depthless" subjectivity is not subjectivity in the real sense of the word[27]; instead, it is no better than a metamorphosizing exteriority of one's real selfhood, of which Don DeLillo has developed a sharp awareness. So, in *Americana*, DeLillo presents

---

[27] See Note 2 about "subjectivity" and Note 26 about "de-legitimatization".

to his readership one of his best known terms—"universal third person"[28], a type of subjectivity on which all the aforementioned characters of a postmodern subjectivity are concentrated.

To film a documentary of his personal history, David Bell invites Glenn Yost, one of his friends, to act as his father Clinton. In one scene of the documentary, David and "Clinton" engage in a talk on "universal third person":

> "How does a successful television commercial affect the viewer?"
>
> "It makes him want to change the way he lives."
>
> "In what way?" I said.
>
> "It moves him from first person consciousness to third person. In this country there is a universal third person, the man we all want to be. Advertising has discovered this man. It uses him to express the possibilities open to the consumer. To consume in America is not to buy; it is to dream. Advertising is the suggestion that the dream of entering the third person singular might possibly be fulfilled." (270)

The "third person" consciousness permeates into a commercialized America, which cancels off its subjects' legitimate concern with their self and reduces their effort in rebuilding their real subjectivity to establishing their self as

---

[28] "Universal third person" is a saying Don DeLillo works out to represent, in *Americana*, his characters' despair towards the postmodern conditions whose alienating power is so strong as to make a mockery of all their endeavors to rebuild "a legitimatized self" (synonymous with "authentic self", see Note 29) and so, numb their senses. To regain in their subjectivity, stability, singularity, wholeness and depth, which are all traits of an "authentic self", contemporary Americans, of whom the *Americana* characters are typical, should resort to a media-dominated culture, which counts as the greatest "object" in the postmodern times, and expect to have it do a job it is best at—creating a public image, after which, all Americans can remold their self so that "legitimacy" or "authenticity" can be recovered. Nevertheless, their dream can not come true in the real sense of the word because "legitimacy"—an end they strive so hard towards—is delusional, and besides, their chosen means—mediatization—is by itself what should have been held culpable of their loss of "a legitimatized self".

a standardized and universalized "third person". Therefore, sarcastically, their subjectivity-rebuilding effort takes them nowhere but into a worse situation in which their meaning of life can be dissolved no further. No matter how pathetic the situation is, it happens as in *Americana*, David-like American young men all dream that they could become "the Marlboro Man"—a world-famous American TV commercial image, which stands for masculinity, strength, independence and heroism.

Don DeLillo is sure to understand that what worsens their subjectivity crisis is American people's own role of working as media's accomplice in erasing their true self or meaning of life, which is illustrated by what "Clinton" continues to say, "The third person was invented by the consumer, the great armchair dreamer. Advertising discovered the value of the third person but the consumer invented him." (271) DeLillo hereby suggests a vicious cycle from which contemporary Americans can hardly free themselves. On the one hand, the subjects volunteer to abandon their original selfhood as it is they themselves who "invented the third person"; on the other hand, the invented "third person" in TV commercials drives the American subjects to alienate from their true selfhood and create or copy more "third person" images. So, in this sense, DeLillo tries to suggest that the meaning of an American subject's life, in contemporary America, is cornered into a dead end, from which, no secular means could set it free.

Under his father's influence, David Bell chooses TV program production as his start of career, which is proved fatal in augmenting the destructive effect of the "third person" images upon his genuine self. One of David's musings on his job could help gauge the depth of the abyss into which his life-value has been plunged:

> There were times when I thought all of us at the network existed only on videotape. Our words and actions seemed to have a disturbingly elapsed quality. We had said and done all these things before and they had been frozen for a time, rolled up in little laboratory trays to await broadcast and rebroadcast when the proper time slots became available. And there was the

feeling that somebody's deadly pinky might nudge a button and we would all be erased forever. (23)

What he is musing on has suggested that David, a TV network executive, has come to recognize that freedom of his body is a deceptive superficiality that hides a horrifying truth underneath—the "third person"-centered image culture has de-legitimatize contemporary Americans' subjectivity to the degree that their being could "all be erased forever" by a gentle "nudge" of the "third person's" "deadly pinky". David helps reveal a truth that so much absorbed in the images from the "videotapes", Americans' sense of existence has "elapsed", which conforms to Robert Nadeau's reading of *Americana* as an illustration of the idea that an "authentic or unique self has been trivialized out of existence" (Nadeau, 1981: 165) in the postmodern conditions. This is all the reason why David Bell, in the later part of the story, travels to the American West where he works hard to retrieve an "authentic self"㉙ by making a documentary film about his personal history.

The postmodern American society is built upon consumerism, unprecedented in both magnitude and scope. Consumerism is also the solid pedestal on which a monumental culture of image erects itself. However, besides the media-engineered image culture, consumerism has another means to de-legitimatize contemporary subjectivity—mass culture, an equally vicious force that could

---

㉙ "Authentic self" is a phrasal term that Charles Taylor elaborates on in his *A Secular Age* as a subjectivity characteristic of "The Secular Age". According to him, as a side effect of secularization, "authentic self" is a god-like subjectivity that comes as a result of human beings' ardent belief that reason, whose strength is increased a lot by the Enlightenment, can help them exert their free will in shaping the objective in whichever way that pleases them and reduce the intrusive force of the objective upon self formation to nil. So, in "A Secular Age", a self is "authentic" in the sense that the dynamic and two-way interaction between "subject" and "object" has come to a halt and in the meantime becomes one-way as reason teaches all modern subjects a lesson that a subject, armed with sophisticated weaponry reason comes to present, can exert shaping influence upon all objects at free will so that he can assert his "authority" or "authenticity" and never allow the objective to change its status of passivity in the relationship between "subject" and "object".

turn the nature of "the human predicament" from a psychological crisis to an arbitrary effacement and a willful re-formulation of a selfhood's outer contour. According to Fredric Jameson, mass culture is elevated to a height that it has never reached before because the postmodern culture, in a way, characterizes itself by "effacement in it of the key boundaries or separations, most notably the erosion of the older distinction between high culture and so-called mass or popular culture" (Jameson, 1992: 165). It is all due to the rise of mass culture in postmodern America that Bucky Wunderlick, the hero of *Great Jones Street*, can enjoy his highly profitable stardom of a rock-and-roll singer on the condition that he should surrender his right to shape his outer appearance to the market, which has both determined and consumed his subjectivity.

Bucky tastes his high celebrity with relish until one moment in his concert when he is scared by the eruptive fervor of his fans that transforms to the blood-stained violence. Upon the sudden halt of the concert, Bucky vanishes from public view and retires into his moderately furnished apartment hidden deep in New York's Great Jones Street. However, Bucky's withdrawal cannot contain consumerism-driven mass culture that has since long overwhelmingly flooded his private life and shaped the fragile exteriority of his subjectivity to meet the commercial interests of his bosses. In other words, the entirety of his self has been commodified and even his voluntary withdrawal is of no exception in this respect, which could be verified by what Globke, Bucky's performance agent, tells Bucky when he tries to convince the latter of fulfilling a quick comeback:

> You can jam, you can whistle, you can hum, you can do top-forty AM schlock, you can just stand there and shout at the audience. It doesn't make any difference what you do. The idea is get you out there, get the whole mystique going again, make them wet their pants, make them yell and scream. (198)

Globke is frank to Bucky about the working mechanism of mass culture, which, as he has explained, requests a subject to surrender his basic right of formulating his public image to the market that will arrange him an image or an outer contour of subjectivity, and the contour is going to change forever as a "mystique" to the profit-maximizing demand of the market. Bucky has developed certain understanding of the extent to which his image has been commodified, and so when Globke comes to his Great-Jones-Street apartment and asks him what reply he is going to make to the rumors concerning his hiding place, Bucky grants Globke full liberty in making up whatever the latter likes. "Whatever you write will be true. I'll confirm every word." (21) Obviously, Bucky is keenly perceptive of the harsh reality that his subjectivity, either its inner essence or outer appearance, has to be processed by the market and cannot originate from his "authentic self".

To a certain degree, Bucky Wunderlick, as a pop music star, suffers some double de-legitimatization of his subjectivity, or to put it another way, Bucky feels from the depth of his heart the disintegration of his subjectivity just as David Bell does and besides, he does not even have the weakest possible control of the shaping job of his subjectivity's outer contour. What causes Bucky to endure more pains at the loss of his life-value is the market, whose running mechanism is symbolized by DeLillo's description of how Globke looks like. As Matthew Luter suggests, from the very moment when Globke debuts in the novel, DeLillo describes him as a human exemplar of "artificiality"—"his synthetic clothing and all-consuming impulse toward monetary profit" (Luter, 2012: 19). "Artificiality" is part of Globke's personality too, which is evidenced by "his synthetic clothing". In the novel, Globke plays his role of a peeping hole, through which the market's unconstrained power of synthesizing a subjectivity's outer appearance could be clearly seen. The market can, at its own free will, choose from its bounteous source of components the ones it needs to frame up a subjectivity that could best suit its monetary interests. Anthony DeCurtis, one of DeLillo's canonical critics, calls this running mechanism of the market "consumer ethos", which, in his regard, is universal and so fully embodied in the text of *Great Jones Street*:

> What DeLillo depicts in *Great Jones Street* is a society in which there are no meaningful alternatives, in which everyone and everything is bound in the

cash nexus and the exchange of commodities, outside of which there stands nothing. Everything is consumed, or it consumes itself: murder or suicide, exploitation or self-destruction. (DeCurtis, 1991b: 140)

"Outside of which there stands nothing" is DeCurtis's way of saying what DeLillo tries to thematize in *Great Jones Street*—that one's subjectivity has been kidnapped by the market-ruled consumerism, whose intrusion into the deepest recess of private life cannot be resisted even by means of retirement or withdrawal.

If consumerism works as a power engine that energizes the running mechanism of an image culture, technology is an inexhaustible source of fuel that replenishes the tank of the power engine. As a close observer and critic of postmodern America, Don DeLillo throws into relief what a role technology plays in giving rise to an absurd interaction between subject and object in his National-Book-Award winner—*White Noise*. "A thoroughly postmodern, dehistoricized America" (Duvall, 2008: 7) in *White Noise* is an ideal breeding ground for the interactional absurdity whose nature could be at least partly revealed by Bran Nicol's delineation of the *White-Noise*-represented world as one that is increasingly "divorced from the real as a result of the persuasive power of technology and systems of representation" (Nicol, 2009: 184). "Systems of representation" is just another way of calling American media, which is one of the products of the unparalleled technological advancement in postmodern America and therefore is the main contributor to the high-pace increase of technology's "persuasive power". More importantly, what technology "persuades" postmodern Americans to believe is that technology, though human-made itself, should decide what a subject sees or perceives as truth, and so, he should be contented to abandon all his initiatives in cognizing the world. The great absurdity in the interaction between subject and object is thus caused, which, in every sense, amounts to a zero interaction, or in other words, is an insurmountable barrier erected between subject and object. Doubtlessly, such an absurdity is symptomatic of a de-legitimatized subjectivity.

Technology assures the postmodern subjects of the necessity of giving in their active role in observing and understanding the world by convincing them of "the truth" that it is technology that constructs their selfhoods. In *White Noise*, after the social unrest caused by the "airborne toxic event" quiets down a bit, the government dispatches a team of technicians to test the health conditions of those residents in the affected area. Jack Gladney, the hero of the novel, is unfortunately among the most exposed and he narrates in first person the testing procedure. The technicians use a complex computer network installed with a grand-scale data-base to check the degree of the victims' exposure to the poisonous emissions and their chances for survival. The computers know everything about a person after he has been victimized by the "toxic event". The technicians punch in the name and the information "comes back pulsing stars and you are the sum total of your data" (141). It could be inferred from the scene DeLillo's understanding of technology's basic logic that since it can determine the very composition of subjectivity and make it no more than a "sum total of data", any subject should do nothing else but agree in all sincerity to give in their right of perceiving the objective on their own, or they should succumb to accepting the fact that technology has nullified the two-way interaction between the subject and the object and the subject has no alternative but to perceive the world and their selves through a "lens" that modern technology offers them.

The first technological category that Don DeLillo mocks at is photography, which he represents by one of his best plot designs in *White Noise*. Once upon a time before the "airborne toxic event" breaks out in the vicinity of their neighborhood, Jack Gladney is invited by Murray Jay Siskind, one of his colleagues in College-on-the-Hill, to go on a trip to "tourist attraction known as the most photographed barn in America" (12). Standing with Jack before the barn, Murray, on behalf of his creator Don DeLillo and his fellow Americans, makes an incisive comment on what photography and other image-producing technologies can do to the human cognizance of the world:

> What was the barn like before it was photographed? What did it look like, how was it different from other barns, how was it similar to other

> barns? We can't answer these questions because we've read the signs, seen the people snapping the pictures. We can't get outside the aura. We're part of the aura. We're here, we're now. (13)

The photos taken of the barn are "the signs", which, once watched, would cut off the immediate ties between the subject and the object, throwing the former into a status of life in which one's concept of reality is invalidated or in Jean Baudrillard's terms, the boundary between reality and its representation is blurred. "The signs" are what Baudrillard tends to call "simulacra" and he holds that there are three "orders of simulacra". Judging by Murray's elaboration on the "barn-and-photo" relationship, Baudrillard would agree that his and Jack Gladney's America has made its way up to the third order:

> In the third order of simulacra, which is associated with the postmodern age, we are confronted with a precession of simulacra; that is, the representation precedes and determines the real. There is no longer any distinction between reality and its representation; there is only the simulacrum. (Felluga, 2012)

In postmodern America, Jack-and-Murray-like Americans cannot, in any way, gain access to the real since it has been preempted or "preceded" by simulacra, which, as Baudrillard argues on another occasion, constitute a new reality—hyperreality that is even more real than the real. (Baudrillard, 1983: 133) Hyperreality brings forth some apocalyptic damage on a subject's active cognition of the world, as Murray tells Jack that they are no longer in a position to tell the differences or the similarities between the photographed barn and other real barns. Fredric Jameson calls this postmodern symptom "a new kind of depthlessness" in contemporary subjectivity. (Olster, 2011: 80) To a great extent, the "depthlessness" means no more than a thorough de-legitimatization of the subjectivity. Besides, Murray's conclusive statement—"We are here, we are now"—resonates with Jameson's diagnosis of the second pathological symptom of a subjectivity in the postmodern conditions—a crisis in historicity, as he argues that "late capitalism has created a 'perpetual present' where time is dominated by the free-floating rhythms of the new electronic media" (Nicol, 2009: 10). The "perpetual present" de-historicizes the subjectivity so as to despoil it of both its past and future, or to put it another way, make it a history-free shell, both empty and useless.

Hampered by a depthless, de-historicized and thus fake subjectivity, American subjects cannot fulfill normal perception of what is outside them without recourse to hyperreality, both constituted and controlled by the image-saturated media. Even Jack Gladney's kids are of no exception in this respect. Heinrich, Jack's 14-year-old son, engages himself in a talk with his father on his way to school after his days of a sick leave are over:

> "It is going to rain tonight."
>
> "It's raining now," I said.
>
> "The radio said tonight." ...
>
> "Look at the windshield," I said. "Is that rain or isn't it?"
>
> "I'm only telling you what they said." (22 –23)

The mediatization of Heinrich's cognitive schemata opens up a gaping hole between his self and reality, whose width is so unbridgeable that hyperreality has hardened an individual's will to deny the truthfulness of a reality as visible and touchable as rain. The design of the plot helps Don DeLillo warn that the postmodern conditions, as an advanced stage of secularization, will aggravate its destruction of subjectivity, if not curbed by any proper means. In another tell-tale episode that occurs after the "airborne toxic event", Jack and his wife Babette disagree upon whether their daughters have truly developed certain symptoms of an "airborne-toxic-event"-caused disease:

> "So the girls can't hear. They haven't got beyond déjá vu. I want to keep it that way."
>
> "What if the symptoms are real?"
>
> "How could they be real?"

> "Why couldn't they be real?"
>
> "They get them only when they are broadcast," she whispered. (133)

It can be seen in the man-to-wife dialogue that Babette does not intend to do any more self-deception as she, than her husband, is more frank about what havoc mediatization could wreak with their and their daughters' inborn right to determine how their own health and surroundings should be looked at and understood. Nevertheless, neither Babette nor Jack can do anything to change the harsh fact that the media can even decide whether they think they are ill or not.

With their de-legitimatized subjectivity, Jack and Babette can feel nothing but a great fear of death that goes worse day after day. "Who will die first" becomes a heated subject they cannot avoid talking of in their quotidian life. Exposure in the "airborne toxic event" makes Jack's fear of death escalate into so full a scale that he pushes Babette to confide in him where to obtain "Dylar", supposedly a death-fear-killing capsule, only to learn that to get herself some capsules of "Dylar", Babette has an affair with its producer Mink and so, cuckolds her husband. That Jack is cuckolded by his wife Babette and Mink can be a metaphor DeLillo works out for the truth that in the postmodern conditions, one's subjectivity or meaning of life has been cuckolded by the technology-fueled mediatization.

No caged bird would feel content to live with shackles and fetters with no resistance, which is true to most of the DeLillo characters. Mired deep in a cultural milieu that takes a great toll on the legitimacy of an American subjectivity, some of them dream of and work towards killing off their dread at the loss of their meaning of life by practicing either a nostalgic regression to modernity[30]—a rock-solid belief in reason and its promise of leading one straight to logos—or modernism—a reaction Western arts make to the advent of

---

㉚ For a detailed explanation of the term's contextual meaning, please see Note 8.

modernity, which, they believe, can help them all regain stability and wholeness of their subjectivity and so issue out a legitimate claim for their value of life again. The somewhat backward recourse to modernity and modernism, the earlier developmental stages of the secular society and its culture, can do nothing else but to "repress"—as William Connolly has claimed—the pressing truth that the postmodern culture, a higher stage of the secularity's development, has intruded into and will keep encroaching on the once sacred terrain of subjectivity, making the DeLillo characters' compulsive return to modernity or modernism some feeble and futile self-repression or at its best, self-deception.

In *End Zone*, Gary Harkness' flaming desire for redemption from the de-legitimatization of his life-value is ignited by an accident in a college-football-league game, in which, Gary, with some other teammates of his, crushes one of their opponents underneath their heavy and muscular bodies, resulting in the player's tragic death. Harassed much by a strong sense of guilt, Gary cannot endure the sheer randomness and vulnerability of life any more, both of which he has just witnessed and experienced in this sporting accident. Upon profound meditation, Gary Harkness decides to rely on logos to fulfill his self-redeeming ambition, because as for him, singularity, wholeness and permanence of logos can function precisely as an antidote to the pathological de-legitimatization of his subjectivity in the postmodern conditions, and so can force his consciousness of his imminent death, which looms large in his heart after his opponent's death, to fall into oblivion, at least for the time being.

Gary's choice of retreating to study at and play college football for Logos College, which is remote from postmodern American civilization and situated in the Texas desert, is a maneuver highly symbolic of his hardened determination to grip a saving hand from logos. As its name suggests, Logos College lays its very foundation on one and easy principle—logos, which comforts Gary a lot and is at least partly the reason why he drops off from other prestigious colleges and comes to play for the College. The College's rocky belief in logos is crystallized in Tom Wade, its founder, who "built it out of nothing. He had an idea and he followed it through to the end. He believed in reason. He was a man of reason. He cherished the very word" (6). Logos is therefore chosen by the founder to name his college.

Wade the founder, does set a tradition for the College that none of his followers seem to fail, among whom, Emmett Creed, the head coach of the College's football team, obviously exerts the profoundest impact upon Gary Harkness and so affords him great logos-fed consolation. Mr. Creed has entertained in his bosom no other "creed" than reason. He is adored by Gary and all his fellow players for his fame "for creating order out of chaos" (8) and it is him who sets logos as the very basis on which the team-building job proceeds. To Coach Creed, the team's progress in strength relies on whether he is able "to instill a sense of unity" (8) in his players. Emmett Creed's deep conviction in the omnipotence of logos shapes American football in a way that pleases Gary a lot. Under Creed's instructions, Gary loves to see the end zone on the football pitch as a terrain of finality, in which reason domineers and helps set the Gary-like Americans off on a "right" track to rebuild his subjectivity. Gary Harkness stresses what he intends to obtain from playing football as he says, "It was important to come upon something that could be defined in one sense only, something not probable or variable, a thing unalterably itself." (69) Football, metaphorical for the end zone of his life, is "something that could be defined in one sense only", which is not "variable" or "alterable". The American football, in Gary's eyes, can help him rebuild his selfhood in the way that its "ideal" state can be achieved because:

> Football players are simple folk. Whatever complexities, whatever dark politics of the human mind, the heart—these are noted only within the chalked borders of the playing field. At times strange visions ripple across that turf; madness leaks out. But wherever else he goes, the football player travels the straightest of lines. His thoughts are wholesomely commonplace, his actions uncomplicated by history, enigma, holocaust or dream. (4)

Gary accepts his football as a logos-informed sport that can dissolve all the "complexities" or "dark politics" within "the chalked borders of the playing field". As a result, a player, upon leaving the field, would necessarily re-frame his subjectivity to make it "wholesome", "commonplace" and "uncomplicated", since it has been re-outlined with "the straightest of lines". Gary Harkness's illusion about a logos-informed subjectivity is largely fed by the American football, which does not work so well if Gary's unique perception of the English language does not come to its assistance. Besides playing American football to rebuild an integrated self, Gary Harkness works hard to eliminate the arbitrariness of the English language and coaxes himself into accepting a belief that to endow language with a meaning that is in all time singular and stable by establishing a one-to-one correspondence between a signifier and its signified is to assert a similar self just as singular and stable as his "re-constructed" language is.

To fulfill his "re-construction" of language and "re-constitution" of his "new" self, Gary chooses to work extra hours with Major Stanley, his teacher and friend, who teaches him an optional course called "Aspects of Modern Wars". What fascinates Gary the most about the course is that Major Stanley can, with almost no variation, teach all his lessons with a fixed set of terms, which, is able to affirm Gary's conviction that an arbitrariness-free language can be produced. Among all the terms he's learned from Major Stanley, those about the nuclear war count as the most attractive to Gary, about which he does not even try to deny:

> I became fascinated by words and phrases like thermal hurricane, overkill, circular error probability, post-attack environment, stark deterrence, dose-rate contours, kill-ratio, spasm war. Pleasure in these words. ... A thrill almost sensual accompanied the reading of this book. (21)

Beyond any doubt, Gary's "pleasure in these words" is all caused by his understanding of them as some constituents of another American-football-like end zone, or as Tom LeClair comments, "a finality for the language game" (LeClair, 1987b: 118), in which all the destabilizing factors in language and his subjectivity construction are presumed to be ended. In a word, Gary feels an "almost sensual thrill" upon the alleged fulfillment of a dream Derrida calls "an end to play" (LeClair, 1987b: 118), the "play" that is so random and irrational as to deconstruct or de-legitimatize one's subjectivity.

American football and the English language, the two saving hands of modernity㉛ that Gary Harkness holds on to resist the de-legitimization of his subjectivity, do him no good other than to objectify his subjectivity by sheer reason and so, cause him to hallucinate about a uniform and stable subjectivity, which, of course, is an illusion Don DeLillo would soon crack.

The modernization or rationalization of Western civilization can be abstracted as a process of logocentrism tightening its grip of the human minds, lying at whose root is a basic logic of binary opposition. Ever since logocentrism gains momentum after the Enlightenment, binary opposition has shot off its ramifications into various fields of human civilization. For example, secularism, either in its epistemological or social sense, establishes itself by following the logic of binary opposition—reason vs. faith or "the secular" vs. "the religious". Analogous to secularism in its logic foundation, Cold War Mentality, a phantasmal presence whose origin rests in a policy of containment the American government enforced during the Cold War against the Soviet Union, cannot linger and still take a strong hold on American minds without its obsessive persistence in a "Us vs. Them" logic, which by itself is a political derivative of binary opposition and origin of all antagonistic bilateral relations

---

㉛ Modernity, here in this very paragraph, refers to an alleged "ultimate truth" an American mind as rationalized and secularized as Gary Harkness's is obsessed with. The "ultimate truth" means exactly what the term logos is intended to mean in the book—a basic and irreducible truth about a god-free world of materiality or physicality, which, to Gary Harkness, if accessed with sheer reason, can endow him with an unchanging and singular subjectivity or meaning of life. Also, in his very eyes, "football and language", if "reconstructed" in a way he sees fit, will become two most handy epitomes of reason in his personal life, and so, can offer him such an "access" to "the ultimate truth" and it, in return, can help singularize and stabilize his self, which is to explain why he is so preoccupied with the two.

between members in the international community. Bred out of a common logic, secularism and the Cold War Mentality, both of which are subservient to logos, execute logocentrism with no remorse and as a result, both stick to an ideal that one of the two opposites must assume a role of dominance over the other. Secularism evicts the religious from off the boundaries of public consciousness and settles reason down in a ruling position to keep running the secular life of mankind. With the Cold War Mentality, the American government and its people take for granted a "truth" that the justice of their cause is self-evident and all other causes, especially one as un-American as the Soviet Union's, must be evil and need to be annihilated or at least contained.

However, many of the characters in Delillo's fictional world assume that the Cold War Mentality, or to be more exact, the logic of binary opposition that it entails, could "help" accomplish their ideal about a singular, stable and unified self. Sister Edgar, the heroine of the Epilogue of *Underworld*, is an obstinate follower of the Cold War logic and pushes its limits to the farthest possible point at which she assumes that the wholeness of her subjectivity is retrieved and her life-value regained, but on the contrary, it turns out that what she achieves is nothing but her pathological obsession with a logic, which is supposedly conducive to the uniformity and stability of a subjectivity, but in fact both unfulfillable and non-redemptive.

Sister Edgar is an aged nun, who is committed to charitable work of poverty-relief with younger Sister Gracie in the Bronx. Edgar and Gracie work hard to fund their purchase and distribution of foods for the destitute residents of the Bronx by offering to Ismael Munoz and his city graffitists the information they have garnered about the deserted cars that are scattered almost everywhere in the district. Don DeLillo sets all his plot designs and characterizations of the story against the historical background of the 1990s, which witnessed USSR's collapse and the end of the Cold War, and so, it is understandable that DeLillo should talk of Sister Edgar's close relationship with the Cold War by saying, "Edgar was a cold-war nun who'd once lined the walls of her room with Reynolds Wrap as a safeguard against nuclear fallout." (245) Sister Edgar's "self-preservation" technique betrays her age, about which it could at least be speculated that Edgar must have been already an adult when the "Cold" military competition between the two superpowers was most likely to turn "hot". It is indisputable that all fear and earnest desire for precautionary means against USSR nuclear attacks originate in the "Us vs. Them" logic. Martin Buber (1878—1965), an Austria-born Israeli philosopher, when commenting on the Cold War in a 1952 speech delivered in New York, theorizes as follows: "The human world is today, as never before, split into two camps, each of which regards the other as the embodiment of falsehood and itself as the embodiment of truth." (qtd. in Freidman, 1988: 303) The clear-cut logic of "falsehood vs. truth" helps the Cold-War-era America draw the portrayal of its Soviet enemy and justify its foreign policy of containment, which exerts profound impact on American people's mindset both during and after the Cold War, which is exemplified by Sister Edgar's Cold War personality. It is George Frost Kennan (1904—2005), an American diplomat, who 70 years ago first brought forward the Containment in a written document as a probable strategy against the Soviet threats. Dispatched as a charge d'affaires to the American embassy at Moscow, Kennan, upon the request of American State Department, gave an account of how he viewed the USSR as a nation and what tactics the USA should adopt in addressing its diplomatic ties with the country by sending the State Department an 8,000-word-long telegram. Based on his presumption that "the Soviet Union will never reach any compromise or agreement with its opponent" (qtd. in Liu, 1993: 55), Kennan refutes any advice about achieving a peaceful coexistence between the two superpowers and thus places all his emphasis on the policy of containment that would be adopted in dealing with America's largest "Them" camp on the earth. The Containment is by and large a political and military derivative of the Cold War Mentality, whose ideological importance, should not be underestimated either.

In fact, a close reading of Kennan's long telegram will manifest his stronger propensity to exercise the policy of containment on shaping the American ideology in such a way that "the greatest risk we all face" can be averted so that "we should not allow ourselves to become just like our opponents". (qtd. in Liu, 1993: 66) In order not to "become just like our opponents", the USA must spare no effort in keeping its own "spirit" and "morale", on which George F. Kennan elucidates: "Any resolute and effective measure that can solve the problems of our own society and strengthen our people's confidence, discipline, morale and collective spirit should be counted as a diplomatic victory against Moscow, whose value could amount to one thousand of diplomatic notes and joint communiqués." (qtd. in Liu, 1993: 65) According to Kennan, to "keep" is to "strengthen", and what needs strengthening, first of all, is American people's "discipline". It follows that Kennan's policy of containment is aimed at re-charting the USA's cultural or ideological map so as to establish the American-style liberty and democracy as a uniform and unchallengeable character that all American nationals should develop in themselves. Protected by the "well-defined and stable" subjectivity, American people can stand at a safe distance from the Other, by which Kennan, his peers and also his superiors in the American government can fulfill their task of alienating, demonizing and antagonizing the USSR. Catering to contemporary American governmental authority's identification of the Soviet Union as its arch-rival, Kennan's dualism-based strategy of containment has determined to a great extent the general route by which postwar American foreign policy, culture and ideology should develop. Even today, about 30 years after the USSR's dissolution, the Cold War Mentality, with "antagonism" and "containment" as its two key words, still functions a lot in the American realms of politics and culture. To throw more light on the probable effects upon American people, Martin Buber propounds the term "existential mistrust". In his representative work *I and Thou* (1970), he argues that the logos-centered secularism empties the human minds of any reliance on the spiritual and so causes in them "existential mistrust" in not only their own value of life but also that of all the "others" different from themselves. (Buber, 1970: 33) It could be inferred from what Buber speaks of "the existential mistrust" that the Cold War Mentality that the USA has applied to itself for more than half a century should be held culpable of the increasingly deepened "mistrust" in the American minds, which, has made American life impossible without a so-called "paranoid narrative" as Patrick O'Donnell has argued. O'Donnell believes that the break-up of the Soviet Union does not alleviate American people's mistrust in and fear of the Other; on the contrary, they continue to rely on the paranoid narratives in their attempts to rewrite their history in a way that lends order to chaos. (O'Donnell, 2000: 46) Implied in O'Donnell's observation on "the paranoid narrative" is the logic by which American people adopt their mistrust in and fear of the Other to align themselves in a national subjectivity, unitary, whole and stable, that can help them overcome their fear or paranoia. However, Don DeLillo knows better that to transform a disintegrated subjectivity to an integrated and orderly one by some "paranoid narrative" is nothing but another hallucination, in which Sister Edgar has been for a long time submerged and in the meantime groping her way out.

The "paranoid narrative" that Sister Edgar is living with is represented by DeLillo's comic-strip-like depiction of her mysophobia. After getting off bed in the morning, Sister Edgar washes her hands like practicing a ritual as important as her morning prayer:

> At the sink she scrubbed her hands repeatedly with coarse brown soap. How can the hands be clean if the soap is not? This question was insistent in her life. But if you clean the soap with bleach, what do you clean the bleach bottle with? If you use scouring powder on the bleach bottle, how do you clean the box of Ajax? Germs have personalities. Different objects harbor threats of various insidious types. And the questions turn inward forever. (237 -238)

Sister Edgar's insatiable desire for a germ-free life works as a metaphor for Americans' hard determination to insulate themselves from all un-American others. Or, in other words, Americans must wrap themselves up tight as Sister Edgar does so as not to "become just like them". Sister Edgar's mysophobia is also reflected in her pursuit of a "germ-free" use of the English language. Born into minor ethnical groups, Ismael Munoz-led graffitists speak "unclean" English, which, just like germs, exacerbates Edgar's discomfort. "They spoke an unfinished English, soft and muffled, insufficiently suffixed, and she wanted to drum some hard g's into the ends of their gerunds." (243) Her pathological fear lowers down Sister Edgar's tolerance of any objects that cannot meet American standards, especially the language use. If non-American elements should be mixed into standard American English, her defense of the demarcation line between what's American and what's not will be broken through, which is sure to increase, by a large margin, Sister Edgar's fear. In addition, the reason why Sister Edgar should abandon the corporal punishment she has committed herself to in disciplining her students can also epitomize the exclusive-of-all-others logic of American paranoid narrative: "Edgar stopped hitting children when the neighborhood changed and the faces of her students became darker. All the righteous fury went out of her soul. How could she strike a child who was not like her?" (238) The "paranoid narrative" has convinced Sister Edgar that American educational tool of discipline should be wielded to and only to the benefits of American students like Sister Edgar herself, white, probably Anglo-Saxon and Protestant, but not to the others, non-white, Spanish-speaking and possibly Catholic. So it could be concluded that Sister Edgar's "righteous fury" is dispelled as a result of her condescending gesture towards the Other; and the "fury" is something that she is more than contented to let go as she is much encouraged by an all-exclusive uniform and stable American subjectivity.

The "paranoid narrative" consolidates the wholesomeness of a unifying American subjectivity; nonetheless, no matter how much temporary and illusive comfort it could offer Sister Edgar and her fellow Americans, it cannot work as a crane that lifts the American subjects from their abyss of meaningless life, about which Don DeLillo will reveal by his design of a heartbreaking plot in the latter part of the story.

As an American subject who lives in the postmodern conditions, both Gary Harkness and Sister Edgar rest all their hope for reconstructing a none-postmodern subjectivity on their active slip back to the logos-centered modernity, which, as they might have expected, can help them regain a singular, whole and stable subjectivity. Different in profession from both the two characters, Bucky Wunderlick, a high-fame rock-and-roll singer, searches in his own domain for a measure that can ensure the wholeness or integrity of his subjectivity, and what he manages to obtain to redeem his meaning of life is his modernist rock-and-roll music. The distinctive character of Bucky's subjectivity-reconstruction means is reflective of how deeply, Don DeLillo, an artist himself, is concerned with a young artist's hard but fruitless struggle in a postmodern and subjectivity-unfriendly culture.

Like other practitioners of modernist arts, Bucky Wunderlick asserts his right to shape his own subjectivity by cutting off all the physical contact between himself and the market that usurps his right to form his own selfhood. He completes his cut-off job by his voluntary retreat to his confining Great-Jones-Street apartment, a perfect retreat in his own regard. As for Opel Hampson, Bucky's lover, Great Jones Street that lies in the wastes of New York City's Lower East Side is the very proof of his retreat's perfection as she comments, "Great Jones Street, Bond Street, the Bowery. These places are deserts too, just as beautiful and scary as a matter of fact, except too cold for some people." (90) The desert-like Great Jones Street is such an insular environment, in which Bucky can be fully engrossed on composing a kind of rock music, faithful to his own selfhood whereas irrespective of any market requests upon the formation of his stardom. Bucky's odd admiration for the Micklewhite Boy, one of his neighbors, is also an indicator of his obsessive chase after an "object-free" and "true-to-self" form of art. The Micklewhite Boy has been for years wheelchair-ridden by a disease, rare and indefinable. More than that, the boy cannot move or speak, and so, in most of his neighbors' eyes, he is no better than a walking dead whose fat body bloats as time passes by. However, Bucky Wunderlick grows more and more infatuated with the boy instead of placing on this wretched creature any due pity. To Bucky, he is attracted to the Micklewhite boy because he lives as a full embodiment of "what we'd always feared, ourselves in radical divestment" (161). Bucky is also "drawn into what I felt was his ascendancy, the helpless strength of his entrapment in tepid flesh, in the reductions of being" (161). As for Bucky, the "radical divestment" that normal people should fear is precisely what an artist like him should cherish with heart and soul, since what should be divested off him is all the intrusive elements that the market forces into his subjectivity. In this sense, Bucky should have assumed that the Micklewhite Boy's life, as an exemplar of "the reductions of being", is a living symbol of a status of life Bucky craves for, in which a complete "wordlessness", or in his case, a musical type that is despoiled of any discipline, form and content, can assure him of a chance to escape from commodification and recompose a new self at his own will.

As a matter of fact, to master commerce, some time before his retreat to Great Jones Street, Bucky Wunderlick has already put his artistic ideal into practice. During a vocation he spends in a mountainous area, Bucky finishes a set of recordings that have never been released and known only as "the mountain tapes". These tapes are a musical counterpart to the Micklewhite Boy because the music in them is almost as "wordless" as the boy is, except for one single lyrical line "pee-pee-maw-maw". The mechanical repetition of "pee-pee-maw-maw" in the tapes is "unperformable" on stage, and Bucky is not worried even if the tapes should be at last grabbed away from him since they are just too true to his selfhood to be released to the market. As a result, Bucky believes that the wordless music in the tapes that helps him "achieve maximum expressive power through minimalist lyrical material" (Luter, 2012: 16) can enable him to regain his right of shaping his subjectivity without American commercialism meddling in a business he regards as completely his own. About his self-reconstruction project, Bucky announces with much confidence: "I had centered myself, learning of the existence of an interior motion, a shift in levels from isolation to solitude to wordlessness to immobility." (85–86) The "shift in levels" is the measure Bucky takes to orchestrate his music to follow his own free will, and through doing so could he feel on top of the world again, as he claims later: "The artist sits still, finally, because the materials he deals with begin to shape his life, instead of being shaped, and in stillness he seeks a form of self-defense." (126)

Bucky Wunderlick assumes that his rock-and-roll music can defend his subjectivity as a stronghold that can withstand the attacks from the market. However, as will be narrated in the end of the story, the seemingly unbreakable line of defense Bucky sets up between his so-called integrated self and the market turns out to be no less flimsy that it is before, when the market pulls itself up and launches against him a new round of attack.

Gary Harkness, Sister Edgar and Bucky Wunderlick do all they can to earn their full initiatives in reconstructing their subjectivities by "repressing" the basically irresistible impact on their selfhoods the postmodern conditions have exerted. Gary Harkness and Sister Edgar fulfill their "repression" of their postmodernized selves by means of their headlong reversion to modernity that is supposed to unify and stabilize their once splintered subjectivities, whereas Bucky, an artist who is standing in the vanguard of American popular culture, commits himself to an unexpected retreat at the peak of his fame and allows his rock-and-roll music to relapse into a market-unfriendly variety of the modernist arts in the hope that his determination to cut the ties between subject and object could entitle him to an utterly self-made subjectivity. These three characters' common practice of rebuilding "an authentic self" through repressing the encroaching force of the postmodern culture distinguishes them all from David Bell, Don DeLillo's first full-length-novel hero, who dares to confront the postmodern culture and engage it in constructing his selfhood, which is not diametrically different in nature from the ideal one Gary, Edgar and Bucky all try so hard to rebuild.

David's desire for self-redemption can suggest how resolute he is in rebuilding his "authentic" selfhood: "The city was full of people searching for the man or woman who would save them." (110) As one among the "people" waiting to be saved, David chooses from all the resources available to a TV network executive, film, though part of the image culture as TV is, as his measure to re-assert his real self. Having asked for a long leave on the excuse of filming a documentary on the Navajos' life, David Bell invites some of his best friends and recruits two or three acting professionals, and with them, starts off a West-bound journey to make a film on his personal history. According to Fredric Jameson's trenchant criticism, the postmodern society in which David Bell is stranded is "bereft of all historicity, and the past as 'referent' finds itself gradually bracketed, and then effaced altogether, leaving us with nothing but texts" (Jameson, 2005: 18). As for David-like American individuals, despoiled of "historicity" or "the past as 'referent'", they can not even launch off their reconstruction of subjectivity when it is still dehistoricized, flat and depthless. It could be thus inferred that David Bell's film-making endeavor in his westward pilgrimage is the very first step he takes, as Mark Osteen has observed, in his "quest for stable identity and perfect originality" (Osteen, 2000a: 8-9). Osteen also agrees that "In *Americana* DeLillo provides multiple frames for his protagonist's quest, and the most powerful of which is film history" (Osteen, 2000a: 8-9). In his critical essay on *Americana*, Randy Laist argues that certain qualities peculiar to film tell the distinction between itself and TV, and it is the distinction that compels David to choose the former as his measure for self-redemption. On the distinction, Laist elaborates as follows:

> Television is infected with the numbness of everyday life, of intangible signals in a kind of time that has no memory, and of the fusion of consciousness with a piece of furniture. Movies, however, seem larger than life, they have a kind of physical existence, and they persist in collective and personal memory. (Laist, 2008: 56)

The "physical existence" of a movie that helps it "persist in collective and personal memory" is, in David's regard, an ideal tool with which he could recover the historicity in his subjectivity, and meanwhile, to be "larger than life" can also quench his thirst for transcending the physical limits of his mortal life. Since his early boyhood, David Bell has developed a vague awareness of film's salvific power:

> When I was a teenager I saw Burt in *From Here to Eternity*. He stood above Deborah Kerr on that Hawaiian beach and for the first time in my life I felt the true power of the image. Burt was like a city in which we are all living. He was that big. Within the conflux of shadow and time, there was room for all of us that I knew I must extend myself until the molecules parted and I was spliced into the image. Burt in the moonlight was a crescendo of male perfection but no less human because of it. Burt lives! I carry that image to this day, and so, I believe, do millions of others, men and women, for their separate reasons. Burt in the moonlight. It was a concept; it was the icon of a new religion. (12 –13)

Burt Lancaster, a Hollywood superstar, is the first movie image, from which, in David Bell's inexperienced eyes, emanates "a new religion"—like power of redemption or "the true power of the image". David's unconditional readiness to be "spliced into the image" and "carry the image to this day" betrays his will to reach a somewhat compromise between his selfhood and the image culture—an indispensable component of postmodern America—and so, is suggestive of a posture of "engagement" with the postmodern conditions that he will take to reconstruct his subjectivity.

As his creator Don DeLillo has claimed in an interview with Tom LeClair: "Probably the movies of Jean-Luc Godard had a more immediate effect on my early work than anything I'd ever read" (qtd. in LeClair, McCaffery, 1983: 15) David Bell admits that he is a "child of Godard and Coca-Cola" (269), which is a witty transmutation of Godard's famous description of his characters in *Masculin Feminin* as "children of Marx and Coca-Cola". David's proclamation of his indebtedness to Godard, a French-Swiss movie director identified with the 1960s French film movement "New Wave", can suggest that his "engagement" with the postmodern conditions is not only a simple selection of film as some scaffolding upon which the rebuilding process of his subjectivity could be started off, but also a self-willed implementation of the postmodern movie-making techniques that could at last complete the entire process, play his full originality and thus, rebuild his selfhood. Among those New-Wave movie-making techniques, David Bell gives his special favor to parody and self-reference and applies them both to the filming of his autobiographical documentary. The mother-and-son relationship is a key constituent of his personal history that David Bell tries hard to reminiscence and review in his documentary. To better delineate the image his late mother has left on his mind, David does not choose to arrange in his movie any realistic filming of the basic facts about her; instead, he takes from Jean-Luc Godard the technique of parody to modify his memory of the mother in a reasonably creative way. In the film, having known that she is going to die soon of cancer, David's mother, the role played by Sullivan, David's best friend, is gently swaying on a swing, wistfully reminiscing about all the things past. David Cowart, another of Don DeLillo's canonical critics, is so observant and resourceful as to recognize that to design the scene, David imitates a well-known scene in Akira Kurosawa's 1952 production of *Ikiru*, in which, an aged and dying cancer patient Watanabe sways on a swing in a park, meditating on his soon-to-end life, while snow is drifting in the wind. It is undeniable that David's choice of parody in developing before himself a mental picture of the deceased is an indicator of his determination to achieve certain originality in the movie-making process, which, in his regard, could help renovate his worn-out subjectivity. Besides, at both the start and the end of the documentary, David, in filming "David's" two personal statements, makes a skillful use of self-reference, another New-Wave technique. David the Director assigns the role of David to Austin Wakely, an actor. "David" speaks all his lines before a mirror, which reflects "David", the operating camera and real David who is running the camera. A repeated use of self-reference in David's documentary works as a reminder to the director that he has to distance himself from the movie images in case that he should lose his "authentic self" again in this subjectivity-rebuilding process that is still very much dependent on the chosen images; and these images, if not cautioned against, will exert some insidious impact on his assertion of full originality.

No matter what innovations he could manage to accomplish in the making of his autobiographical documentary, David Bell, as has been suggested in his resort to self-reference twice in the movie, cannot proceed in his quest of an "authentic self" without any misgivings about his ability to "violate the endless circuit of the signifying chain" (Cowart, 2003: 133) of images, which in all probabilities might cause "complexity, or even impossibility, of determining the truly authentic subject" (Cowart, 2003: 133). David Bell's continuation of his westward journey upon the completion of the documentary, his resignation from the TV network and final settlement on an isolated island can at least in part prove that his ideal for an authentic subjectivity has never come true.

All of the four characters aforementioned, David Bell, Gary Harkness, Bucky Wunderlick and Sister Edgar, have been attempting to reform their subjectivity and render it wholesome and stable again within the dimension of the reasonable. Neither "repression", a blunt defiance of the postmodern condition with recourse to either modernity or modernism, nor "engagement", a creative use of some applicable techniques bred out of the postmodern conditions, has transcended reason's bounds that have delimited their secular life. So, as Don DeLillo would imply by his arrangement of what at last becomes of Gary, Bucky and David, neither "repression" nor "engagement" can fulfill what they are supposed to fulfill. However, DeLillo, as a novelist who "never abandons hope in life" (Zhu, 2013: 54), cannot refute an argument that those failures in re-establishing their "authentic self" might lead to some deeper crises. Nonetheless, it is the crises that can ignite the flaming hope of breaking free from reason's delimitation and blazing a new trail to certain spirituality that can affirm one's meaning of life, which is exactly what Sister Edgar does to set all his readers an example at the end of *Underworld*.

Gary Harkness, a super college-football-league star, seems to continue his daydream about logos with two supportive forces in his real life—American football and the English language—or to be more exact, the nuclear war jargon he has learned from Major Staley, who teaches him "Aspects of Modern Wars". A closer reading of *End Zone* will make it evident that it is not only American football of itself but also its unique jargon that satiates Gary's desire towards logos to a degree, which, he believes, can help construct an "authentic self" he has since long dreamed about. In an interview, Don DeLillo confirms that language is indeed his first thematic concern in writing *End Zone*: "I began to suspect that language was a subject as well as an instrument in my work" (LeClair, McCaffery, 1983: 81).

As far as Gary is concerned, American football embodies a category of discourse that is so tightly under the control of logos that it can put him on a "right" track to integrate and stabilize his once disintegrated self. Gary's confidence with American football's logos-centered and self-redeeming power originates in what Emmett Creed, his head coach, instructs him about. Creed never even tries to challenge the American football's role of an only legitimate way of expression in his and his players' lives; and so, he opposes strongly when his player should decide to learn another language: "I've never seen a good football player who wanted to learn a foreign language." (163) To him, only one voice should be heard beside the football pitch: "Hit somebody. Hit somebody. Hit somebody." (28) The simple and uniform American-football discourse that Coach Creed personifies and practices, together with all the nuclear war terms Major Staley imparts to him, implants in Gary's young mind several "joyous visions" (223) in which language is no longer arbitrary and can help him rebuild his authentic self, as logos-informed as nuclear war jargon is. Nevertheless, no matter how much "joy" the "visions" can overwhelm Gary with, it is bound to end both quickly and tragically because Gary's deliberate interpretation of language as a bunch of absolute and direct correspondences between the signifiers and their signifieds is no more than a mistaken reduction of its complexity and a spiteful enslavement of it to logos.

Jacques Derrida, in his *Writing and Difference*, has come to realize that there is certain language user who "seeks to decipher, dreams of deciphering a truth or an origin which escapes play and the order of the sign, and which lives the necessity of interpretation as an exile" (Derrida, 1978: 292). Pitiably, Gary Harkness is such a hallucinating "decipherer" as Derrida has pictured, who tends to terminate the actually unstoppable "play" in language, or in other words, establishes language as an entity that subsists on its own and beyond any "interpretation". In doing so, Gary transports himself into his self-made "exile", in which, he fails to fixate his subjectivity in any change-proof and logos-ruled landscape and what's worse, loses his subjectivity with no trace of it remaining. Sometimes plagued by a faint sense of being cheated by logos, Gary feels that his subjectivity is still in flux because logos might be one of "the darker crimes of thought and language" (54). This shallow perception of the "criminal" character of logos throws Gary into a severe predicament in which he even starts to admit that language is a game: "The language game is so to say something unpredictable. I mean, it is not based on grounds. It is not reasonable (or unreasonable). It is there—like our life." (73) The idea that language might be "unpredictable", "groundless" and "unreasonable" compels Gary to be growingly suspicious of whether language is truly reliable in affording his subjectivity certain fixity.

Doubts and misgivings gnaw at him. Even immediately after he talks of nuclear wars with Major Staley in jargon, he can still be bothered by a scene he encounters on his way back to Logos College:

> It was three yards in front of me, excrement, a low mound of it, simple shit, nothing more ... I wanted my senses to deny this experience, leaving it for wind and dust ... shit everywhere, shit in life cycle ... everywhere this whisper of inexistence. (88 -89)

In this surreal plot, "shit" is scattered there by Don DeLillo in a landscape, so much renovated and reformed by reason, as a reminder to both Gary and his readers that "excrement", "inexistence" or unreasonable beings are right there in life, and therefore, logos could be easily invalidated or devastated and cannot offer substantial help to one's self-rebuilding work that can reward him with happiness. Reminded time and again, at the end of the story, Gary still cannot reconcile himself to the harsh truth that logos does not work in building him an ideal self and thus tries to exercise reason to its extreme of controlling his basic physiological need—eating:

> In my room at five o'clock the next morning I drank half a cup of lukewarm water. It was the last of food or drink I would take for many days. High fevers burned a thin straight channel through my brain. In the end they had to carry me to the infirmary and feed me through plastic tubes. (241 – 242)

While his body is going on a voluntary fast, his mind is instead feasting on logos, which can lead him to no place but death.

Artistic modernism stretches out a saving hand to Bucky Wunderlick in the sense that it erects an apparently impenetrable barricade between his self and the intrusive market, which should work as a prerequisite for his successful reconstruction of an unmixed and genuine self as far as Bucky is concerned. Deplorable to Don DeLillo, his creator, is that Bucky cannot recognize even faintly how specious his plan is since his voluntary separation of his self from the postmodern conditions is no better than a willed surrender of his right of subjectivity-construction to the market, or to put it another way, the subjectivity-construction job, which, as Bucky sees it, has been taken back to himself by his self-banishment, is still right under the manipulation of the market.

Happy Valley, a mystic organization, sends its envoy Bohack to pay Bucky a visit, whose acrid criticism of Bucky' withdrawal from public sight is what Don DeLillo intends to say about the market's underhanded while ubiquitous effect upon one's selfhood:

> Demythologizing yourself. Keeping covered. Putting up walls. Stripping off fantasy and legend. Reducing yourself to minimums. Your privacy and isolation are what give us the strength to be ourselves. We were willing victims of your sound. Now we're acolytes of your silence. (194)

Bohack helps DeLillo warn that the marketization of Bucky's stardom is going under way even when he retreats to "privacy and isolation"; and whether he sings and produces any sound on stage or keeps his "silence" back at home, Bucky still submits his image to be consumed by "us". If a reclusive and "silent" style of life is not actual realization of his ambition for modernist music and so cannot help too much in retaining the purity of his self, Bucky Wunderlick still tries to convince himself that the subjectivity-redeeming value of his "mountain tapes" is indisputable, only to realize that his self-deception cannot go too far when the "tapes" are at last "taken". Stolen and delivered to the hands of Globke, Bucky's agent, the "mountain tapes" cannot escape their fate of being released to the market where they are warmly received and thus thousands of copies are sold. The "mountain tapes", as an epitome of Bucky's most cherished originality in his own field of business, are expectedly entrapped in an endless cycle of reproduction again, which comes into being in an age of modernity and is upgraded and accelerated in a postmodern age. On the mechanical reproduction's erosion of originality or authenticity in art, Walter Benjamin has long before given a world-famous remark: "That which withers in the age of mechanical reproduction is the aura of the work of art" as "reproduction detaches the reproduced object from the domain of tradition" (Benjamin, 1969: 221). "Aura" refers to art's originality, which is so sacred as to deserve to be called so in Benjamin's regard. Besides, if mechanically reproduced, "aura" will "wither", which causes an artist's subjectivity to decay as it is consumed or usurped by commercialism. There is no wonder that Bucky should mourn on his loss of "the mountain tapes" by claiming that he would "never be able to reproduce the complex emotional content of those tapes, or remember a single lyric" (164).

An irremediable depression almost kills Bucky Wunderlick as he has been seriously thinking of committing suicide. He abandons the idea because his resolute luster of will is dimmed by Watney, Bucky's English counterpart, who denigrates his suicidal plan as he says to Bucky:

> One's death must be equal to one's power. The OD or assassination ... means little unless it reverberates to the sound of power. The powerful man who achieves a gorgeous death automatically becomes a national hero and saint of all churches. No power, the thing falls flat. Bucky, you have no power. (231 –232)

Watney is so right in saying that Bucky's death would be granted no power to influence any aspect of society in any possible manner because his modernist music and alleged self-centered construction of subjectivity are all going on in a reality-free vacuum, or in other words, a "true-to-self" modernist-art practitioner like Bucky, in lack of realistic concerns, cannot fulfill any subjectivity construction in the true sense of the word as the subjectivity, which Bucky is pursuing in great earnest, is emptied of content, powerless and so cannot even be labeled subjectivity at all.

Both Gyorgy Lukacs and Daniel Bell speak very ill of a modernist artist's assertion of subjectivity. When asked to comment on modernist art, Lukacs chooses to voice his derogatory standpoint on it by criticizing a modernist artist's subjectivity. Lukacs does not think that any creator of modernist art is "a coherent subject", "because they have blocked out any objectivity through which subjectivity can be dialectically realized" (Lukacs, 1995: 147). Bell scolds a modernistic self as one "that had been emptied of content and which masqueraded as being vital through the playacting of Revolution" (Bell, 1976: 144). As the two learned scholars have put across, Bucky Wunderlick cannot acquire any substance in his subjectivity in a process short of a dialectic or reciprocal movement between object and subject. In sum, at his very best, Bucky might destruct a market-shaped self, but he never has worked out any means to build a satisfactory new self.

While commenting on the writing purport of *Americana*, Mark Osteen observes that "DeLillo provides multiple frames for his protagonist's quest for stable identity and perfect originality". However, none of these "frames", "the most powerful of which is film history", end well because they all do nothing more than to "expose this quest as a chimera, and originality as merely the echo of an echo". (Osteen, 2000a: 8 – 9) From Osteen's description of what David Bell accomplishes in his quest for "identity" and "originality" by "chimera" and "the echo of an echo", it follows that David is destined to failure since there is a huge discrepancy between the goal he sets for his "quest" and an "identity" he at last constructs through various means, among which filming a documentary on his personal history is "the most powerful".

The subjectivity David Bell rebuilds through his documentary-making enterprise in his trying westward journey is indeed a "chimera"-like composite, since his movie-making endeavor, though counted as an active posture in which David engages himself with the postmodern conditions, is still an exemplar of "pastiche", an artistic maneuver diagnosed by Fredric Jameson as part of the postmodern culture's "pathological conditions, (for example) schizophrenia, hysteria, nostalgia, paranoia, and a 'waning of effect'" (Nicol, 2009: 9). The New Wave movie techniques—parody and self-reference—both help enhance the "waning of effect" or the deterioration of originality because the former teaches David to borrow and to patch up ready-made fragments from other renowned movies like *Ikiru* so as to make his documentary a decent product of pastiche, whereas the latter, as one of the most often used techniques in the field of postmodern movie-making, is a parody in its own right and so could do him no good other than to reduce what David produces to an unwanted collage. More importantly, collage, as a movie-making technique David Bell also applies to the making of his documentary, is strongly suggestive of his own subjectivity, which is not only patched-up and composite but also floating in quick flux. As Philip E. Simmons comes to realize, American writers like Thomas Pynchon and Don DeLillo might have seen the mass culture as practically the only condition out of which people can build their selfhoods. (Simmons, 1997: 53) Elizabeth Deeds Ermarth adds that in the mass culture, a subject has to claim his subjectivity in "this gap between the potential capacities of a differential code and any particular specification of it" (Ermarth, 2000: 411). To a great extent, the "originality" David Bell achieves in his documentary-making job stems from his "particular specification of" "a differential code"—an evergrowing body of ready-made movie images, and therefore his "originality" is at most an embezzlement of one or several programmed codes. Ermarth also believes that in the postmodern conditions, the code systems are multiple and "code-multiplicity means that we no longer have only a subject-in-process, or even a subjectivity-in-process, but something more like subjectivity-in-processes" (Ermarth, 2000: 411). It could be inferred that an appropriation of one code system should involve a "subjectivity-in-process", while an embezzlement of code systems, which is more likely to occur in the mass culture, will increase the floating speed of a subjectivity as it is "in-processes". In this sense, what David manages to reconstruct in his documentary is an "identity" that is not stable at all, and his "originality" is very much distanced from a dreamed state of perfection.

A huge gap, which feels so unpleasant to David Bell, between a self he aims to rebuild and his movie-reconstructed subjectivity plants in the depth of his heart an insistent longing to flee from his own life and so, upon the completion of his autobiographical film, David drops out of the trip, abandons his travel companions and continues to go west alone into his own wilderness "to smash my likeness, prism of all my images, and become finally a man who lives by his own power and smell" (236). His long-term employment of multiple code systems allows David Bell to be conscious of his "likeness" to a multitude of images he borrows, and he comes to understand that he is no better than an aggregation of "all images" he embezzles from various sources. In a word, even David himself feels that he is not yet sufficiently himself. In consequence, wrapping up his lone journey to the West, David quits his job of TV network executive, leaves New York for an island near the "equatorial loin" of Africa and settles down there. (347) It is on the isolated island that David narrates in first person his entire subjectivity-reconstructing process. The first-person narration could reflect David Bell's intent to rebuild a subjectivity that can live up to his expectation by a literary means. Literature can be a new realm of art in which David yearns for a full assertion of his creativity. Nevertheless, the last glimmer of hope in David's yearning heart is extinguished as he cannot help feeling:

> It was literature I had been confronting these past days, the archetypes of the dismal mystery, sons and daughters of the archetypes, images that could not be certain which of two confusions held less terror, their own or what their own might become if it ever faced the truth. (377)

Even in literature where one's originality is supposed to be most freely exercised, David Bell can see nothing but "archetypes" or "images", or their "sons and daughters". No matter how seemingly courageous he is in flourishing these literary "archetypes", he is in great "terror" of not being himself, and so his subjectivity is still a copy of an endless cycle of "images".

In sum, David Bell's reconstructed self is a "postexistential self", a term coined by Curtis A. Yehnert when he tries to give shape to a subjectivity developed when a subject is engaged in his interaction with the postmodern conditions. Yehnert defines "the postexistential self" as "a concept of subjectivity grounded not on a separation of psyche and socius but on a dialectic between form and formlessness" (Yehnert, 2001: 365). It is not hard to find that "form" refers to "socius", "formlessness" and "psyche". Born out of the ever-going interaction between "form" and "formlessness", the postmodern self, as Yehnert continues to argue, is "neither solidified nor reified, but remains in a state of flux" (Yehnert, 2001: 365). Accordingly, it is more than understandable that David Bell sets out for a utopia, and when he realizes that it is never reachable, he goes out and returns to a life of self-exile.

Like David Bell, Gary Harkness and Bucky Wunderlick, Sister Edgar, one of the protagonists in Don DeLillo's colossal work *Underworld*, once struggled in vain within the domain of the secular for an allegedly genuine self, stable, uniform and free of change. What tells her apart from the other 3 male DeLillo characters is some luck DeLillo grants her in encountering an event, which enlightens her on a hard-won truth that a light of hope of setting one free from his subjectivity crisis will be ignited if he dares to stride out of the reasonable and to venture back to the religious. The return of the religious is to be fulfilled on the prerequisite that it is first postsecularized, which, as is recurringly intimated by DeLillo in the novel, should work as an antidote to the intoxicating effect of the subjectivity reconstruction on an individual. More notably, through his ingenious design of plot, DeLillo tends to suggest that a crisis in one's life, which is exemplified by what Sister Edgar experiences, will trigger off his awakening process of his once dormant religious consciousness, with which he could gain an entry into a new domain of belief and subjectivity is no longer a problem at all.

Sister Edgar's final resolution of her subjectivity crisis starts with a direful event in her life, which helps melt away her Cold War Mentality and reboot her religious faith that has been in a hibernation-like state for ages. The 12-year-old girl Esmeralda Lopez is a wretched homeless girl. As her mother is a heavy drug addict, fatherless Esmeralda is in bad lack of parental care and so she wanders like an apparition in the Bronx, seeking for anything deserted to feed and clothe herself. Sister Gracie, Edgar's colleague, tries to offer her a helping hand a couple of times, but the girl escapes with no exception because she is a very fast runner. DeLillo gives Esmeralda a verisimilar portrayal:

> A lanky kid who had a sort of feral intelligence, a sureness of gesture and step—she looked helpless but alert, she looked unwashed but completely clean somehow, earth-clean and hungry and quick. There was something about her that mesmerized the nun, a charmed quality, a grace that guided and sustained. (244)

The enchanting angelic quality in Esmeralda that "mesmerized" Sister Edgar cannot save the poor little girl from a bloody downfall in the miserable secular world. One morning, when Gracie and Edgar first meet on the day to start their work off, the former declares in great despair: "Somebody raped Esmeralda and threw her off a roof." (814) Taken aback, Sister Edgar sees that all the prayers she lavishes on the girl have failed, and so, she is thrown into an abysmal crisis in her life. Nevertheless, it is the blood-soaked death of the angel-like girl Esmeralda that might function well as an impetus for Sister Edgar's conversion to a new formula of faith, which could free her from a losing battle she has been fighting for a logos-informed subjectivity under the very guidance of logos's basic logic—binary opposition. This implied meaning Don DeLillo invests in Esmeralda's violent death could be revealed in the light of some religious researchers' theorization on Martin Buber's term "holy insecurity".

Having first put forward the term "holy insecurity", Martin Buber does not elucidate on it too much. Luckily, two researchers on his religious theory, Maurice Friedman and Daisetz Teitaro Suzuki propose their own understandings, which both throw much light upon what the term could probably denote. Friedman defines "holy insecurity" as a moment of "high tension and intense experience" (Friedman, 1988: 188), whilst Suzuki, a great Japanese religious scholar, concretizes Friedman's "intense experience" by his "Great Doubt", which is a time "when the finely balanced equilibrium tilts for one reason or another" (Suzuki, 1994: 259). Friedman's and Suzuki's explanations of the term work together to give it a clearer shape—"holy insecurity" should be a moment in one's quotidian life that collapses his regular mindset or overthrows his set cognitive schemata. Accordingly, it is not far-fetched at all to say that angelic Esmeralda's fall deserves to be called a "holy insecurity" moment in Sister Edgar's life when her "finely balanced equilibrium tilts". Having seen that Gracie fails in all her attempts to help the girl, Sister Edgar still tries to comfort herself and Gracie by saying: "She'll be all right. She can take care of herself. She's quick. She's blessed. She'll be all right." (250) However, her self-consolation or self-deception cannot hold water too long as very soon the terrible news arrives. As a result, it is rather understandable that Edgar, who is not cautioned against possible arrival of any bad news about the girl, is too flabbergasted to keep her mental "equilibrium" at the moment of "high tension". What's more, "a charmed quality" or "a grace that guided and sustained" that Sister Edgar has seen in the girl since the two's first encounter "mesmerizes" Sister Edgar so much that to her Esmeralda is no less than an angelic being, which could also deepen Sister Edgar's feeling of "insecurity" by a large margin.

The word "holy" of "holy insecurity" connotes what effect such a moment in one's life could produce on him. Based on his research on Zen Buddhism, Suzuki sees the "holy" effect on an individual at the moment of "Great Doubt" as a "mental revolution", in which, as Friedman has claimed, one "feels the shackles of causal awareness fall off him" (Friedman, 1988: 118). Friedman argues further on that "after the shackles of causal awareness fall off, he finds within himself that myth-making faculty through which the world's processes are perceived as meaningful beyond causality" (Friedman, 1998: 118). With his design of the tragic termination of Esmeralda's young but pathetic life, DeLillo could have meant to afford Sister Edgar and all his readers an opportunity to recognize that violence inheres in the Cold War logic of "Us vs. Them"㉜ and so, secularism, which also runs on a similar logic basis of binary opposition, can never on its own cure the American society of its pestilence-like violence. However, it is also such a horrible exertion of violence on a girl as helpless and angelic as Esmeralda that plunges Sister Edgar into a deep crisis, in which she will see how reason's supposedly overwhelming explanatory power fails. Having been informed of Esmeralda's death:

> She feels weak and lost. ... All terror is local now. ... She believes she is falling into crisis, beginning to think that all criterion is a spurt of blank matter that chanced to make an emerald planet here and a dead star there, with random waste between. (816 -817)

㉜ The statement here can serve as a summary of the symbolic value that Don DeLillo attaches to the death of angel Esmeralda. What her death is symbolic of can be seen in light of Rene Girard's theorization on "scapegoating". Rene Girard (1923—2015), a French historian, literary critic and philosopher of social science, claims in his writings that "scapegoating is a deliberate act of collective substitution performed at the expense of the victim and absorbing all the internal tensions, feuds, and rivalries pent up within the community" (Girard, 1972: 7), and he goes on to argue that "the sacrificial victim" must be carefully chosen because he cannot be one of "those near us" and has to be "the creature we can strike without fear of reprisal, since he lacks a champion" (Girard, 1972: 13). Though Rene Girard might have gone too far to generalize "scapegoating" as the foundation of all civilized societies, for an American society delineated in *Underworld*, whose regular operation is still riveted on its Cold War logic of binary opposition, "scapegoating" might function just as well. Angel Esmeralda, whose "otherness" can be well evidenced by her surname "Lopez" and a Spanish-speaking worn-out neighborhood in Bronx she wanders all day long in, is, by Girard's definition, an ideal candidate for "scapegoating" as she is not one of "those near us", does not have "a champion", and so cannot commit any act of "reprisal". Therefore, according to Rene Girard, the ruthless slaughtering of Esmeralda can be intended by DeLillo to symbolize an act of sacrificial victimization, into which, all "tensions, feuds and rivalries" in an "Us-community" can be "absorbed".

It can be inferred from Sister Edgar's musings that to her, Esmeralda's death cannot be justified by any reasonable means, and so reason loses its charm of offering all needed explanations and becomes "random waste". Nonetheless, as Suzuki sees it, Sister Edgar's "crisis" can be "a turning point" (Suzuki, 1994: 259) of her life, at which a cause-and-effect chain has broken loose and so, she should now set herself ready to re-enter the terrain of the sacred, from which she has been an outsider though she is a Christian-belief practitioner in appearance㉝. On the effect "holy insecurity" could yield, Martin Buber observes: "Religious reality comes when all security is shattered through mystery" (qtd. in Friedman, 1988: 155). To Sister Edgar, the inexplicable murder of Esmeralda, an innocent angel in her eyes, is such a "mystery", which has "shattered" her "security" though and gets her eyes wide open again for the coming of a "religious reality" though. Edgar is therefore situated in a position to establish herself as a real believer but not just a belief practitioner.

In a nutshell, Sister Edgar's readiness to re-embrace her long lost religious faith can help dissolve a binary opposition between the secular and the religious, the cornerstone logic of logos, and as a result, to a great extent, help dispel from her mindset the Cold War Mentality, which also establishes itself on the basis of binary opposition between "Us" and "Them" and thus is homogeneous with secularism in fundamental logic. With her Cold War Mentality melted away by her readiness to re-embrace the spiritual, Edgar suspends her reconstruction project of a logos-informed subjectivity, which, in DeLillo's regard, will count as the first step for re-initiation of a much more feasible plan to have one's subjectivity crisis resolved—to restart his faith in the spiritual and then entrust it with the ultimate resolution of the subjectivity problem or the final endowment of

---

㉝ Enslaved by a Cold War logic of binary opposition as a sufferer of serious mysophobia, Sister Edgar does live as a practitioner of religion rather than a true believer in it, at which, Don DeLillo hints by one telltale detail. At the start of the novel's Epilogue, the Sister admits that "Prayer is a practical strategy, the gaining of temporal advantage in the capital markets of Sin and Remission" (237). To her, "prayer" is no more than a utilitarian paradigm by which one can gain some "temporal advantage", or cheap self-comfort, from a religion in which "Sin and Remission" can be both "marketed" as "capitals".

meaning on his life and in the meantime, terminate all his trials of constructing his self with any reasonable or secular means.

Paul Tillich, one of the most celebrated American theologians, once said to the effect that limitation of its span is all the reason why life is ridiculous, and therefore every human being should live with a strong existential angst and equip his mindset with an unrelenting ambition to learn life's meaning or value, or to be more specific, to seek for the reason why he should live once and only once for a limited span of time. The DeLillo characters of the aforementioned novels discussed in this chapter of the book all struggle in a way that betrays their belief that realization of one's meaning of life depends on or even equals their establishment of a subjectivity as an answer to a most fundamental question about existence—"Who am I?" Especially after the Enlightenment, the accelerating secularization of the Western society has been taking its toll on its subjects' subjectivity-constructing endeavor, and as a result, assertion of their life's significance becomes a Mission Impossible which seems not to stand any chance of being fulfilled while his existential angst is going deeper and deeper.

In the first place, the purportedly religion-free secular discourse sets up logos or reason as the sole and indisputable criterion against which subjectivity construction is standardized so as to achieve a subjectivity that is unitary, change-proof and controllable. The logos-informed subjectivity is an "authentic self", which DeLillo's novel protagonists like David Bell, Gary Harkness and Sister Edgar all chase after in earnest. Furthermore, the cause-and-effect chain, as one of the logic derivatives of logos, teaches all subjects a simple lesson on subjectivity construction that all he needs to do is to exercise full control over "causes" to ensure an expected "effect"—"an authentic self". "Causes" are the means by which the subjects attempt to rebuild their subjectivity. Both the English jargons that Gary Harkness is obsessed with and the Cold War Mentality that Sister Edgar indulges herself in originate from their once unshakable belief in logocentrism. Even David Bell's movie-making endeavor, a form of art that seems to be so multi-faceted, self-reflexive and avant-gardist, is still a patchwork of logos's products—images that are mass produced in a logos-dominated age of mechanical reproduction. Built in a chain of cause-and-effect whose two ends are under the tight control of logos, a contemporary self becomes a "buffered self", a term Charles Taylor treats with meticulous care in his *A Secular Age*. According to Charles Taylor, a "buffered self" is like a stepping-stone upon which mankind strides into "an authentic age", an age of reason-guided self-control. Charles Taylor suggests that a "buffered self" is a self that is safeguarded from or impervious to all the irrational or the unreasonable, which are hostile to or destructive of logos's role of a dictatorial controller of subjectivity construction. Nonetheless, most pitiably, "a buffered self" or "an authentic self" is nothing but an illusion, whose fragility and fraudulence have been evidenced time and again by the DeLillo characters' failures in their pursuit of selfhood.

David, Gary and Sister Edgar at first feel rather happy with their control of the "causes" or measures available to them, only to be stung with strong humiliation as they all at last come to realize that these "causes" have been in fact controlling and manipulating them, and therefore, distancing them farther and farther away from their goal of building an "authentic self". Besides, the logic chain of cause-and-effect that these characters follow in their subjectivity construction has been snapped off since the "causes" fail to acquire them the "effect" as they have promised. Their subjectivities are still shaped or determined by some factors out of their reach so that the elusiveness of "an authentic self" has never been lessened no matter how hard they have tried. What those characters end in—David's reclusive life on an isolated island, Gary's voluntary fast and Sister Edgar's serious mysophobia—can testify to the falsity of the subjectivity's nature decided and the measures to achieve it propounded by the secular. So it could be concluded that through his characters' failures, Don DeLillo tries to suggest to his readers that it is time to break free from the confining domain of absolute reason or abandon the logos-informed construction of one's subjectivity, if he still is determined to construct a subjectivity, which is both respectful to and confirmative of his meaning of life.

As Laura Barrett argues, Don DeLillo suggests more than once in his works that to resolve the subjectivity problem, one should first of all "refrain from seeking solutions" (Barrett, 2001/2002: 111). What Barrett truly intends to say is that DeLillo persuades his readers to "refrain from" solving the problem only because he can see no hope of achieving any satisfactory solution within the dimension of the reasonable, and as a result, Barrett claims that she sees in DeLillo an ardent request to go beyond reason or in her own terms, an ideal of "subscribing to a faith in mystery" (Barrett, 2001/2002: 111) after reason is given up as an option. To put it more accurately, DeLillo's strong approval of "a faith in mystery" is his belief in the spirituality, which is in total reflective of his heartfelt inclination towards the religious. To DeLillo, as is implied in his characterization of Sister Edgar, a belief in the spiritual once re-activated can break loose "the shackles of casual awareness" and help a subject "find within himself that myth-making faculty through which the world's processes are perceived as meaningful beyond causality". (Barrett, 2001/2002:111) "That myth-making faculty" is a sincere trust in the spirituality or an awakened religious consciousness, whose greatest potential lies in helping a subject perceive all "the world's processes as meaningful beyond causality". It follows that if one can see all the things in the world as meaningful, he should meet no difficulty in seeing his own existence as meaningful too, and so, in this way, a non-constructed and non-control-oriented self is constructed and life's value realized accordingly. In a word, Don DeLillo implies that to go "beyond causality" into the terrain of the religious should be the only feasible project of life-meaning-affirmation in the contemporary conditions.

As for DeLillo, the spiritual is a solid foundation on which one can rest his subjectivity or life-value; however, Christian God and the gods in the world's other institutional religions have since long lost their footings on Westerners', especially Americans' minds, which could be most shockingly evidenced by Sister Edgar's skepticism towards God. So, the spirituality that DeLillo tends to warmly embrace should be different from or even deconstructive of any institutional divinity like Christian God. Besides, in *Great Jones Street*, Bucky Wunderlick's self-banishment from the secular cannot save him from his fatalistic subjection to commercialism, by which DeLillo can suggest that no living soul should ignore the glimmering of a redemptive light in the secular because though too much rationalized, the secular is still saturated with the phenomenal incarnations of the spiritual. In the sense, DeLillo should agree that the secular and the spiritual should conjoin to form an integrated whole—secular spirituality, whose redeeming strength is well worth all pursuing efforts of a contemporary subject.

In conclusion, DeLillo's artful representation of various embodiments of secular spirituality and probable measures to pursue it in his half-a-century-long literary endeavor establishes him as a postsecular writer in the realm of American fiction, and postsecularism, a burgeoning branch of Western academics, can in return develop for DeLillo's readers a much profounder understanding of his novels.

CHAPTER THREE

Incarnations of Secular Spirituality

—Transcendence and Immanence

Having been laid down as the very cornerstone of postsecularism, secular spirituality seems to be rather paradoxical because it integrates transcendence and immanence into a whole, which distinguishes postsecularism from other ready-made Western theological and sociological theories. Don DeLillo, as a postmodern novelist whose distinctiveness consists in his determination to establish his literary identity of not only problem raiser but also solution proposer, is keenly aware of how significant the fusion between transcendence and immanence is as for any attempt to resolve the existential crises of contemporary Americans. To convince his readership of the feasibility of his postsecular strategy to solve their problems, DeLillo has no alternative but to exhibit, in his works, as many secular incarnations of spirituality as possible, in which transcendence and immanence are truly fused, or in other words, a spirituality incarnate offers immediate access to all hands of the mortals reaching out for salvation.

If in writing his earlier work *End Zone*, DeLillo comes to "suspect that language was a subject as well as an instrument in my work" (LeClair, McCaffery, 1983: 81), he gives full play to the potential of the "subject" in enhancing the philosophical profundity of his *The Names* by exploring in the novel the possible ways in which spirituality could emanate itself from language—a secular form of existence, in whose texture certain spirituality has been embedded though it has been neglected for so long a time. In *The Names*, DeLillo presents by his exquisite design of plot two diametrically different outlooks on language. The first aims at a false spirituality that can provoke cultic violence, whereas the second, deconstructive of logos and its derivative grand narratives about language, can take speakers of a language right to the spirituality incarnated in so secular a medium as language.

The plot development of *The Names* is centered on a cult that calls itself "The Names". The cult is so called because its members choose and bludgeon to death its victims whose names' initial letters match those of the place where they are first found, and the chosen victims of the cult are almost unexceptionally the crippled, the old or the infirm. Asked to document in written form all that the cult does, James Axton, the hero of the novel, is granted a chance to meet Andahl, a core member of the cult, who terms himself and other cultists as "abecedarians ... Learners of the alphabet. Beginners" (210). The label "beginners" these cultists append to their identity marks off their purposeful refusal to see more in language than a simple aggregate of alphabetic letters because the way the letters combine and work to make language communicative scare them a lot.

The cultists slaughter the innocent as they live in fear, and they live in fear because their dream of putting "an end to play" (LeClair, 1987a: 118) will never come true. As Jacques Derrida has seen it, language is a circular "play of differences that involves syntheses and referrals that prevent there from being at any moment or in any way a simple element that is present in and of itself and refers only to itself. Whether in written or in spoken discourse, no element can function as a sign without relating to another element which itself is not simply present" (Derrida, 1981: 26). It follows from Derrida's view on language that it is born as an endless play of signs because a sign, consisting of a certain number of letters, cannot perform its communicative function without persistent referral to another sign, and the referring process comes in an endless circle, which will make all the meanings conveyed float like the quicksilver in a very speedy flux. If language, an entity that determines human form of existence, is not fixed as a pillar against which the cultists can lean their meaning of life, they cannot tell distinction between themselves and other lower species, nor can they grip tight any means to justify their continual survival on the earth. As a result, Andahl and his fellow cultists do have a "magnificent" goal to achieve. By matching the name initials of their prospective victim with those of the place where he is first found, and killing him with no remorse, the "abecedarians" endeavor to not only smash the ever-going referral chain within language but also establish "an inexorable equivalence between word and world" (Bryant, 1987: 19). The perfect match in initials between the slaughtering site and the victim help the cultists achieve the equivalence, or the absolutely direct reference from the words to the world, and by doing so, the cultists can appease their rage and frustration over the indeterminacy in both language and life, though a lot of innocent blood is thus expended.

As Paula Bryant observes, the cultists' is "a perverse version of Wittgenstein's logical positivist search for one ideal language that will redeem confusion by being both static and orderly" (Bryant, 1987: 19), which counts no more than an illusion because language that can live up to the cultists' expectation never happened in the past and will never happen in the future. Nonetheless, the cultists of "The Names", volunteering to blindfold themselves about language's true nature, see in their cultic practices a certain hint of mystical spirituality. Amy Hungerford reveals that in *The Names* "the cult demonstrates the dangerous limit case of a belief that language is mystically powerful by virtue of its abstract material patterns" (Hungerford, 2006: 367), which is evidenced by what Andahl tells James Axton, "We are here to carry out the pattern" so that words can behave the way "numbers behave" (210). "The material patterns", resulting from the cultists' arbitrary initial-letter matches, seem to break loose the confines of logos with their seeming randomness and therefore cheat the cultists into believing that they are a probable source of the spiritual. However, a closer look at the "spiritual materiality" in language that the cultists worship in hot craze, will disclose its fraudulent nature because being a "pattern", the so-called spirituality originates from a DIY rule that the cult makes and practices out of a logos-inspired desire to control or master all that have not been controlled yet, no matter whether it is controllable or not in nature. So, what the cultists pay tribute to is nothing but a self-made embodiment of some fake spirituality, which is in fact created out of their perverse exertion of reason and therefore cannot be more false. The worship of a false spirituality can, in an effortless way, transform into a form of religious fanaticism and so there is no wonder that "The Names" should sacrifice the human lives, though crippled and infirm, to their self-made "spiritual materiality".

Fortunately, in *The Names*, DeLillo does not allow any innocent blood to be spilt in vain. The blood-dripping sacrifices the cult practices are what DeLillo designs, as Amy Hungerford claims, to suggest, though in a macabre way, the very necessity of finding an "alternative that retains the mysticism of the cult while making mystical language beneficial to human life rather than destructive of it" (Hungerford, 2006: 367). To make language "mystical", and meanwhile, let it be "beneficial" but not sacrificial, DeLillo in the novel switches to the other outlook at language, which represents how he views language and is the one that offers to save his hero of *The Names* from falling into the trap the cult sets for him.

In *The Names*, the cult intends its cold-blood destruction of innocent lives to work as a measure to attain to their ultimate goal of recovering full arbitrariness of language or unobstructed reference from word to world, which most shockingly manifests that they have been so obsessed with meaning a language is supposed to convey. DeLillo suggests that the cultists' life-sacrificing obsession with meaning is a symptom for their pathological admiration for logos. So, aiming at achieving a fixed and unalterable meaning by means of logos-stimulated discipline and control, the cultists cannot break free from the confining realm of reason nor gain access to the spirituality incarnated in some aspects of language other than meaning. DeLillo hints at where to locate the spiritual in language by a phrasal noun he talks of in an interview—"automatic writing". "First you look for discipline and control," DeLillo explains, "You want to bend the language your way. But there's a higher place, a secret aspiration. You want to let go. The best moments involve a loss of control. It's a kind of rapture." (DeLillo, 1993: 282) Apparently, it is the cultists of *The Names* who are keen to "bend the language" in their own way so as to sacrifice the blood of the chosen victims they have never met before. Unlike them, DeLillo, as one who uses language for art's purpose, appreciates "a loss of control" of language, or to put it simply, he says no to any measure of imposing meaning upon language or establishing direct word-to-object referencing relationship. To him, the abandonment of a meaning-oriented view on language can take one to "a higher place" where his "secret aspiration"—re-embracing spirituality incarnated in language—can be realized, and so he can indulge himself in "a kind of rapture".

On another occasion, DeLillo expands on his argument about "automatic writing". He states that to be "automatic" is not to press meaning upon language but "to let language press meaning upon me", and only by so doing can one come to discern the very aspect of language—"the materiality of words"—that incarnates the spiritual. About what counts to him as "materiality of words", DeLillo explains in detail as follows:

> There's a rhythm I hear that drives me through a sentence. And the words typed on the white page have a sculptural quality. They form odd correspondences. They match up not just through meaning but through sound and look. The rhythm of a sentence will accommodate a certain number of syllables. One syllable too many, I look for another word. There's always another word that means nearly the same thing, and if it doesn't then I'll consider altering the meaning of a sentence to keep the rhythm, the syllable beat. I'm completely willing to let language press meaning upon me. (DeLillo, 1993: 283)

"A rhythm I hear" is what inspires DeLillo to give a start in writing a particular sentence, and it is manifest that the start is not in any way concerned with meaning. It is this meaning-free start that "drives" DeLillo to be engrossed on "the materiality" or "a sculptural quality" of words. To be more specific, "the materiality" refers to the "sound and look" of a word, or in more academic terms, the phonetic and morphological characters of a language, which, in DeLillo's regard, are created by the inspiration mankind receives from the unknown or the irrational that is by nature, linked straight up to spirituality. To put it another way, as for DeLillo, language's materiality or physicality is not made within the borders of the rational and to the fullest possible degree "sculpted" by the spiritual that has been offering an inexhaustible supply of inspiration to mankind, and besides, it is "meaning" or the semantic aspect of language that has been keeping mankind's eyes off the spiritual in language for so long a time.

Amy Hungerford, a specialist in DeLillo studies who has been working on the novelist's persistent concerns with the spiritual as a subject in his works, believes that, to DeLillo, language is a medium, through which one can gain access to the spirituality: "By him, language is conceived as a retaining medium that frees the person from the strictures of reason to reach a mystical relation to the material world and to what transcends the material world." (Hungerford, 2006: 375) As far as DeLillo is concerned, language, his most faithful pal who helps him succeed, is a miniature of "the material world", in which he sees a "mystical" quality in its "materiality" and thus opens a window to "what transcend the material world"—the spiritual that inspires the making of 26 letters in English and incarnates itself right in them. David Bosworth at least partly agrees to Hungerford's judgment on DeLillo's view on language as he remarks: "Time and time again, with perhaps excessive thoroughness but undeniable eloquence, DeLillo impresses upon us his view that what matters about language is its 'pattern,' its deeper rhythms and syntax, the design behind the signs rather than what they signify." (Bosworth, 1983: 30) "The design behind the signs" is the designless physicality of words or signs that is the imprint of the spiritual. Bosworth is right about what he says except his choosing the word "pattern" to tell what DeLillo cares about language because the word might confuse his readers since what the cultists take innocent lives to worship is also "pattern" in language, as Andahl has admitted to James Axton. However, the "patterns" that DeLillo cherishes the most are all ready made in a language as a result of mankind's free play of the inspiration from the spiritual and thus not at all contaminated with any amount of artificiality. However, the cultists who are bound tight in "the strictures of reason" superimpose a rule upon language with an illusion that direct reference or fixed meaning can be recovered. Different from the cult's morbidly stringent "pattern", DeLillo's is a patternless "pattern", which is exemplified by a 9-year-old boy's short composition DeLillo presents in full length near the end of *The Names*.

Deeply intrigued by its ideal to kill "the flux of existence" (Bryant, 1987: 19), James Axton is drawn nearer and nearer to a threatening prospect of becoming a new recruit of the Andahl-led cult. He at last has a narrow escape as his fatal slip into the cultic trap is curbed in time by his encounter with his 9-year-old son Tap's short story titled "The Prairie". DeLillo places Tap's story in the penultimate chapter of *The Names*, which is a fictional adaptation of what the boy hears from his mother's co-worker Owen Brademas who tells his early experience of Pentecostalism—to be specific, his failure to speak in tongues. Orville Benton, which is how Owen is called by Tap in the story, pushed by both his parents and his pastor to surrender himself to the Holy Spirit, is straining himself hard to speak in tongues but fails and so flees the church into deep night and heavy rain. Religious in thematic concern, Tap's story draws its salvific power from its intense representation of the spiritual in language, and so in this sense, the story is clearly a sample of "automatic writing" DeLillo has been in warm support of.

Compared with adult writers, a child writer is much easier to be "automatic" because DeLillo sees in children "some especially valued, and often mystical, state of consciousness or being" (Hungerford, 2006: 368) as Amy Hungerford argues. It could be inferred that "the mystical state of consciousness" is "especially valued" because children will have much more immediate access to the spirituality, and as Hungerford continues to explain, "the mystical state of consciousness" can be planted in a child's mindset as it has not been too much framed by rationalistic conventions. So, in Tap's case, driven by "the mystical consciousness", he flouts the logos-informed language rules and so enjoys "automatic writing" by his misspellings that are seen in almost every single sentence of the entire narrative. Misspelt in general, Tap's story bounces off the strict limits of logos and lives in its own right as a "little narrative". Its "littleness" is first seen in Tap's spelling of "yield" as "yeeld" when he tells of how young Orville is urged to speak in tongues. Stronger "littleness" can be discerned in Tap's wording of the story's ending:

> Tongue tied! His fait was signed. He ran into the rainy distance, smaller and smaller. This was worse than a retched nightmare. It was the nightmare of real things, the fallen wonder of the world. (339)

Tap's misspellings like "fait (fate)" and "retched (wretched)" can take the readers away, at least temporarily, from their focus on the meaning of a language since the misspelled words, which flout the lexical conventions so as to be deconstructive of meaning, "call attention to letters" or "the materiality of words".

As the very first reader of Tap's "little narrative", the boy's father, with all his attention summoned and focused on the physicality of letters, cannot help but agree to Amy Hungerford's observation that in his son's short story, "the spiritual reality of language can be perceived" (Hungerford, 2006: 370). As Paula Bryant suggests, "the perceived spiritual reality of language" in Tap's short writing is a "liberating message" (Bryant, 1987: 25) the son imparts to set his farther free from his obsessive concern, just like those cultists', with the never-to-be-fulfilled mission of fixating the meaning of language. Having realized "the possibility of human transcendence hidden in the ordinary" (Hungerford, 2006: 371) by reading his son's story, James Axton experiences an upheaval in his view on language, which is evidenced by what he speaks of when he stands in face of the Parthenon, a temple dedicated in Athens to Athena:

> The Parthenon was not a thing to study but to feel. It wasn't aloof, rational, timeless, pure. I hadn't expected a human feeling to come from the stones but this is what I found, deeper than the art and mathematics embodied in the structure, the optical exactitudes. (330)

To James Axton, the Parthenon, as an incarnation of human reason, is a symbol for language, which is equally or even more monumental. Greatly touched by "the spiritual reality", he recognizes in "the materiality" of his son's writing, James cannot see language as an "aloof and rational" being any more; but instead, an unexpected "human feeling" summons him to penetrate through the rational make-up of "art and mathematics" and other forms of "exactitude" to a profounder dimension of the spiritual, in which logos cannot hold its footing and the irrational rules in its stead so that language in particular and human life in general is made meaningful, both unconditionally and meaninglessly.

James Axton thus prevents himself from being indoctrinated by the sacrificial and pathological tenets of the cult by daring to embrace the spiritual incarnated in the materiality of language. His ending, as for DeLillo, is a perfect starting line off which the novelist sets out to exhibit further the unparalleled competence of secular spirituality in helping one realize his self-redemption.

Up till now, *Libra* has been the only commercial success that Don DeLillo has ever achieved in career, whose time-honored appealing strength should be largely attributed to its tentative solution to the possibly grandest mystery in American history—John F. Kennedy's assassination. To unveil what might be behind the event of great historic importance, DeLillo gives full play to his literary craftsmanship in designing a much commended double-plotline structure for the novel. The "officially recognized" lone assassin Lee Harvey Oswald's life is depicted in chapters marked by place names, which constitute a "small" or personal history of the "lone assassin". In the other plotline, Win Everett, a retired CIA agent, leads his crew in plotting against the American president, and all the relevant chapters are marked by the dates, which amount to a "big history" of the conspirators planning their president's death. In "small history", DeLillo reveals how Libra, the seventh sign of the zodiac Lee Harvey Oswald is born into, affects, in a most mysterious and profound fashion, the developing course of his life that ends up in the assassination site at Dallas. More significantly, through an unobtrusive arrangement of plot, DeLillo lets Oswald known to and selected by the conspirators to be the mission performer so that "small history" and "big history" meet to gather a tremendous force to turn a new leaf in the America history, and further on, DeLillo comes to suggest what is spiritual about the power that intertwines the two "histories". The spiritual power that welding the two plotlines or "histories", together with an astrological effect of Libra on Oswald's course of life, puts DeLillo in a position to assert that history can incarnate the spiritual too, and the spirituality, a mysterious power that runs through the secular, will save Americans from "a world of randomness and ambiguity" into which JFK's assassination throws them.

In September 29, 1963, Lyndon B. Johnson, JFK's successor, called upon a commission of top-notch American specialists to investigate into the former president's assassination, which got itself an unofficial name "the Warren Commission". One year later in September 24, 1964, the Commission submitted its 888-page report to President Johnson. Called by the American public as *The Warren Report*, the report, in an assertive tone, reassured the madly curious public of the "fact" that Lee Harvey Oswald was a "lone assassin" and Jack Ruby also acted all on his own when he shot Oswald to death 2 days after the assassination. Imaginably, the lone-assassin theory must have given rise to a seemingly never-to-cease controversy, which, to a great extent, reflects how fiercely the two epistemological modes—contingency and conspiracy—competes in the mindsets of contemporary Americans who find themselves helplessly trapped in the postmodern conditions.

Conclusively identifying Oswald as the "lone assassin", *The Warren Report* is meant to convince the public that JFK's assassination, not motivated by any rational powers, is a case of sheer contingency. Under the help of the contingency theory, the American government can disengage the American public from any grounded trial of probing into certain governmental department's possible involvement in the tragic ending of Kennedy's life. However, an incessantly upgraded controversy that first arises from the report suggests that American people do not buy the theory at all. They have since long developed a much stronger proclivity to accept conspiracy theory as valid in explaining all that befalls them, no matter how ridiculous it might sound. Gordon S. Wood holds that people's unconditional trust in the explicative power of conspiracy theory originates in their determination to live as faithful followers of logocentrism since it teaches them to make "a rational attempt to explain human phenomena in terms of human intentions and to maintain moral coherence in the affairs of men" (Wood, 1982: 429). Nonetheless, in contemporary America, no matter how hard the conspiracy theory tries to master the postmodern confusions by "attributing events to the concerted designs of willful individuals" (Wood, 1982: 411), it is going to fail and be dismissed by Fredric Jameson as "a degraded attempt to think the impossible totality of the contemporary world system" (Jameson, 2005: 38). Destructive in nature of "totality", the postmodern conditions would convert the conspiracy theory, a "well-intentioned" mode of thinking, into "cultural paranoia", about which O'Donnell has explained quite a lot. Agreeing to Fredric Jameson's understanding that the conspiracy theory is attuned to the realities of "late capitalism", O'Donnell argues that "cultural paranoia", derived from the conspiracy theory, is "a mode of perception", with which people tend to "interconnect the multiple stratifications of reality into a network" (O'Donnell, 1994: 182) so that they can "make order out of chaos" (O'Donnell, 1994: 204).

With their bold but futile defiance of "the multiple stratifications of reality", contemporary Americans desire to perceive their national history in the conventional way of reposing it on a "classical representational scheme or system" (Johnston, 1994: 338) that is bestowed upon them by logos. Running contrary to what they have expected, the "classical scheme or system" can do nothing but to throw them into an endless cycle of one "reasonable" theory being replaced by another, and by so doing sink them down to an abysmal paranoia which cannot at all be cured with any "reasonable" means. It is exactly the way in which logos's possessiveness exercises itself fully in abducting the history into its own domain where reason urges one conspiracy theory to reproduce itself with no stop so that American people's fear can never be dispelled. Having developed a keen awareness of the paranoid mechanism of the conspiracy theory, Don DeLillo, through both his plot designs and characterizations in *Libra*, illustrates to his readers his interests in "effects that cannot be represented within such as system" (Johnston, 1994: 338). These "effects", as have been first implied in Lee Harvey Oswald's "small history", are indeed produced "without such a system", or in other words, far off the domain of the reasonable and therefore, should have come from the dimension of the spiritual, which, though neglected for so long, can reveal a more essential aspect of the human history and thus be able to cure contemporary American subjects of their paranoid cognizance of their historical events.

Don DeLillo confirms with one of his interviewers that it is astrology that lends the novel its title: "But finally when I hit upon this notion of coincidence and dream and intuition and the possible impact of astrology on the way men act, I thought that Libra, being Oswald's sign, would be the one title that summarized what's inside the book." (DeCurtis, 1991a: 55 – 56) DeLillo's self-assurance in calling "Libra" a summary of all that is in the novel suggests that Oswald's sign, as the concept of an ancient study on the spiritual carried out through a close observation of heavenly bodies, can count, as far as DeLillo is concerned, as a spiritual source of effect upon the assassin's personality and also his course of life. The astrological characterization of Oswald can break loose the stringent confinement of a logos-inspired totalistic perception of a certain individual, which, in Fredric Jameson's regard, is "unthinkable" against the historical backdrop of "late capitalism" and its cultural derivative—the postmodern conditions, and so at least counteract the insidious effect of the conspiracy theory that has been hovering around Americans' perception of the assassination mystery for decades.

DeLillo, as a keen observer of contemporary American culture, has developed in himself deep insights into a fact that Lee Harvey Oswald's real personality is never a reachable truth since Americans all tend to picture their own Oswald through various sources available, as he writes in *Libra*: "He is not an actor so much as he is a character, a fictional character who first emerges as such in the year of 1957. Oswald seems scripted out of doctored photos, tourist cards, change-of-address cards, mail order forms, visa applications, altered signatures, pseudonyms." (24) As DeLillo has described in the novel, Americans' understanding of Oswald as a historical figure cannot be formed without their wide use of an extensive range of images, which constitutes a cultural essential of postmodern America, and more importantly, all these imaging efforts directed at Oswald are aimed at establishing him as an assassin, who plays his due role in the plot against JFK, so as to solidify the basis of the conspiracy theory. The self-evident contradiction between the American public's means of constructing Oswald's subjectivity—patching-up of his media images and thus postmodern by nature, and their construction result—a personified hinge upon which a logos-informed conspiracy theory revolves, results in an irresolvable paradox that renders Oswald's identity, as John Johnston has claimed, "entirely relational and perspectival" (Johnston, 1994: 335). To be "relational and perspectival", Johnston argues further on, is symptomatic of Oswald becoming no better than a simulacrum, behind which there is everything except "an original". To put it another way, through being imaged for millions of times, Oswald has been reduced into "a double or copy" of nothing, whose subjectivity is in the way thrown into "a state of resonance"; and in such "a state", one "solely reasonable" explanation about his subjectivity will be forever "resonated" by or repeated in another "solely reasonable" explanation. (Johnston, 1994: 335) Such an endless imaging of Lee Harvey Oswald as one of the greatest plotting figures in the American history extinguishes contemporary Americans' flaming hope for pleasing themselves by "a fantasy logic". Skip Willman sees "the logic" as one that is "represented by the ideologically charged conspiracy theories of the JFK assassination", and Don DeLillo, as a "writer in opposition", has managed to weaponize his best-seller *Libra* to counteract the ill effects of "a fantasy logic". (Willman, 1998: 431) The weapon implied in Willman's argument is the seemingly "discredited and 'irrational' notion of astrology" (Willman, 1998: 431)—Oswald's personality, shaped to be a human incarnation of the Libran spirituality. By resorting to and believing in the Libran spirituality as the decisive force in shaping Oswald's personality, without his mindset being any more yoked by a "paranoid narrative", one can develop an ultimate understanding of what is behind Oswald's seemingly unreasonable "climax" of life—his involvement in the assassination of the president. Affected by Libra that resembles a scale in shape, Oswald will tip himself towards any source of influence that exerts a bit heavier impact on him, which could best explain why he can be so easily recruited by any conspiratorial group and committed to any maneuver they assign to him. To see the shaping power of Libra in Oswald's personality and course of life is an approval of secular incarnation of the spiritual in a personality, which can cure one of "cultural paranoia" and afford one much more freedom than what "the imaginary resolutions" and "the comforting 'guarantees'" of the conspiracy theory can promise. (Willman, 1998: 431)

In addition to calling an end to contemporary Americans' self-indulgence in "the fantasy logic" of the conspiracy theory by which they come to cognize Oswald's persona and the role he plays in the JFK assassination, Libra, as DeLillo continually suggests in the novel, can work as a spiritual power that would have resisted a force as irresistible as the contingency and saved Oswald from falling into a trap that the conspiratorial clique has set for him. In *Libra*, through Clay Shaw, one of its characters, DeLillo labels Oswald "the negative Libran", and dozens of hints dropped throughout the novel suggest that his "negativity" lies in his purposeful denial of Libran traits of personality and his obstinacy in obstructing his innate tipping tendency by "his continual search for a fantasy space wherein he imagines that these troubling social contradictions or dichotomies (individual vs. collective, public vs. private) will be overcome" (Willman, 1998: 426). Embedded in the confounding texture of the postmodern conditions, Oswald, a young Libran, entertains himself in an illusion of "overcoming these troubling social contradictions" by, as Amy Hungerford realizes, "memorizing and alternately obeying Marxist theory and the Marine Corps manual" (Hungerford, 2006: 353). However, his persistent search for a elixir-like theory that can terminate his oscillation, does not alleviate his pains by even the slightest degree, about which, Lentricchia comments that all the chapters about him form "a plotless tale of an aimless life propelled by the agonies of inconsistent and contradictory motivation" (Lentricchia, 1991a: 202). Lentricchia's viewpoint is supported by Oswald's self-lamentation over his inability to give a clear shape to his "aimless life":

> He feels he is living at the center of an emptiness. He wants to sense a structure that includes him, a definition clear enough to specify where he belongs. But the system floats right through him, through everything, even the revolution. He is a zero in the system. (357)

Having been informed by logocentrism for all his life, Oswald cannot concede to the sacredness of the oscillations in a Libran character, which, if recognized, will place him in "an emptiness" that is to be cherished as an open and tolerant posture to embrace all the possibilities, and thus shake off him all obsessive concerns with any "structure" or "system". By living contently as a Libran, Oswald might still be "a zero in the system", but meanwhile he can score a full mark in the test his life asks him to take because his Libran personality will become a point upon which all wholesome and healthy sources of influence can converge. This can be the original intention of DeLillo titling the novel, which, unfortunately, never dawns upon Oswald. As a result, he goes with no remorse to a conspiratorial "system" awaiting him ahead by chance.

In *Libra*, a clear distinction between "small history" and "big history" is neatly drawn by David Ferrie, a delegate from the Win Everett-led clique sent to nudge Oswald into taking part in the conspiracy to shoot the President, who tries to enlighten the chose mission performer by saying: "Think of two parallel lines ... one is the life of Lee H. Oswald. One is the conspiracy to kill the President." (338) The individual and secret life of Oswald is "small history", whereas the conspiracy of the JFK assassination is "big history" as it is a well-organized and logically-devised plot which is supposed to exert profound impact upon the course of the American history. To DeLillo and his fellow Americans, who have been predisposed to re-embrace the redemptive strength of the spiritual, a unique and bold understanding of what welds the two histories together will play a decisive role in granting them immediate access to the dimension of the spiritual.

To make it more clearly seen that it is some power, transcending the domain of the rational and thus being spiritual in nature, that works as an adhesive binding "small history" and "big history", Don DeLillo places a fictional role who works at the intermissions between the two separate plotlines of the novel and is commissioned by DeLillo to deconstruct the apparently unchallengeable conspiracy theory and to knock at the door to the once abandoned domain of the spiritual. Nicholas Branch, a historian hired by CIA into its project of writing the "secret history of the assassination of President Kennedy" (15), cannot draw any conclusion on a rational basis as CIA expects him to, though his investigation has been continuing on and on for years, during which he has read a sea of diverse and troublesome data. His research, instead, leads him to a final judgment, not acceptable to CIA at all, that "the conspiracy against the President was a rambling affair that succeeded in the short term due mainly to chance. Deft men and fools, ambivalence and fixed will and what the weather was like" (441). Disappointed with the reason that works as a guideline in his study on the JFK assassination, Branch turns to the irrational diction of "rambling" and "chance" to denote reason's failure in affecting the course of history since he has come to discern that a factor, as chancy as "weather", can be much more decisive in shaping JFK's destiny. However, Nicholas Branch's frustration at his forced destruction of reason can be alleviated if he could have read what John Johnston has come to contribute in his critical essay on *Libra*, in which he argues for the sublimity of a mysterious force that changes the course of history. John Johnston first calls the force "the historical sublime" and proceeds to define it as "a superlinearity" or "the third line" in contrast with the two visible lines of plot development in *Libra*, as he claims: "In any case, it would appear that the articulation of this Superlinear 'third line' is more essential to the novel's structural design or plan, inasmuch as its logic seems to determine the novel's convergent double plot structure and its thematic resonance of parts." (Johnston, 1994: 322) Accordingly, the reason why the double plot lines can converge is that "the third line" intertwines the two lines and it is "Superlinear" because it runs way up above the simplistically linear contour of historical development by its own logos-free logic. So, it can be inferred that the "superlinearity" is just a re-wording of the contingent, "the articulation" of which is done by David Ferrie too when he addresses Oswald:

> What bridges the space between them? What makes a connection inevitable? There is a third line. It comes out of dreams, visions, intuitions, prayers, out of the deepest levels of the self. It's not generated by cause and effect like the other two lines. It's a line that cuts across causality, cuts across time. It has no history that we can recognize or understand. But it forces a connection. It puts a man on the path of his destiny. (338)

As a well-informed insider in the alternating process that is going on between "small history" and "big history", David Ferrie makes, on behalf of DeLillo, a convincing judgment that "the third line" running through history, with no dependence on the logic chain of "cause and effect", can be something profoundly different, which is closely linked up to the spirituality in the sense that it can be "generated" by nothing but itself.

David Ferrie might not have known about an incident that occurs before he is sent to talk to Oswald and is so contingent as to enhance the "superlinearity" of "the third line". Oswald first comes, in a most random way, to the conspirators' eyesight, when George de Mohrenschildt and Lawrence Parmenter, two of Ferrie's close pals in the clique, meet and mention Oswald's name, which results in his being chosen as the "patsy" to perform the final act of assassination. However, David Ferrie does know something vital and he tells it to Oswald when JFK's visit to Dallas is drawing nearer:

> We didn't arrange your job in that building or set up the motorcade route. We don't have that kind of reach or power. There's something else that's generating this event. A pattern outside experience. Something that jerks you out of the spin of history. (384)

It is indeed a coincidence that Kennedy's motorcade should pass right in front of the Texas School Book Depository where Oswald is working before the assassination, and as Ferrie honestly puts it, nobody can make such a perfect arrangement since it exceeds the reach of reason's power. In the way, Ferrie helps DeLillo suggest that one has no alternative but to approve of the presence of some spirituality in the fabric of history, which, as "a pattern outside experience", goes beyond any means of rational representation. In accordance with Immanuel Kant's elaboration on the sublime, a conclusion can be drawn that it is the ineffability of the "pattern" that determines its sacredness, as Kant suggests: "In the case of the logical estimation of magnitude, the impossibility of ever arriving at absolute totality by the progressive measurement of things of the sensible world in time and space was cognized as an objective impossibility." (Kant, 1952: 108)

Spirituality is such "an objective impossibility", whose immeasurable "absolute totality" is, in *Libra*, crystallized as a sublime force of "coincidence" that changes both Oswald's and JFK's course of life. So, "coincidence" is a way in which human beings can perceive the will of the spiritual, and if established, this spiritual mode of perceiving the phenomenal can cure one of his "cultural paranoia", as Frank Lentricchia announces: "The true paranoid does not believe in chance or accident ... DeLillo, by his insistence on the chancy appearance of Oswald, presses us to rethink the question of Oswald outside the framework of conspiracy." (Lentricchia, 1991a: 203) DeLillo does more than simply to put his thinking readers "outside the framework of conspiracy" because once "outside", they will defy the conspiracy theory as a paranoid logic and so, live in full contentment and with a strong sense of life's meaning. As for Oswald, DeLillo also offers the way in which he can be saved by the historical sublime:

> I think you've had it backwards all this time. You wanted to enter history. Wrong approach, Leon. What you really want is out. Get out. Jump out. Find your place and your name on another level. (384)

The speaker of the utterance, David Ferrie, claims that what motivates Oswald to go on in his life is to "enter history". To "enter history", as far as Oswald is concerned, can be understood as his determination to place himself in clearly a reason-bound system of cognition that can help him suppress his Libran personality and define who he is with no error or uncertainty. Knowing that Oswald can never succeed in this attempt, Ferrie suggests that he should "get out" or "jump out" of his self-confinement in reason and give a warm hug to the redeeming power of the spiritual. However, most pitiably, David Ferrie misleads, just as some religious fanaticism does, Oswald's budding sense of the historical sublime to a sacrificial or violent end, to which Don DeLillo disagrees with his strong conviction that "on another level"—a level at which the spirituality, especially the secular spirituality prevails—there is no blood spill, but only blossoming embodiment of "humanistic qualities such as love, compassion, patience, forgiveness, responsibility, harmony and a concern for others". Last but not the least, his fervid yearning to reach "another level" should be what motivates him to present the astrological impact upon Oswald's "small history" and the spiritual force that intertwines "small history" and "big history".

In *Libra*, Don DeLillo has exhibited his marvelous capability of dealing with the subjects of historic significance, which outdoes *The Warren Report* in revealing something secret and mythic hidden so deep underneath the turbid currents of the American history and so sends off an irresistible charm to both his readers and critics. DeLillo's revelation in *Libra*, as the foregoing argument suggests, is imbued with the decisive shaping power of the spiritual, which has been envisioned by him since long and is to surface out again in his much more voluminous work *Underworld*. Unlike *Libra*, to make it clearly seen how the spirituality can be incarnated in every unimpressive detail of Americans' quotidian life, DeLillo in *Underworld* is representing an American "underhistory"—a much more petty, trivial and obscure course of historical development than what is documented and publicized by the US authorities. Among all those "underhistorical" facts in *Underworld*, consumerism and what best epitomizes it on American soil—city life—stand out as the two that best immanetize the spirituality and thus are presented as the greatest incarnations of the secular spirituality in the work.

In *Underworld*, readers can at least see one of the two essentials that Martin Beck Matustik proclaims as indispensable to postsecular philosophy—loneliness and beauty, and it is in the character of Esmeralda that DeLillo represents the latter. The fallen angel Esmeralda, though raped and killed, is portrayed as a symbol of hope "intimated as beauty that manifests itself in the midst of the tragic" (Matustik, 2008: 189). The murdered girl lies blood-soaked "in the midst of the tragic"; however, the "beauty" of her angelic spirit shines lights of hope off upon those who live in bad thirst for the spiritual comfort because the "beauty" "manifests itself" in their secular daily life. The manifestation or incarnation of Esmeralda's spirit complies well with DeLillo's intention of setting Sister Edgar and her fellow Americans free from the Cold War Mentality through re-opening a passage to the realm of the spiritual. To do so, DeLillo has to increase the visibility and accessibility of the secular spirituality by choosing to land Esmeralda's spirit on a billboard in the Bronx, which is indisputably a sign for American consumerism.

Consumerism, as the domineering component of recent American history, is the most secular aspect of life, and therefore, when chosen as the very vehicle on which Esmeralda's spirit lands, can most effectively convince his readers that what DeLillo tends to embrace is a spirituality that integrates transcendence and immanence into a whole and so is undoubtedly secular in essence. Shortly after Esmeralda is raped and thrown off a rooftop, some heartening news comes to

Sister Edgar that the murdered girl's spirit projects itself upon a billboard situated at the Bronx. A flood of the Bronxian residents crowd to and gather on the site and worship before the billboard, which is described as:

> An advertising sign scaffolded high above the riverbank and meant to attract the doped-over glances of commuters on the trains that ran incessantly down from the northern suburbs into the thick of Manhattan money and glut. (818)

"An advertising sign" at the Bronx, placed right in the middle between "the northern suburbs" and downtown New York, is designed as a metaphorical image that marks off the transition from agricultural thrift to commercial luxury in the American society, which, as a result, works considerably well as a reminder of how an entity, as secular as commercialism, can perform so soundly in incarnating the spiritual. DeLillo, then, pictures in greater detail what is on the billboard to push forward his readers' preliminary understanding of the immanent character of Esmeralda's spirit:

> The billboard was unevenly lighted, dim in spots, several bulbs blown and unreplaced, but the central elements were clear, a vast cascade of orange juice pouring diagonally from top right into a goblet that was handheld at lower left—the perfectly formed hand of a female Caucasian of the middle suburbs. Distant willows and a vaguish lake view set the social locus. But it was the juice that commanded the eye, thick and pulpy with a ruddled flush that matched the madder moon. And the first detailed drops plashing at the bottom of the goblet with a scatter of spindrift, each fleck embellished like the figurations of a precisionist epic. (820)

DeLillo's verisimilar delineation of so familiar a content in the advertisement throws into bold relief the secularity or immanence of a site on which a spirit is soon to be incarnated. Furthermore, in the novel, DeLillo does not even try to conceal the truth that the juice advertised on the billboard is Minute Maid, one of the best-known American brands, which is, with no doubt, the most recommendable epitome of American commercialism and so elevates the immanence of the entire picture to a level of "epic-like precision". It is the "precisionist" drawing of immanence in the incarnation site of Esmeralda's spirit that more strongly affirms the secular spirituality as both a source of Esmeralda's "beauty" and the theoretical core of the postsecular thoughts.

To Don DeLillo and other New York natives alike, the metropolitan cityscape of imposing beauty offers itself as an ideal background for whichever form of art that is meant to represent whatever is going on in the city. However, *Underworld* the New York cityscape does more than what a simple geographical background is supposed to do inasmuch as it, manipulated by the DeLilloesque craftsmanship, collaborates rather actively with American commercialism in bringing the secular spirituality into the forefront of New York residents' perception and thus, helping establish in them a postsecular mode of faith.

After he informs his readers that murdered Esmeralda's spirit has reportedly showed itself up on the billboard in the Bronx, DeLillo draws their attention, in an unaffected manner, to the cityscape of the Bronx, in which the mythic billboard is situated. DeLillo's impressing description of the landscape intimates how familiar he is with the Bronx—his place of birth:

> Two hundred people wedged onto a traffic island in the bottommost Bronx where the expressway arches down from the terminal market and the train yards stretch toward the narrows, all that industrial desolation that breaks your heart with its fretful Depression beauty—the ramps that shoot tall weeds and the old railroad bridge spanning the Harlem River, an openwork tower at either end, maybe swaying slightly in persistent wind. (94)

Bronx, as the most uptown region in New York, has witnessed the slow but steady downfall of American industrial civilization, which is therefore set by DeLillo, born as a Bronxian, as a living specimen of "industrial desolation" seen in a series of his well-chosen images like "traffic island", "train yards", "narrows", "ramps" and "railroad bridge". The decay of the Bronxian landscape, from which "tall weeds shoot", helps Don DeLillo make more obvious the failure of the industrialization—the product of an expanding dominance of reason in a secularized American society—to keep, to American people, its promise of a prospect of both peace and prosperity. By so doing, DeLillo aggravates the "holy insecurity" brought about by the cold-blood slaughtering of Esmeralda and to an extent, the rationalistic "chain of causality" is shrugged off further on from the poverty-stricken Bronxians' cognitive schemata, which predisposes them to re-open their once closed bosom to harbor a new formula of religious belief. The Bronxian surrounding, as DeLillo has pictured, is both corrosive of reason's dominance and conducive to faith's establishment. It is against this geographical backdrop that the commercial billboard can best perform its assigned role as the very medium upon which Esmeralda's spirit is projected.

Nonetheless, the projection or incarnation of a spirit cannot be fulfilled without a dynamic process being activated, which is to suggest that the desolate Bronxian cityscape of "Depression Beauty" and the billboard are both too much static, so their collaboration in taking the spirituality back into the residents' lives has to involve some more assistance, still secular in nature. The commuting trains that the Bronxians take to go to downtown New York will work as the third party or "the projector" to help incarnate Esmeralda's spirit:

> The headlights swept the billboard ... when the train lights hit the dimmest part of the billboard, a face appeared above the misty lake and it belonged to the murdered girl. (821)

If not "swept" by "the headlights", the billboard cannot complete the mission of landing the hovering-overhead spirit of Esmeralda of its own accord because the commuting train, close in nature to the Bronxian cityscape and the billboard, is naturally a catalyst that can give full play to the joint force of the two. On the one hand, the train, running on the track day and night with basically no stop, is an indispensable constituent of the New York cityscape. On the other hand, as DeLillo has poignantly revealed in a former line, the passengers aboard the train are heading for "Manhattan money and glut" (818), which tells a fact that the running trains, together with the advertising billboard, are just like the bolts and nuts that make up the colossal engine of American commercialism and keep it running forever. As a result, the commuting train is taken by DeLillo as a perfect connector to unite the static forces of the cityscape and the billboard, and more importantly, switch it from "static" to "dynamic" in executing the final projection of the spirit.

The cityscape, the billboard and the commuting train, maneuvered with DeLillo's writerly genius, set up a triad whose tripled secularity renders the poor Bronxians' faith in Esmeralda's spirit very much postsecular in nature.

The Bronxian cityscape, the billboard and the headlights of a commuting train work to combine their respective secularity in putting much stress upon the immanent nature of the spirituality thus incarnated. What's more, Don DeLillo does not omit in the novel the necessity of working out the plots demonstrative of the fact that to be immanent will never discount the comforting power of the spiritual, and besides, the comforting power in return can facilitate DeLillo's seemingly effortless endeavor in validating the existence of the secular spirituality.

When approaching the end of *Underworld*'s "the Epilogue", DeLillo takes Sister Edgar and her fellow Bronxians to the very incarnation site of Esmeralda's spirit, where they convene as a temporary community of faithful spectators waiting in earnest for the forthcoming opportunities of witnessing the spirit. To film the first communal witnessing of the incarnation, DeLillo chooses to take a distant view of the entire community by adopting Sister Edgar's eyes as the lens:

> Then she saw it, an ordinary commuter train, silver and blue, ungraffitied, moving smoothly toward the drawbridge. The headlights swept the billboard and she heard a sound from the crowd, a gasp that shot into sobs and moans and the cry of some unnameable painful elation. A blurted sort of whoop, the holler of unstoppered belief. ... A dozen women, clutched their heads, they whooped and sobbed, a spirit, a godsbreath passing through the crowd. (821)

The visible and the audible, for example, murdered Esmeralda's "face", "a gasp", "sobs and moans", and "the cry", are all meant to describe the community's warm response to the incarnation event, or in other words, function concertedly as an indicator of "some unnameable painful elation" that is seething in all the hearts of the crowd when they are most heavily impacted by the incarnated spirituality. More importantly, the surging emotions, which strike their once tranquil chords of heart and impel "a dozen women" to "whoop and sob", are all vented out in celebration of "a spirit" whose name is not "Godsbreath" but "godsbreath". DeLillo's intentional de-capitalization of the three-letter holy word can be interpreted as a proof of his unquenched thirst for the spirituality, deinstitutionalized and therefore postsecular in essence.

When the commuting train comes by for the second time, DeLillo grants a close-up to Sister Edgar, whose idiosyncratic perception of the projected image of Esmeralda's spirit can help advance DeLillo's literary endeavor in verifying the existence of the secular spirituality and its consoling impact upon its believers. Seeing that Edgar is "a nun in a veil and long habit", all the other spectators make way for her in awe and respect, and so:

> When the train lamps swung their beams onto the billboard, she saw Esmeralda's face take shape under the rainbow of bounteous juice and above the little suburban lake and it has being and disposition, there was someone living in the image, a distinguishing spirit and character, the beauty of a reasoning creature—less than a second of life, less than half a second and the spot was dark again. (822)

Though in "less than half a second" darkness falls upon the incarnation "spot" on the billboard again, Sister Edgar and other onlookers alike have got sufficient time bathing themselves in the soothing comfort that comes off from the spiritual that "takes shape under the rainbow of bounteous juice". Sister Edgar testifies to the verity of the spirituality by confirming her discernment of "being and disposition" in it, which are both "distinguishing and reasoning". Esmeralda's spirit is "distinguishing" because it is immanetized in and fused with the secular life, which differentiates it from all the world's institutionalized spiritualities, for example, Christian God. In the meantime, it is "reasoning" since its comforting strength or tremendous impact upon a heart that is in ardent pursuit of salvation will not be neutralized by its immanence and de-institutionality, and therefore it is well worth religious devotion of Sister Edgar and all other standers-by.

To briefly conclude all the foregoing arguments in this section on *Underworld*, Kathryn Ludwig can be quoted again as she presents such a cogent comment that these Esmeralda-related plots in the novel "point us not to supernatural, extra-worldly versions of the religious but to earthbound (borrowing McClure's term), relational articulations of the infinite within the finite" (Ludwig, 2010: 58). Equivalence can be established not only between "the infinite" and the spiritual but between "the finite" and the secular as well. What is worth reading again about Ludwig's argument is that the incarnation or "articulation" of "the infinite" in "the finite" is not absolute, definite or conclusive but "relational", which is a character of Don DeLillo's postsecular belief, as is derived from the Western school of postmodern thoughts on religion.

New York, as his very place of birth, has most profoundly impacted Don DeLillo's development of personality and selection of literary motifs for his works. Among all the roles New York plays for the USA and the rest of the world, its most respected role as the world's financial center places DeLillo at close quarters to witness how a certain variety of spirituality can emanate from late American capitalism, which has leapt all out of a sudden into a new phase of development and been highly technologized by advanced computer network at the turn of the 21st century. Techno-capital, thus created, travels and gathers at a lightning speed in cyperspace, and gives late capitalism in America a brand new life—cybercapitalism, which is a new form of existence that computer science helps traditional finance metamorphose into by connecting every single financial activity across the globe in a nebula-like network. As Don DeLillo has seen it, cybercapitalism, running itself in a most ostentatious way in New York, is in its own right a carrier loaded with the spiritual that causes Eric Packer, the hero of his *Cosmopolis*, to experience all the upheavals of his life within one single day and take the initiative in gripping the saving hands of a cybercapitalistic spirituality that are reached out to him.

Techno-capital, which lays out the general contour of the 21st landscape of American capitalism, can never come into being without the computer-network technology developing at an incredible speed in the last decade of the 20th century. Vincent Mosco, in his published work on the sublimity of cyberspace, labels the 1990's technologization of capital as "the digital revolution", which he summarizes as: "Powered by computer communication, we would, according to our myths, experience an epochal transformation in human experience that would transcend time (the end of history), space (the end of geography), and power (the end of politics)." (Mosco, 2000: 2 – 3) Don DeLillo, as a well-informed insider in New York, the world's center of techno-capital, would love to agree that "the digital revolution" is of formidable strength in "ending" both history and geography. However, he might not be happy to assent to the idea that the political power is ended therewith, as he claims in one of his published essays, "Technology is our fate, our truth. It is what we mean when we call ourselves the only superpower on the planet. The materials and methods we devise make it possible for us to claim our future. We don't have to depend on God or the prophets or other astonishments. We are the astonishment." (DeLillo, 2001: 37) What DeLillo tends to believe is that technology, and network technology in particular, sharpens America's competitive edge and to a great extent help cement its status of "the only superpower" in the world. Besides, DeLillo, at his most daring again, owns to the public that he sees in technology a spiritual quality with no recourse to "God or the prophets" since it originates in a, relatively speaking, newly developed aspect of the secular civilization and like Christian God and gods in other institutional religions, transcends all limitations of and so puts an end to both "history and geography".

DeLillo, with much spontaneity, extends his cognition of secular spirituality from inside technology to another field of secular life that derives from technology—cybercapitalism whose organic life cannot be made possible without techno-capital functioning as its cell. Cybercapitalism, as for Eric Packer of *Cosmopolis*, is his selected profession that brings him an early success of becoming a billionaire at the age of 28 and is also what New York, through which young Packer is passing on errands by his luxury limousine, is symbolic of. In the novel, DeLillo succeeds in representing how a spirituality that is immanentized in cybercapitalism changes Eric Packer's course of life as he comes to discern the spirituality by feeling what Immanuel Kant calls "a negative pleasure" when examining cybercapitalism at its full scale. DeLillo's experiential perception of cybercapitalism is "negative" because, as a novelist whose main goal is to represent the world, techno-capital is basically unrepresentable no matter how much effort is spent. As Joseph Tabbi claims, techno-capital, being one outcome of technology-made "crisscrossing networks of computers", "has come to represent a magnitude that at once attracts and repels the imagination" (Tabbi, 1995: 16). Jean Baudrillard specifies that the "magnitude" techno-capital is to "represent" by his semi-ironic use of such terms as "autonomous" and "free-floating" (qtd. in Shonkwiler, 2010: 250), which can be proved by Eric Packer's headlong plunge into bankruptcy within a time span as brief as a couple of hours in a day. The fact that Eric's failed investment in yen throws him into bankruptcy suggests that techno-capital is "autonomous" and "free-floating" to the extent that it establishes cybercapitalism as "a space essentially asymmetrical" (Levinas, 1969: 216). Cybercapitalism is "essentially asymmetrical" as it fails any effort to master it by refusing to set up absolute equivalence between one's carefully planned strategy and the actual result one at last gains. In this respect, as is illustrated in *Cosmopolis*, Eric Packer, who is once so confident with his high expertise in investment, is of no exception. The "autonomous", "free-floating" and "asymmetrical" quality of cybercapitalism is the main contributor to its very unrepresentability, in which the sublime lies according to Kant.

Kant claims that the sublime is something that is manifested through magnitude and ineffability, and can exhaust the powers of enumeration or speech to give any representational account of it. Accordingly, Kant goes on to argue that the sublime "is to be found in an object even devoid of form, so far as it immediately involves, or else by its presence provokes, a representation of limitlessness, yet with a super-added thought of its totality" (Kant, 1952: 90). Cybercapitalism is exactly such "an object devoid of form" produced against the postmodern conditions and therefore should be rightfully admitted as part of "a postmodern sublime", which is defined by Fredric Jameson as "enormous and threatening, yet only dimly perceivable, other reality of economic and social institutions" (Jameson, 2005: 38). The "otherness" of this "economic and social reality" consists in cybercapitalism's incarnation of the spiritual that is both within and above the plane of the secular. The "otherness" is thus spiritual in essence and manifested by cybercapitalism's "enormous" unrepresentability, and especially by asymmetry, a necessary constituent of its unrepresentability, which is so "threatening" as to foil any personal struggle to master cybercapitalism.

The implication from Kant's theory on the sublimity of cybercapitalism is agreed to by Alison Shonkwiler in his study on *Cosmopolis*. Shonkwiler calls what he has read out of the novel "the financial sublime" and defines the term as "the full range of mystifications of capital—technological, political, and otherwise—that makes it difficult or impossible to distinguish the actuality of money from the increasing unreality of global capitalism" (Shonkwiler, 2010: 249). It can be seen that cybercapitalism is synonymous with "global capitalism" and "the increasing unreality" refers to its spiritual character that comes to be realized as technology "mystifies" the capital and so, renders it utterly unrepresentable. "The financial sublime" is approved by Doug Henwood too, a renowned expert in the field of Wall Street studies, who concludes that cybercapitalism is such a financial system "that seems overwhelming at times, almost sublime in its complexity and power" (qtd. in Shonkwiler, 2010: 252). In *Cosmopolis*, DeLillo, through his *Ulysses*-like narration of the decline of Eric Packer's fortune from "riches to rags" within one single day, attests to the sublimity of cybercapitalism whose force of unrivalled magnitude should have emitted from the spirituality incarnate and also been evidenced therein by techno-capital's "accelerating dynamics of instability, circulation, and asymmetry" (Shonkwiler, 2010: 249).

It goes without saying that *Cosmopolis* is DeLillo's representational effort towards the unrepresentable—spirituality incarnated in cybercapitalism because to him, his bold confrontation with the unrepresentable will not result in "the end or 'exhaustion' of the novel"; instead, it might perform the novel's "most vital politics" (Shonkwiler, 2010: 279)—to "celebrate" what transcends the material world and reduces time and space to oblivion, which is exemplified by all that Eric Packer chooses to do after his investment in yen does not live up to his expectation.

With no expertise in finance, Don DeLillo is incapable of conducting any systemic study on Wall Street, but his increasingly sharp critic's eyes afford him deepest possible insight into the spirituality's presence within cybercapitalism, which DeLillo is going to re-affirm with his readership through his demonstration of the redemptive effect the spirituality yields upon its believers, for example, in *Cosmopolis*, Eric Packer's jubilant welcome of his death, which is accepted by himself as a certain form of salvation. Packer's self-redemption stands no chance of being fulfilled without dissolving his self under the guidance of the cybercapitalistic spirituality.

Like Gary Harkness in *End Zone*, Eric Packer, a star that shines with dazzling brilliance and splendor in his own realm of business, is once determined to assert his meaning of life by reestablishing an unmixed authenticity in his identity-construction with all means and resources available to so young a Wall Street tycoon as him. As another Gary Harkness exerting himself at the cutting edge of cybercapitalism, Eric Packer works out his strategy of resistance against reason's control of his identity construction by not resisting at all and still following his reason-driven impulse—control or mastery. Like what he does in *End Zone*, DeLillo suggests in the novel that Packer's insatiable desire for mastery is what distances him from self-redemption before he is at last bathed in the saving raindrops of the spiritual. Eric Packer quenches his thirst for mastery in his idiosyncratic way. Dissimilar to Gary Harkness, Packer tries to exert absolute control over his self by "his dependence on what is other than himself as well as his absolute will to master and consume that otherness" (Chandler, 2009: 245). To treat all the other people around him as puppets and to pull their strings at his own will, Packer is so quick-witted as to see that he needs first of all to, abandon all the rules and regulations that are supposed to harmonize his relationship with the others. "Contempt for inherited ethical formulations and social mores (that) underlies very level of Packer's behavior" (Chandler, 2009: 243) is first vividly seen in his belief that he is someone to whom traffic laws cannot be applied:

> The light was red. Only the sparsest traffic moved on the avenue ahead and he sat in the car and realized how curious it was that he was willing to wait, no less than the driver, just because a light was one color and not another. But he wasn't observing the terms of social accord. He was in a patient mood, that's all, and maybe feeling thoughtful, being mortally alone now, with his bodyguards gone. (158)

The red traffic light means nothing to Eric Packer, whose skillful manipulation of techno-capital and resultant accumulation of great wealth has planted an illusion so deep on his mind that he stands on the top of the world and it should be he, a God-like figure, who should endow meanings on all the objects he sees. Therefore, DeLillo is so accurate in identifying him as a non-observer of "the terms of social accord" and indicating that "a mood", "patient" or not, is all that pushes him into actions, including exercising masterly control over his self through "consuming the otherness".

Having wanton extramarital affairs with women is one of the ways which, help assert his individual freedom. He flouts his marital tie with his wife by seeing her rarely and never even thinking about leading a normal life with her at home. Eric Packer's numerous cases of infidelity are truthful illustration of how he exerts stringent mastery over his identity by controlling the others. However, compared with his whimsical slaughtering of his chief of security, Torval, these are far less extremist and violent. In a talk between Packer and Torval, the latter, who has just been given a message that Benno Levin, fired from Packer's firm, is going to avenge himself on his ex-boss with a pistol in hand, warns Packer of the lurking threat that might endanger his life. Packer shifts the subject of their conversation from Levin to weaponry most unaffectedly, and insists that he should take a quick look at Torval's handgun, with which, out of the blue, Packer shoots him to death for no good reason:

> He shot the man. A small white terror of disbelief flickered in Torval's eye. He fired once and the man went down. All authority drained out of him. He looked foolish and confused. (146)

Eric Packer's willful violation of accepted social rules has prepared him so well for this blunter defiance of other people's value of life and by so doing, the billionaire must have obtained tremendous pleasure because he has "drained all authority out of" Torval and injected it to himself, or in other words, he has claimed and won full authority over his subjectivity by precipitating, in his coldness and caprice, an abrupt ending of someone else's life. His undisturbed mental tranquility after he takes Torval's life can reveal how much hardened his will is to devour other subject's authority to assert his, as he tells the kids who has just witnessed the murder to go on with their basketball game and thinks to himself: "Nothing so meaningful had happened that they were required to stop playing." (146) As Aaron Chandler has commented, Eric Packer's random consumption of others' lives helps him "erect barriers to his selfhood for the pleasure of annihilating them" (Chandler, 2009: 245). "The barriers" enclose Packer in a somewhat sacred terrain of self that will not be trespassed into and furthermore, he is so willed as to quench his bloody thirst for asserting his full authenticity by demolishing these "barriers" just built up.

Eric Packer's morbid desire for self-assertion cannot be appeased a bit before he is knocked down by an incident of "holy insecurity" and thus, grants himself a chance to fulfill a redeeming embrace of the spiritual. Before his disastrous investment in yen, life has hinted to him once at the fact that something, which never caters to his impulsive desire for control and mastery, is for all time hidden and it is part of a much grander design than reason—the dimension of the spiritual. His report of regular physical exam suggests that he has got the asymmetrical prostate. The much earlier-than-expected problem with his prostate is already so strong a proof that dead ends are everywhere if one seeks after his value of life by obstinate exertion of his will towards mastery and control. Pitiably, the physical "asymmetry" does not work too well as a reminder to Eric Packer, who, does not learn about what hidden asymmetries mean to him until he is routed in the techno-capital market. An early accumulation of colossal wealth at 28 develops in Packer an illusive sense of security that he, unlike other investors, is immune against all risky vacillations of the currency market, or to put it another way, he is never ever mentally prepared for a sudden loss of all his fortune. So, witnessing, on the computer screen, how his financial empire collapses into ruins in the blink of an eye while seated with calm and ease in his well-equipped limousine, Eric Packer for the first time in his life rushes headlong into "holy insecurity" and he comes to realize his "inability to account for hidden asymmetries" of the world's financial market after he loses all his fortune with his failed investment in yen. Nevertheless, "holy insecurity", as has been provoked by the techno-market's asymmetry unknown to him before, has enabled, as it does with Sister Edgar of *Underworld*, a spiritual truth to dawn upon Packer that there exists in cybercapitalism certain spirituality, whose irresistible divine power is felt by Eric as he sees the devastating effect of the market's uncontrollable asymmetry upon his hard-won fortune.

Immersed in "holy insecurity", Eric Packer finds himself summoned again by the spiritual to prepare himself for a ready acceptance of what is to become of him since his regained trust in the spiritual offers him all the answers he needs to his questions about subjectivity or meaning of life. Like Sister Edgar in *Underworld*, Packer breaks loose from the secular chain of causality and begins to see that his physical being in the visible world is gifted with a meaning ever since its start. As a result, he is more than content with cleansing himself of all the leftover impulses for mastery and control and entrusting cybercapitalistic spirituality with his self construction, which can be seen in DeLillo's description of a bankrupted Eric Parker:

> Eric's delight in going broke seemed blessed and authenticated here. He'd been emptied of everything but a sense of surpassing stillness, a fatedness that felt disinterested and free. (136)

"Blessed and authenticated" by the spiritual he has just re-embraced after his fortune plummets downward, Eric Packer has "emptied" himself of his rationality-driven obsession with masterly control of his identity, and to enjoy his "fatedness"; and to be "disinterested and free" is suggestive of his fulfillment of the highest-level self-redemption—his renunciation of all efforts to build a logos-informed self. Such a self has to be renounced since Packer has blazed a spiritual passage towards redemptive self-formation. The redemptive effect of his renunciation reaches its peak when Packer, well informed of Benno Levin's plan to shoot him, still follows his death drive with no fear at all. Having shot Torval, his chief of security, to death, Packer has his gun in possession. However, he volunteers to disarm himself and wait in calm for his death if it is inevitable:

> He'd tossed the weapon in the bushes because he wanted whatever would happen to happen. Guns were small practical things. He wanted to trust the power of predetermined events. The act was done, the gun should go. (147)

Learning his meaning of life by following the lead of the spiritual, Packer has aborted all his initiatives in constructing a logos-informed self and resultingly, he "trusts the power of the events" predetermined by the spiritual just as his meaning of life is, and lets his death drive go free even if Benno Levin's claim on his life is not justifiable when examined from a rationalistic point of view.

At the end of the novel where Eric Packer has been mortally wounded, he still does not forget to philosophize, in his fading mind, on the spirituality incarnated in cybercapitalism, which leads him towards salvation that at last takes shape in his calm acceptance of an early death:

> It would be the master thrust of cyber-capital, to extend the human experience toward infinity as a medium for corporate growth and investment, for the accumulation of profits and vigorous reinvestment. (207)

"Infinity" is indeed a land of promise, where though his self is dissolved with no trace left, his soul is forever caressed by the gentle saving hands of the divine. This land of promise is right there in the secular, to which Don DeLillo would love to lead his characters who have just gained their access to secular spirituality.

CHAPTER FOUR

Means of Pursuit of Secular Spirituality

—To-dos and Not-to-dos

Identified as a new mode of faith, postsecularism does not merely concern itself with the whereabouts of secular spirituality but also strives to draft a map of routes through which its pursuers can finally get to their goal. In the map, postsecular thinkers chart out both the routes that lead its pursuers straight to secular spirituality and other winding courses, if chosen, might take its pursuers to deviate from their decided destination. DeLillo's oeuvre is such a postsecular map of routes, in which the novelist, through his consummate artistry in plot design and characterization, marks off both "to-dos" and "not-to-dos" in the progress of drawing oneself nearer and nearer to secular spirituality. First of all, in *Underworld*, Don DeLillo, with his full cognizance of the immanent and thus poststructuralist nature of secular spirituality, suggests that a pursuer must learn to individualize his means of pursuit as secular spirituality is a divine being immanetized in the secular world, whose existence cannot be validated if not felt by an individual. In *Falling Man*, DeLillo looks further into one's individuation of his means of pursuit by implying that it is in effect a project of reconstructing one's mode of perception on the world and the human life. In *White Noise* and *Underworld*, DeLillo stresses the indisputable importance of communality for all the pursuers—a certain number of worshippers of common interests in a secular spirituality should gather at a particular site and observe some improvisatory rituals together so as to strengthen the consolatory effect that the secular spirituality can produce upon its believers. Don DeLillo's in-depth meditation on to-dos and not-to-dos draws the finishing stroke of a postsecular picture in his works.

Martin Beck Matustik, one of the major contributors who work to lay down the basis of postsecular thoughts, tends to call postsecularism and its related arguments as "the religious" and he articulates it not as religious texts or institutions, but as "the uncanny", which he defines as: "impersonal fields that exceed secular experience and ... corresponding personal and interpersonal modalities of 'excess'" (Matustik, 2008: 17). As could be suggested by the relevant hints he drops throughout his fictional writings, Don DeLillo could do no more than to partly agree to Matustik's definition. DeLillo would love to affirm that secular spirituality is "the uncanny" because it can make any effort to shape it or institutionalize it in vain, and besides, it for sure is an "impersonal field" since it is there of its own accord in a terrain that is way up above any "secular experience". Nonetheless, DeLillo would not concede to Matustik's argument that secular spirituality goes beyond "personal modalities of 'excess'"—personal endeavors to exceed his physical being to reach and embrace secular spirituality, because the divine could lose its claim for existence if it cannot be felt or dawn on an individual believer. Out of the aforementioned concerns, DeLillo, first in *Underworld*, implies that to attain to the plane of the spiritual, one needs to decide on their own means of pursuit, and further on in *Falling Man*, he elucidates on the two indispensable aspects of the individuation job.

Kathryn Ludwig, in her Ph. D. book on a postsecular criticism of contemporary American fictions, reaches an agreement with other contributors to postsecular thoughts that it is postmodern philosophy that postsecularism originates from, on which Ludwig states: "Another way to consider the notion of 'secular' in 'post-secular' is to interrogate secular characterizations of postmodernism, the theoretical context into which (or, arguably, out of which) the postsecular emerges." (Ludwig, 2010: 13) Postmodernism is "the theoretical context" where "the postsecular" comes into being, and more importantly, it does not matter whether "the postsecular emerges" "into" or "out of" the context. In other words, postsecularism starts itself off with the poststructuralist genes it inherits from postmodern thoughts on religion, which helps affirm individuation of one's means of pursuit as the very prerequisite or starting point in their pilgrimage to secular spirituality.

Don DeLillo, in *Underworld*, has worked to manifest that individuation is in essence a thoroughgoing change in one's consciousness. Having been informed that murdered Esmeralda's spirit has developed itself an image upon a billboard, Sister Edgar and Sister Gracie hold a hot debate on the "supernatural" phenomenon, in which Gracie seems to slight these spectators' faith in the "ghost" by saying:

> It's how the news becomes so powerful it doesn't need TV or newspapers. It exists in people's perceptions. It becomes real or fake-real so people think they're seeing reality when they're seeing something they invent. It's the news without media. (819)

"It exists in people's perceptions" is with no doubt the keynote speech DeLillo intends Gracie to deliver on how much individuation weighs as the very first step that takes one closer to the spirituality. DeLillo's clearly-drawn portrayal of Gracie's posture as an unbeliever in any earthly spirituality indicates his pity on her being too much institutionalized by rigid Christian doctrines and cannot conceal the truth that he cannot consent to Gracie's scornful dismissal of the self-invented means to approach the secular spirituality. To DeLillo, secular spirituality is such a "reality" and to gain access to it, one has no alternative but to "invent". "Invention", in DeLillo's regard, is nothing to feel ashamed of, since when "invented", the passage of faith leads straight to the spirituality that is much more comforting and consolatory than any institutionalized divinity which hangs high overhead and never touches down on the ground of life.

To "invent" is to revolutionize one's consciousness of both their life and the world, and in this sense, "invention" can be nothing else but a turning moment in one's life, which Martin Buber defines as follows:

> Inner transformation simply means surpassing one's present and factual constitution; it means the person one is intended to be penetrates what has appeared up until now, that the customary soul enlarges and transfigures itself into the surprise soul. This is what the prophets of Israel understood by the turning in their language of faith: not a return to an earlier, guiltless stage of life, but a swinging around to where the wasted hither-and-thither becomes walking on a way, and guilt is atoned for in the newly arisen genuineness of existence. (Buber, 2000: 186)

So it follows that "genuineness of existence" is such a guilt-free state of one's life, which cannot be attained to without their success in conducting "inner transformation" and resultingly completing his reunion with some spirituality. By "surpassing one's present and factual constitution", Martin Buber suggests that "transformation" is a "beyond" movement and it is precipitated by sheer individualistic effort, and furthermore, he suggests that "the surprise soul", sublimated from "the customary soul" and "enlarged and transfigured" to be reunited with the spiritual, is an indicator of the individualistic nature of both the spirituality's means of pursuit and its very effect upon the believers. It could be concluded, on the basis of Buber's explanation of "turning", that a postsecular faith is essentially individualized, in both process—paving the way to the spiritual, and final goal—a reunion with the spirituality or a "genuine state of existence". John McClure, who cannot be more insightful towards individuation of both means and end in postsecularism, would complement Martin Buber's arguments by stating that a postmodern belief is utterly individualized as the starting point that triggers it off is individualistic too. McClure, more than once in his writings, claims that "turnings" occur on the precondition that one first experiences what he calls "holy terror" (Ludwig, 2010: 45). The term is close in meaning to Martin Buber's "holy insecurity" and is discussed in detail in Chapter Two of the book. In *Underworld*, Don DeLillo, in turn, enriches both Buber's theorization on individuation and

McClure's extended research on "holy terror" by illustrating that "terror", which starts individuation of a postsecular pursuit of faith, can be most intensely felt by someone whose social identity is marginal.

In *Underworld*, Sister Edgar and Sister Gracie, in a talk conducted to decide whether they should go and watch with their own eyes Esmeralda's spirit on the billboard, exchange their ideas on to whom the spirit should appear:

> Sister Gracie: This is something for poor people to confront and judge and understand if they can and we have to see it in that framework. The poor need visions, okay?
>
> Sister Edgar: You say the poor. But who else would saints appear to? Do saints and angels appear to bank presidents? (819)

"To confront and judge and understand" is to evidence that Gracie must have conceded that individuation is the very passage that leads one to certain spirituality. Besides, both she and Sister Edgar agree that the new mode of faith pursuit is most likely to take place in "the poor" because they are the ones that "need visions" to alleviate their pains and sorrows in the secular life, which is for sure not shared by "bank presidents" who, as a result, stand a slim chance of visualizing "saints and angels" in their life. "The poor" are the subjects of contemporary American society, whose marginality in social identity is largely economic in nature. DeLillo draws a clearer picture of "marginality" by offering Sister Edgar a chance to develop a panoramic view of Esmeralda's believers:

> She let her eyes wander to the crowd. Working people, she thought. Working women, shopkeepers, maybe some drifters and squatters but not many, and then she noticed a group near the front, fitted snug to the prowed shape of the island—they were the charismatics from the top floor of the tenement in the Wall, dressed mainly in floppy white, tublike women, reedy men with dreadlocks. (820)

The witnessing audience, jobless or not, are all "the poor" who suffer privation a lot and therefore are struggling on the margin of American society. They are much more susceptible than "bank presidents" to "holy terror", multitudinous in both kind and number, and in consequence they are much more predisposed to not only start but also strengthen their individuation in their pursuit of a postsecular faith. What's more, more marginalized than all the others in the crowd are "the charismatics", who are economically poor like the rest of the crowd and more unacceptable to the reason-instructed mainstream society as they label themselves as ones who are in total communion with the divine and therefore endowed with extraordinary skills of a magician.

Individuation is "a consciousness revolution" in Habermasian terms, which can be fueled and sped up by one's marginality in identity. In *Falling Man*, a novel written in the aftermath of 9/11 and most closely related to the cataclysmic terrorist attack in his oeuvre, Don DeLillo goes on further to explain what the "revolution" is going to revolutionize.

To rebuild a pavement on which a prospective believer can walk back to the terrain of the spiritual, he has no choice but to eradicate from his mindset his fiery desire to approach logos or his obsessive preoccupation with control or mastery and be ready and willing to live with the truth that much outside there in an unknown dimension is something utterly impervious to human command. Only by one's acceptance of the truth can he humble down his self to be "porous" towards all the mythic and sacred forces and so wins himself an access to spirituality, or else, like Gary Harkness in *End Zone*, he will forever trap his self in a "buffered" state of being—an ingrained hallucination about reason's omnipotence in resolving all tricky human problems, which isolates him at a great distance from a redemptive influence of the spiritual. Thirty-five yeas after the publication of *End Zone*, in his 9/11 novel *Falling Man*, Don DeLillo, offers his readership a chance to neutralize the insidious effect of Gary Harkness's disavowal of mankind's vulnerability by leading them to reaffirm their neglected or unacknowledged vulnerability through his revelation of an unchanged and unchangeable bodily movement—falling, which lays the very foundation for *Falling Man*'s distinctive significance for American literary representation of 9/11.

Before presenting the Falling Man's performance in the novel, Don DeLillo has suggested to all his readers that falling is an ineluctable consequence of gravity, which in its own right is an indomitable force all human minds, no matter how advanced they have been developed to be by reason, have to bow to and is exactly where lies the hope that human beings can regain their lost sense of vulnerability that should take them, with a humbled self, back to the once deserted realm of the spiritual. Keith Neudecker, a 39-year-old lawyer who works in the World Trade Center, escapes from the tower that is on fire and about to collapse soon. He sees every single object falling, and what attracts his attention the most is a floating shirt:

> The world was all this as well, figures in windows a thousand feet up, dropping into free space, and the stink of fuel fire, and the steady rip of sirens in the air. The noise lay everywhere they ran, stratified sound collecting around them, and he walked away from it and into it at the same time. There was something else then, outside all this, not belonging to this, aloft. He watched it coming down. A shirt came down out of the high smoke, a shirt lifted and drifting in the scant light and then falling again, down toward the river. (4)

An inanimate object as light-weighted as "a shirt" is destined to "fall again", though "lifted and drifting in the scant light". The human bodies, which are much more weighty, are sure to fall down more quickly than a shirt does. Inferably, the falling shirt is a much less horrible symbol for a falling human body, whose downfall and being smashed into pieces on the ground works as a reminder of gravity, a natural phenomenon that mankind has to live with and might develop no means to counteract. However, DeLillo does not intend gravity to frighten these life-value pursuers off from their course to redemption; on the contrary, gravity, capable of re-instilling into human minds a sense of vulnerability about their physical existence, is in its own right an incarnation of the spiritual.

As Ralph Waldo Emerson has talked of more than one and half a century before in his well-read essay *Spiritual Laws*, gravity is a law not just natural but also spiritual:

> For, whenever we get the vantage-ground of the past or of a wiser mind in the present, we are able to discern that we are begirt with laws which execute themselves. (Emerson, 1983: 307)
>
> Let us draw a lesson from nature, which always works by short ways. When the fruit is ripe, it falls. When the fruit is dispatched, the leaf falls. The circuit of the waters is mere falling. The walking of man and all animals is a falling forward. All our manual labor and feats of strength, as prying, splitting, digging, rowing, and so forth are done by dint of continual falling, and the globe, earth, moon, comet, sun, star, fall for ever and ever. (Emerson, 1983: 308)

It is self-evident that Emerson is briefing his audience on some natural phenomena so as to make them "able to discern" that gravity is one of the "laws which execute themselves". It is its self-willed execution that elevates gravity way out of the scope of the rational and so, enables it to remain at large from all human means of control and mastery. So, Emerson might have suggested that gravity should be part of the design of the spiritual, through which it, no matter how shapeless or de-institutional, can be still felt in the physical world. Or to put it another way, gravity deserves to be called one incarnation of secular spirituality, which can well reconcile the natural and the spiritual and integrate the two paradoxical entities into a whole, and so, as J. H. Atchley argues in his essay, enlightens human minds upon the truth that "spirit is not otherworldly, and nature is not a derivative from some higher realm of being ... ultimate reality (which, in certain moods, could also be called the divine) is not far away" (Atchley, 2010: 68 – 69). One's affirmation of vulnerability when confronted with gravity, a variety of secular spirituality that operates by its own natural but divine rule, is in the meantime his affirmation of value of life—"a value that does not change when our fates and fortunes do" (Atchley, 2010: 68).

Gravity, whose power is as divine as to pull everyone down to the ground, either animate or inanimate, is right here reminding mankind that "life's value is there, no matter what happens to us" (Atchley, 2010: 68), or in other words, reason is not what is needed to define life's value since every human life is created with a value as is decided prenatally by the spiritual, which gravity incarnates on its own. Emerson, thus, names the life-value affirming character of gravity as "the optimism of nature", which, in Atchley's regard, could be better termed "ontology". (Atchley, 2010: 68)

In *Falling Man*, Lianne Glenn, Keith Neudecker's estranged wife, is characterized by Don DeLillo as a deputy, on behalf of all humans, to learn about such an "ontology" that confers upon human life a value with no interference from reason. Lianne is not there in the towers when the attack occurs and so, in order to help her recapture what her husband experiences and by so doing affirm her vulnerability, DeLillo places her among the crowds who watch Falling Man's stunning performance:

> She'd heard of him, a performance artist known as Falling Man. He'd appeared several times in the last week, unannounced, in various parts of the city, suspended from one or another structure, always upside down, wearing a suit, a tie and dress shoes. He brought it back, of course, those stark moments in the burning towers when people fell or were forced to jump. ... Traffic was barely moving now. There were people shouting up at him, outraged at the spectacle, the puppetry of human desperation, a body's last fleet breath and what it held. It held the gaze of the world, she thought. (33)

The traumatizing effect the performance can exert upon Lianne is so strong as to arouse in her and all other spectators a vehement feeling of vulnerability, which brings them all closer to the spiritual in awe and fear. As she thinks to herself when she later watches Falling Man jump off from an elevated train platform on the 100th Street that "he was a falling angel and his beauty was horrific" (222), Lianne has come to recognize the implicit meaning of the "falling angel's" performance that one's subjection of himself to gravity is all that his "horrific beauty" is meant to hint at. Though "she could have spoken to him, but that was another plane of being, beyond reach" (168), Lianne, throughout the course of the plot development, struggles to "reach another plane of being" that Falling Man has exhibited to her, where she could blend her physical being with the spiritual and in such a way consummate her meaning of life. To do so, Lianne knows that her religious consciousness, as has been awaken by Falling Man's performance, must undergo a more thoroughgoing revolution—secularization of her Catholic faith to serve her own end. The two most deadly traumas in her life help Lianne complete her mission of secularization, with the first functioning as the motive and the second working as the experimental field in which Lianne tests the very effects of her mission.

Before her encounter with Falling Man and his performance, Lianne has allowed her religious faith to hibernate for years, since her mother is a non-believer and her father is a lapsed Catholic. As a result, her life is basically secular, which offers her no breeding ground for the secularization of Catholicism. The advent of the turning point takes place as her father's suicide befalls her, which, together with 9/11, marks off a starting point for her casting a new thought on Catholicism and secularizing it. Lianne's father, Jack Glenn, kills himself after he knows that he is suffering from an early-stage Alzheimer's disease and so makes his final judgment that "he did not want to submit to the long course of senile dementia" (40). To Lianne's great frustration, what at last extinguishes Jack's flame of life is not his disbelief in Catholicism but Catholicism itself. Through her in-depth investigation into her father's religious thoughts, Lianne learns that as a lapsed Catholic, Jack only claims not to practice any Catholic rituals, but in fact, he is still a firm believer in all Catholic doctrines:

> She thought of her father. She carried her father's name. She was Lianne Glenn. Her father had been a traditional lapsed Catholic, devoted to the Latin mass as long as he didn't have to sit through it. He made no distinction between Catholics and lapsed Catholics. The only thing that

mattered was tradition but not in his work, never there, his designs for buildings and other structures, situated in mostly remote landscapes. (68)

That Jack does not "sit through" any Latin mass but is still "devoted to" it manifests the truth that his "lapsedness" is not that thoroughgoing and he is as ever before indoctrinated by the Catholic tenets. As Lianne suggests that "he made no distinction between Catholics and lapsed Catholics", though having not observed any Catholic rituals, Jack still indoctrinates himself exceedingly and chooses to believe the neat demarcation between the two "planes"—God's and humans'. As a result, the genuine essence of the Catholic "tradition"—communion with the divine, does not "matter" to him especially in "his work", which can account for his resolute choice of situating "his designs for buildings and other structures in mostly remote landscapes". As an architect, Jack Glen persists in his peculiar choice of isolated construction sites to build his designs, which can suggest how strong his disbelief in the probability of the spiritual being incarnated in the secular is. As Brian Conniff asserts in his essay, Jack Glen lacks "an imaginative capacity to translate his work into an apprehension of God's presence in everyday circumstances", and so his "represents a kind of faith that does not engage culture, even in the most elevated terms, and even his immediate world" (Conniff, 2013: 59 - 60). Jack's religious belief disengages him from "his immediate world", which, in his regard, is never tainted with even the slightest trace of spirituality and cannot offer him any spiritual comfort after he becomes an Alzheimer's patient and is not worth his continual stay. That is the reason why Conniff should claim that "when the time comes for Jack to face his final illness, it is hardly surprising that his elevated and dislocated sense of the eternal cannot sustain him" (Conniff, 2013: 59 - 60). Badly traumatized by Jack's suicide, Lianne learns a lesson that Catholic faith is of no redemptive value without her going as far as to cross out the demarcation line between the spiritual and the secular. As for Lianne secularization is to situate the divine back into the immediate world so that its saving power could be accessible to every single one in need of help.

Lianne's skepticism towards God—the institutionalized divinity in

Catholicism—sets herself ready to secularize her return to Catholic belief:

> There was religion, then there was God. Lianne wanted to disbelieve. Disbelief was the line of travel that led to clarity of thought and purpose. Or was this simply another form of superstition? She wanted to trust in the forces and processes of the natural world, this only, perceptible reality and scientific endeavor, men and women alone on earth. ... But she didn't want to. ... and there was the sacred art she'd always loved. Doubters created this work, and ardent believers, and those who'd doubted and then believed, and she was free to think and doubt and believe simultaneously. But she didn't want to. God would crowd her, make her weaker. God would be a presence that remained unimaginable. She wanted this only, to snuff out the pulse of the shaky faith she'd held for much of her life. (64 –65)

On the one hand, Lianne is seriously thinking about the probability of secularizing her consciousness completely by establishing herself as a disbeliever who believes only in "perceptible reality and scientific endeavor", but "she didn't want to". On the other hand, by enjoying the sublime beauty of "the sacred art", she grants herself a chance to grasp tight the hands of the divine, but still "she didn't want to". Lianne's "faith" is so "shaky" that she cannot accept Catholic God as the only identity for the divine, because as Conniff argues, God's eternal absence befuddles and frightens her (Conniff, 2013: 59), and even if Catholic God is here with her in her life, His presence might be too overwhelming, which would "crowd her, make her weaker". So, on the basis of DeLillo's revelation of Lianne's state of religious consciousness and Conniff's judgment on it, it could be inferred that what Lianne is searching for is a certain formula of spirituality that is de-institutional whereas incarnated in the secular. Accordingly, secular spirituality can well answer for her spiritual quest, which will not "snuff out" her skepticism and leave her "free to think and doubt and believe simultaneously", as she has requested.

Almost two decades after her father's suicide, 9/11 and its stimulated falling performance of Falling Man traumatize Lianne for the second time, which triggers off her secularizing project of Catholic faith that was conceived but not put into practice when she had her first traumatic experience. A much intensified sense of vulnerability Lianne gains through her witnessing of Falling Man's performance reminds her that spirituality is incarnated in the most immediate and natural phenomenon—gravity, which injects into her heart strong confidence that her mission of secularizing Catholic faith is more than feasible. Though not enabled or compelled to give a well-defined shape to secular spirituality, Lianne decides to take God as one of her temporary options for the divine object in which she places her belief. By doing so, she can draw herself nearer to the spiritual, of which Catholic God is but one possible way of naming. In her attempt to cure herself of the two traumas—Jack Glenn's suicide and the 9/11 attack, Lianne works for her neighborhood as a volunteer whose duty is to direct a writing workshop for Alzheimer's patients. Not surprisingly, in the workshop, the subject under their hottest debate is how to justify God's way in a historical event as cataclysmic as 9/11—"where was God when this happened?" (60) Hearing from her "students" the question, Lianne right away comes to admit that:

> She needed these people. It was possible that the group meant more to her than it did to the members. There was something precious here, something that seeps and bleeds. These people were the living breath of the thing that killed her father. (62)

Lianne's students, similar to her father in both religious background and physical condition, join her in carrying forward her self-imposed mission of landing Catholic God upon their secular life, whose presence in the immediate world can execute some redemptive force to help them all confront and overcome the double threats from Alzheimer's disease and Al Qaeda. In fact, Lianne's secular version of Catholicism should be entitled to a new name tag—postsecularism, whose poststructuralist nature is protective of Lianne's religious skepticism, and so, can work as a strong antidote to the fundamentalist virus Al Qaeda spreads through its indiscriminate exertion of violence. Besides, the pain-soothing property of any institutional religious belief is still inherent in the Catholicism that Lianne and her Alzheimer's-patient students choose to follow, which stimulates Lianne and all her workshop members to conquer their fear of "the thing that killed her father" and even death itself. To a great extent, the group discussion that follows the theoretical route of a secular Catholicism relieves Lianne's tremendous pains at the unprepared-for loss of her father and cures Lianne and her "students" of their national trauma that wreaks great havoc with their mental health. There is no wonder that one member calls the workshop, with much pride, their "prayer room" (63)—a religious community in the real sense of the word.

In a thanksgiving mood, Lianne visits the Catholic Church that one of her Alzheimer students recommends and attends Mass there regularly. By so doing, she does not abandon herself to a Catholic God hovering high above her immediate world; instead, she consolidates her belief in a God who sets his footing right on the secular and in all time, stays fully prepared to serve the interests of all his believers:

> She was stuck with her doubts but liked sitting in church. She went early, before mass began, to be alone for a while, to feel the calm that marks a presence outside the nonstop riffs of the waking mind. ... Church brings us closer. ... It was a comfort, feeling their presence, the dead she'd loved and all the faceless others who'd filled a thousand churches. (233)

Her "conversion" to the secularized Catholicism is to make her grow more and more forgetful about God's name, which is not referred to for even once in the paragraph quoted above from the end of the novel. However, her spiritual communion with "a presence outside the nonstop riffs of the waking mind" is not a bit compromised, which is at least part of the reason why she goes to sit in the church earlier than others. "The calm" she can feel alone is strengthened by being shared with all her Alzheimer's patients that form a miniature Church that "brings us closer". Most importantly, it is "the calm" brought upon her by the "presence" that helps her overcome her fear of death so that when thinking of "the dead she'd loved and all the faceless others", she feels nothing but "a comfort".

In Lianne Glenn, Don DeLillo embodies his ideal for "cultural Catholicism" or "incarnational faith", a phrasal term Robert Orsi brings forward in his *The Madonna of 115th Street*, in which "Heaven was closer to the people and the people never set the two worlds completely apart" (Orsi, 2010: 227). It can be clearly seen that both "cultural Catholicism" and "incarnational faith" are close in meaning to Lianne's secularized Catholicism, a Catholic variant of postsecularism, which represent "ways of knowing and habits of being outside the official precincts and sanction ... of the church ... a form of transfigurative reenvisioning that refuses to quarantine the sacred" (Orsi, 2010: 8 – 9). To DeLillo, Lianne Glenn and other postsecular characters in his fiction, postsecularism indeed works as a "way of knowing" or a "habit of being", which, though not sanctioned by any church or religious institution, never even tries to "quarantine the sacred" so that its followers could gain access to the spiritual in their secular life and be comforted whenever need be.

A religious faith, either as institutionalized as Christianity or as de-institutionalized as postsecularism, cannot be soundly practiced with no dependence on the formation of a worshipping community. For these pursuers of a postsecular faith, they gather in a community of a certain scale, as stimulated by a shared belief in a secular spirituality. In the community, the postsecular believers can effect "the festive", a religious category that Charles Taylor's defines in *A Secular Age*, "which can be observed in certain moments of mass celebration which seem to take us out of the everyday and seems to put us in touch with something exceptional, beyond ourselves" (Taylor, 2007: 546). Manifestly, it is "the festive" the believing "mass" celebrates that not only puts them in close contact with "something exceptional" or the spirituality, but also more powerfully gratifies their sorest desire for the spiritual comfort by dint of their mutual understanding and support in the community. Don DeLillo's keen awareness of a community-of-belief's magnificent ability to facilitate one's pursuit of a postsecular faith has been talked of in the foregoing section on

Falling Man, in which crowds of spectators who watch Falling Man's performance and Lianne Glenn's writing workshop are both typical of a postsecular community. The two communities in *Falling Man* are both born out of 9/11, the American crisis of the greatest severity in its history, as the working mechanisms to alleviate or cure the resulting traumas. A retrospective glimpse at DeLillo's writing history will reveal that *Falling Man* is not his first attempt by which he suggests how a community, in a crisis that occurs out of the blue, could function in solidifying one's belief in secular spirituality and thus dressing one's physical and mental wounds. "The airborne toxic event" in *White Noise* and Angel Esmeralda's pathetic fall in *Underworld* are the other two representative cases in which the sound effect of a postsecular community, though "improvisational and fleeting" (Conniff, 2013: 54), is intensified to an extent that it can no longer be neglected. Besides, known for his fervor for American-style sports, DeLillo, in *End Zone*, also taps the potential of American football as a community that might have offered Gary Harkness a saving hand, which he does not come to grip.

Don DeLillo's plot arrangement in *White Noise* revolves around an ecological crisis known to Jack Gladney and all the others in the neighborhood as "airborne toxic event" because DeLillo might have reached some tacit agreement with Martin Buber, one of the most celebrated Jewish philosophers in religion, that "holy insecurity" in a crisis can set off the development of a community in which the "sacred bond" between the members will bring them closer to self-redemption no matter how short a period their coordinated worshipping activity should last. A professor specializing in Hitler studies, Jack Gladney establishes his family right in the middle of the American social ladder. He and his neighbors, therefore, all lead a middle-class life, so cozy and well-off as to slacken their precaution against the possible outbreak of an unexpected and severe crisis. Consequently, when "the airborne toxic event" befalls the neighborhood and its very severity threatens them to evacuate from their dwelling places, Jack is so dumbfounded as to dissuade himself and his family from believing that they will be impacted:

> "It won't come this way."
>
> "How do you know?"
>
> "It just won't." (110)

Even when an official order for evacuation is passed around, Jack still chooses to turn a deaf ear to the well-clarified threats of "the event":

> "But will we have to leave our homes?"
>
> "Of course not."
>
> "How do you know?"
>
> "I just know."
>
> "Remember how we wouldn't go to school?"
>
> "That was inside. This is outside." (112)

Dread overwhelms Jack Gladney as he sees that it is so pervasive and strong in "the evacuation army" who flood out of the impacted area when he and his family are forced to join them at last. Nonetheless, it is the dread shared between Jack Gladney's family and their fellow evacuees in the long and slow-moving car procession that helps develop a community of faith, in which they can imbibe some spiritual comfort from the direful effect of "the toxic event".

In "The Power of History", a short essay published in *The New York Times Magazine* in 1997, Don DeLillo observes that "we depend on disaster to consolidate our vision" (DeLillo, 1997: 63). In *White Noise*, it is the ecological crisis that works to "consolidate our vision" because, as Matthew J. Packer argues, it is "first of all public, collectively experienced, and therefore binding" (Packer, 2005: 657). A tremendous feeling of "insecurity" floods into the Jack Gladneys' hearts, which not only "consolidates" but also redirects their "vision" towards certain sacred aspect of the deadly crisis, and thus "binds" them all in a makeshift community to worship a secular spirituality shot off from their strong sense of "holy insecurity":

> The enormous dark mass moved like some death ship in a Norse

> legend. We weren't sure how to react. It was a terrible thing to see, so close, so low ... But it was also spectacular, part of the grandness of a sweeping event ... Our fear was accompanied by a sense of awe that bordered on the religious. It is surely possible to be awed by the thing that threatens your life, to see it as a cosmic force, so much larger than yourself, more powerful, created by elemental and willful rhythms. (127 –128)

Though Jack Gladney admits that "the enormous dark mass"—a huge cloud-like aggregation of spilt toxic chemicals that hangs right over the evacuees' heads—is first created in a laboratory, he cannot help coming to recognize the truth that it is nature itself that assists in the development of the mass and ultimately takes it to reach a scale of "grandness", "larger than yourself" and "more powerful" than what human hands can reach out for. So, in every possible sense, "the dark mass", though man-made at first, is "an objective impossibility" in Kantian terms, whose "infiniteness as given" entails mankind's "incapacity for grasping". (Kant, 1952: 108) It follows that what "we"—Jack and other evacuees in the car procession—are witnessing is an incarnation of something sacred or spiritual, whose presence in turn cannot be so easily discerned if no "we"-community is formed to have one's painful thirst for the spiritual echoed and answered. Thanks to the calamitous event, the family crises they have to face in their mundane and private lives are interrupted and these evacuees, quite involuntarily, unite in a sacred bond to seek for the relief for the community as a whole. Furthermore, the bond is sacred because "the impossible object" the victims are watching is holy, which is in the case exemplified by "the dark mass", and its soothing effect cannot be strengthened or even felt as well without the evacuees being bound in a community.

The sacred bond in Jack Gladney's community is turning stronger after "the airborne toxic event" as it expands in size and its "worshipping" activity grows increasingly regular. When "the dark mass" is dispersed at last, all the inhabitants in Blacksmith are so amazed to see that a sunset of unusual splendor has been made as a consequence. The Blacksmithians, from all walks of life, gather, out of their own will, on an overpass, which is rumored to be the best observation site. However, as Jack Gladney admits on behalf of "we", the observers cannot capture their feeling about the sunset:

> It is hard to know how we should feel about this. Some people are scared by the sunsets, some determined to be elated, but most of us don't know how to feel, are ready to go either way. ... What else do we feel? Certainly there is awe, but we don't know whether we are watching in wonder or dread, we don't know what we are watching or what it means, we don't know whether it is permanent, a level of experience to which we will gradually adjust, into which our uncertainty will eventually be absorbed, or just some atmospheric weirdness, soon to pass. (308 –309)

Though "we" claim not to know the exact nature of "our" feeling, DeLillo has indeed dropped sufficient hints by his carefully chosen diction. Words like "scared", "awe" and "dread" are all there to suggest that a feeling close in nature to "terror" prevails in the spectators' hearts, from which "wonder" or "elation" derives. According to Edmund Burke, "terror" can be an indicator of the whereabouts of "the sublime" or the sacred: "What is fitted in any sort to excite the ideas of pain, and danger ... whatever is any sort terrible, or is conversant about terrible objects, or operates in a manner analogous to terror, is a source of the sublime." (Burke, 1958: 39) The sunset of strong brilliance and radiance that "excites" so much terror in the Gladneys is such "a source of the sublime" or another incarnation of the spiritual whose very birth cannot materialize without an earlier development of "the dark mass". The spiritual, which has developed a form visible in nature and able to arouse in the crowds "uncertainty", should be a secular one. An access to the secular spirituality is gained with much ease when a "we-community" is formed up because mutual and tacit affirmation of each other's belief can, by a large margin, increase the strength of such a belief. Communality in "our" "religious service" directed at the sunset, in return, bathes "us" in much stronger a spiritual comfort the lingering grace of the "airborne toxic event" gives; and the sunset also teaches "us" all a lesson that nature, if wrongly used, can cause some irrevocable damage to the human lot.

In *Underworld*, it is not easy for Sister Edgar, who has remained so skeptical of Christian belief throughout her nearly entire career, to melt away Cold War Mentality that has since long frozen her once devout heart. Her self-made belief in Esmeralda's spirit at last helps her reestablish her faith and dissolve the Cold War Mentality, but the belief cannot be so powerful if it is not testified to by many more spectators and believers who gather underneath the billboard together with her. Communality, as embodied in Sister Edgar and other witnesses' close observation and ritualistic worshipping of the "fallen angel's" spirit, endows Edgar-like believers' postsecular faith with a greater saving power. Sister Edgar's reunion with the spiritual well conforms to the belief that the sacred is about community—the cementing of communal bonds, which is held as true by such preeminent scholars in anthropology and sociology as Bataille, Girard and Durkheim[34]. As a de-institutionalized sacredness, secular spirituality that all the postsecular faiths are directed at does require a community of proper size too, which has been agreed to by Jurgen Habermas who agrees that "transcendence from within"—secular spirituality—"is predicated upon an ideal communication community" (Habermas, 2002: 108). Sister Edgar, together with her fellow spectators, is placed in such "an ideal communication community". Sister Edgar's community is ideal because, on the one hand, it is so "improvisatory and fleeting" as not to be as ritualistic or institutional as any religious community is; on the other hand, the marginality of the community members' cultural identity can help coordinate all their efforts in the spiritual pursuit so as to strengthen the communality of the community and

---

㉞ David Emile Durkheim (1858—1917), a French sociologist, social psychologist and philosopher, is revered as one of three "principal architect(s) of modern social science and father(s) of sociology" (the other two being Karl Marx and Max Weber). Durkheim asserts his belief that the sacred is about community or the cementing of communal bonds. Two French scholars of younger generations, Georges Bataille (1897—1962) and Rene Girard (1923—2015), follow Durkheim in his belief, but both push beyond him to claim that rituals in such a sacred community are of a sacrificial nature, which, as postsecularism believes, can only be rectified by a postsecular community with its "improvisatory, fleeting" and marginal qualities.

make it no weaker than that of any believers' community in doctrinal religions. As mentioned before in the Introduction of the book, DeLillo's confidence with such an "improvisatory", "fleeting" and marginal community originates in his Catholic upbringing, his later abandon of Catholic rituals and resulting practice of a "cultural Catholicism".

Before Sister Edgar sees the appearance of murdered Esmeralda's face on the billboard, Don DeLillo first allows her sufficient time to have a thorough contemplation on who are in the "witnessing" community, whose marginality is thus laid bare to his audience:

> She let her eyes wander to the crowd. Working people, she thought. Working women, shopkeepers, maybe some drifters and squatters but not many, and then she noticed a group near the front, fitted snug to the prowed shape of the island—they were the charismatics from the top floor of the tenement in the Wall, dressed mainly in floppy white, tublike women, reedy men with dreadlocks. (820)

Among all these crowd members, "the charismatics" from "the Wall" should have the greatest marginality in their cultural identity. On the one hand, they believe that they have been endowed with certain sacred ability, due to which they will be taken as probable candidates for lunatic asylums. On the other hand, "the Wall" they reside in is the shabbiest building in the Bronx that works as a makeshift home for the homeless, so it is manifest that "the charismatics" constitute the main part of the homeless. However, in the witnessing crowd, their marginality has been shared by "working women, drifters, squatters", whose marginality is no less strong. As a helper of the marginalized, Sister Edgar is not one of them, but when standing among them, she still cannot help feeling that she is a core member of this communal worshipping of Esmeralda's spirit, and she is touched and comforted by the spiritual thus incarnated on the billboard. So when the murdered girl's face appears on the billboard, Sister Edgar, standing among these pious and watchful believers, feels as if they blurt out Esmeralda's name in unison, which is clearly the evidence of her understanding of the incarnation event being incorporated into one "single consciousness" (821) shared by all in the community. The "single consciousness" is to be of singular power in developing in Edgar a new mode of religious faith as "sobs", "moans", and "the cry of some unnameable painful elation" (821) are issued out of the crowd. Besides, those women who "clutch their heads", "whoop and sob" can be regarded as the living evidences of the strength of "a spirit". The strength, as is increased a lot by communality, is so irresistible that Sister Edgar has to admit that "there was someone living in the image, a distinguishing spirit and character" (822). Edgar's self-affirmation is, to a large degree, brought about by the crowd's consensual belief in the genuineness of the spirit, and in turn her re-ignition of faith in the spirituality contributes to the solidification of the communal faith, which develops a virtuous cycle so helpful to Edgar's ultimate dissolution of the Cold War Mentality:

> She felt something break upon her. ... She thumped a man's chest with her fists. Everything felt near at hand, breaking upon her, sadness and loss and glory and an old mother's bleak pity and a force at some deep level of lament that made her feel inseparable from the shakers and mourners, the awestruck who stood in tidal traffic—she was nameless for a moment, lost to the details of personal history, a disembodied fact in liquid form, pouring into the crowd. (822 –823)

Undeniably, "something" that "breaks upon her" is the spiritual whose presence in the secular is reminded by Esmeralda's visage projected on the billboard. All hands in the witnessing crowd who are craving for the spiritual help her gain access to it. It is also "something" itself that dawns on Sister Edgar how effective communality might be in speeding up one's progress towards the spiritual, and as a result, she decides to abandon herself to an unblocked embrace of and an unforced integration into "others", of whom she used to be very much afraid as a sufferer of severe mysophobia. The fists with which "she thumped a man's chest" can suggest that her mysophobia is cured and her Cold War Mentality also melted. Furthermore, "everything felt near at hand" that "something" gives birth to, "breaks upon her" too, which uplifts her spiritual comfort to such a level that her resoluteness in merging into the community is sharpened, as she claims that she is now "inseparable from the shakers and mourners, the awestruck". Her unconditional readiness to be absorbed into the community raises her to a status of believing, in which her identity as an individual believer is eradicated as she becomes a "nameless" and "disembodied fact in liquid form". Sister Edgar's voluntary give-in of her individuality marks off the unrivalled strength of communality in introducing one into the realm of the spiritual and intensifying the resultant comfort, to which Don DeLillo, with all his plot designs and character portrayals in *Underworld*, should have agreed to.

To the present days, *End Zone* is still the only sports novel of Don DeLillo's, which is not unqualified to give its very creator the name of a full-fledged thinker on the issues of paramount importance to contemporary American experience. Now and then, in the fiercest physical contact of the American football games, DeLillo comes to recognize that the real athleticism of the team sport consists in a logos-free play whose communality, stronger than those in other human activities, can take the players all the way to the warm and consolatory bosom of secular spirituality.

The American football, a team sport that America devises all on its own, is born to be communal as every single game involves two competing teams of players who are strong in both physique and mentality. The communality in the American football is capable of, for its players, paving a way to the spiritual and also bettering their emotional comfort thus gained. Such is it because football is a sacred and secular embodiment of the spiritual, whose coming-into-being in the sport is, in turn, made possible by its communality. All sports, team sports in particular, are secular activities imbued with "godsbreath", a compound DeLillo coins in *Underworld*, to which Ignacio L. Gotz attests by arguing that sports are "sets of very physical conditions, with very specific material objects, which, for the properly trained, become vehicles of mystical grace" (Gotz, 2001: 10). All participants in sports games, professional or amateurish, must be "properly trained" so as to form a community, whose members should have in common their interests in the sport and sufficient knowledge on its rules. To put it another way, the necessity of the participants being "properly trained" is predicated upon the fact that the American-football-like team sports all involve a long list of the governing rules. The formulation of these rules is akin to the birth of an artistic work because both of them originate from sheer inspirations, the source of which, further on, can be linked right up to some "mystical grace". Besides, it goes without saying that the "mystical grace" cannot be accessed if no conceited efforts are made by a community of the rule setters since a singled-handed endeavor will never work out in perfecting the competitive system of a sports game. More importantly, the implementation of the determined game rules involves all participants' full exertion of their potential and creativity, and it is self-evident that an individual's creativity, no matter how marvelous it is, should never count in winning a team its victory if it does not interact with the creativity of the other players involved. So, the two communities of the rule setters and the game players both contribute to the embodiment of the spiritual in the team sports. In addition, a team sport is a self-contained system that runs free from the bounds of any secular institutions, and remains intact from interference of any secular convention. In this sense, sports, especially team sports, can, by and large, keep all human-made rules and regulations of secular institutions at bay, and admittedly, this self-containing character can add to its legitimacy of "becoming vehicles of mystical grace", or "vehicles" of the spiritual.

The presence of "mystical grace" in sports is well testified to by sportsmen, with Gary Harkness, the hero of *End Zone*, included. In *End Zone*, Gary Harkness, a star player of the American football, feels that the spiritual comfort he can gain from the sport is much more forcefully strengthened by the sport's communality. Though Emmett Creed, the head coach of the Logos College football team, indoctrinates his players about a strident observation with all the game rules to subject them all and himself to the brutal force of logos,

Gary Harkness could still see at least a bit some free exertion of one's creativity at play, which is in all probabilities, a passage to the spiritual comfort, as he once thinks to himself: "Football is brutal only from a distance. In the middle of it there's calm, a tranquility." (199) It is Coach Creed, an "outsider" standing from time to time "from a distance" off the pitch, who inflicts his players with some biased understanding of the football as a "brutal" sport shaped or ruled by sheer reason, whereas the players like Gary, when placed "in the middle of it", come to feel that some spiritual comfort flows right through all their blood vessels, instilling in their hearts "calm" or "tranquility". Such is it because in the middle of a game, fierce competition between the two teams is sure to force logos to loosen its grip upon the players' minds and an individual player's originality should be exerted to a certain extent; besides, all efforts coordinated in one team to win its victory tend to assemble every individual originality into a communal and much stronger one, which will in return reward the players with some heartfelt enjoyment of spiritual comforts. Having struggled free from the gripping hands of logos, an American football game takes effect upon all its participants just as a parish does with its parishioners, whose communal dedication to the spirituality can strengthen the consolatory effect of their worshipping efforts and therefore, is all that a genuine sportsman is supposed to do under the name of real athleticism. There is no wonder that, though hit with brutal force down to the ground, Gary still feels summoned to a spiritual dimension of calm and order: "There's a sense of order even at the end of a running play with bodies strewn everywhere. When the systems interlock, there's a satisfaction to the game that can't be duplicated. There's a harmony." (199) The "bodies" that are "strewn everywhere" constitute a symbolic scene for the logos-free play of American football, which "interlocks" the two "systems"—the two competing teams involved in a game—and so gives full play to communality's great potential in proffering the players the senses of "satisfaction" and "harmony" that cannot be "duplicated".

If a so-called rule-free play of football by Gary Harkness, his teammates and opponents in an official game is compromised by their compulsory observance of Creed-like coaches' tactics, Gary and his fellow players' spontaneous engagement in a self-organized "game" on a snow-covered pitch after the college football season is over is the very driving force DeLillo sees as essential to the formulation of a real faith community. Even when it is still snowing badly, Gary and his teammates, with a shared intention to answer a common call, gather on the pitch of the campus, playing a game in so casual a way that they do not bother to wear any protection gears or adopt any coach-made tactics: "Nobody cared how many passes were dropped or badly thrown and it didn't matter how slowly we ran or if we fell trying to cut or stop short. The idea was to keep playing, keep moving, get it going again." (193) Since logocentrism, which has taught them to follow the rules for all time as an American football player, is at this moment driven off their minds, communality is cemented in the loosely organized team of these self-invited players, who by doing so increase their sense of belonging and further their affirmation of the spiritual incarnated in the sport. In accordance with what John McClure proclaims in one of his published articles on the postsecular literary criticism, Gary Harkness and other casual players on the pitch form "a creaturely community that suffers, enjoys, and endures" (McClure, 1995: 157), upon which the significance of all self-redemptive efforts is rested and more generally, the practical value of postsecular thoughts is predicated too.

Conclusion

Dietrich Bonhoeffer, a celebrated German theologian and Lutheran priest, when asked what secularization could mean to him, said to the effect that it, to a certain extent, complies with the notion of humankind's "coming of age", which encourages people to live with an "autonomy"—an absolute exertion of their free will with no interference from God or any other gods, or in other words, to take full responsibility for their lives rather than accept in total passivity all that befall them as providence. (qtd. in Toit, 2009: 1256) Nevertheless, Don DeLillo has known, perhaps better than most of his peers in contemporary American field of fictional writing, that such an "autonomy" is bought at a dear price, which mankind cannot afford. As has been exemplified by Gary Harkness, the college-football-star hero of his *End Zone*, mankind procures and asserts their free will or autonomy at the expense of all faith in the divine and by so doing, Gary-Harkness-like figures in modern life would become subservient to reason and plays a game as Gary plays his football, which, in the name of singularizing and stabilizing meaning of one's life, locks them so tight in an endless cycle of referencing and suffocates them all in the bottomless void that reason has promised to free them from. Also, as DeLillo has seen it, man's delusion about "autonomy" can manifest itself with a vengeance in his conscientious delineation of a demarcation line between the objective and the subjective, which is illustrated in *Great Jones Street* by Bucky Wunderlick's retreat from his stardom. Well-intentioned as he is to live in defiance against the corrupting influence of commercialized America upon his rock-and-roll music, Bucky still ends up in a failed project of subjectivity construction, whose allegedly reality-proof nature, empty of any content, cannot escape its fate of being used again by American commercialism to enlarge Bucky's aura as a rock star and so maximize its craved economic interests. These two DeLilloesque specimens of his contemporary Americans—Gary Harkness and Bucky Wunderlick—are both well-devised reminders of how deceitful mankind's "autonomy" could be in his secular life that goes on with no reliance on any variety of faith in the spiritual, because "free will", one exerts with his recourse to either modernity or modernism, as has been seen in personal endeavors of Gary's and Bucky's respectively, can never grant him meaning of life that can be of redemptive value as strong as to dispel his existential angst. To put it another way, DeLillo has come to perceive that "autonomy", a story framed by reason and imparted to the Westerners ever since the Enlightenment, precipitates their "coming of age" on the one hand, whereas on the other, if exerted for too long a time in a way that desiccates all the faiths of a society, it would quicken their spiritual demise when their "coming of age" or "maturity" is passed. To assist his fellow Americans in fulfilling a spiritual rebirth, Don DeLillo cannot help but write further on to add up "post- " as a prefix to "secular" so as to mark off a much necessitated termination of a secular age and welcome the spiritual as a plausible cure back to contemporary American experience.

Postsecularism, an unsystemized school of thought that underpins most of Don DeLillo's artistic designs in his major contributions to the American fiction, is the warmest possible greeting contemporary philosophy, especially, its theological branch, could give to the return of the spiritual to the secular life of mankind. An innovative and deconstructionist ability to mingle religiosity with secularity and integrate them into an organic whole enables it to accomplish two tiers of ethicization, which are so earnestly desired by contemporary American subjects and cannot be fulfilled single-handedly by either religiosity or secularity.

To ethicize an individual being, which is a necessary prerequisite for the attainment of a higher-tier ethicization, can be achieved thanks to postsecularism's committed inheritance of all the traits that a doctrinal religious faith is supposed to own. Institutional religions are born as a response to mankind's inborn desire to transcend their limited self or in other words, define their meaning of life that can be so easily ridiculed by its short span. Once in an interview, Gianni Vattimo asks a question on behalf of the human race: "Why 'being' rather than 'nothingness'?" (Vattimo, Zabala, 2002: 463) To him, this is a question of ultimate significance, to which neither metaphysics nor science can propound a satisfactory answer. As a result, all man-made schools of thought should be "suspended" except religion, which represents mankind's faith in the spiritual. Vattimo's re-ignition of hope in religion is answered by Paul Tillich, who in his *Systematic Theology* declares that "the object of theology is what concerns us ultimately. Only those propositions are theological which deal with their object insofar as it can become a matter of ultimate concern for us". "Us", which Paul Tillich refers to in the citation, is just another saying of "the human race", whose "ultimate concern" with their value or meaning of life can be resolved by and only by a systemic theological study on God according to Tillich. Postsecularism, as a burgeoning school of theological thought that studies god or even gods, if not God, can very well answer for mankind's "ultimate concern" too. A formidable belief in the gods or the spiritual will not fail one's pursuit of life's meaning or value, to which Charles Winquist attests by taking Milan Kundera as an example and saying, "The desire for theological thinking is a desire for a thinking that does not disappoint us. It is not unlike Milan Kundera's gesture of longing for immortality that is at the same time a longing for a relationship to the infinite that does not disappoint us." (Winquist, 1994: 1025) The "relationship to the infinite" that such a great writer as Milan Kundera is "longing for" cannot "disappoint us" because "the relationship" is built upon one's committal trust in the spiritual as an unfailing source of meaning that can never be accessed by anyone who holds absolute beliefs in logocentrism and its derivant—secularism. A most valuable ability to believe will reframe one's meaning of life so that its sacredness can be fully exhibited since every being is born out of gods' will, if not God's will, and so, the divinity must have been shared by every individual being. In this sense, any one who does harm to each and every individual being will be convicted as an offender against the divine and sure to be punished in this way or that. Any subject in the contemporary world, as long as he commits himself to this spiritual or religious interpretation of life's meaning or value, will, for certain, develop a profounder awareness of how spurious "autonomy", a concept about self that the secularization inculcates the modern men with, is and in the meantime, live in awe and fear, especially when given a chance to offend or hurt the divinity of other beings. The "awe and fear" can be a manifest evidence of the first-tier ethicization being fulfilled, which has been explained by John McClure on a few occasions as: "Weak religion 'summons humans back' to their historicity, their finitude, and their fallibility, and it makes a conversion to charity (rather than an anticipation of judgment and eternal life) the core of its message." (McClure, 2007: 13) As one of the first American postsecular literary critics, John McClure agrees with other Western thinkers who contribute to postsecularism in calling it "weak religion" so that its deconstructionist or deinstitutionalized property can be laid bare. Postsecularism, though detached from any institutionalized deity and therefore "weak", is strongly capable of "summoning back" its mortal believers to their "finitude", which is erosive of their self-conceit but in return ignites their fiery wish to transcend their mortal and limited being and deepens their respect to the spiritual as an ultimate source of all meanings. Such a deepened respect will ingrain a great fear in every mind that he could do harm to any other beings so that the divine will is offended, which, according to McClure, marks postsecularism's fulfillment of its first-tier ethicization of all its followers. The thus ethicized individuals, in such a fear that is wholesome to their spiritual integrity, will become "charitable" or concerned with others' concerns with their welfare, which has laid the required basis for postsecularism's second-tier ethicization.

A "charitable" selfhood, one that postsecularism-stimulated respect towards the divinity of all beings has ethicized an individual into, will, in the first place, teaches him to do all that is within his reach of power to safeguard the well-beings of "small Others"—those Others who are geographically close to him, or to be more specific, his fellow compatriots in one particular country. With respect, awe and even fear of hurting small Others by the slightest possible degree, a believer in the spiritual will, beyond any doubt, earn himself some heartfelt admiration and reverence from those Others so that a benevolent reciprocity can be forged within the boundary of a nation, which is of considerable significance to consolidating both the unity and stability of the whole society. If he and small Others should happen to share a postsecular faith in one secular spirituality, they can, with great spontaneity, form a community of belief, in which every member's faith will be solidified through mutual communication and resultingly, their spiritual comfort will be increased by a large margin. A postsecular community, whose size has to be controlled so as to hamper its rampant growth, will gather the ethicizing power of every single believer to form a much greater ethicizing power, which will be even more conducive to harmonizing the cross-personal relationship between the members of a society. Nevertheless, the ethicization of a particular society is by no means a point that postsecularism's second-tier ethicization is to stop by. A deconstructionist propensity of the postsecular thought decrees that all its followers should, without being asked, target their unconditional respect and benevolent deeds towards not only "small Others" but also "big Others", or those Others who are much more alien to them than "small Others" in nation, race and especially belief. Postsecularism, whose hardened will to deconstruct both secularity and religiosity has been most conspicuously reflected in its dedication to secular spirituality—a harmonious combination between two opposing categories in the human epistemology—cannot help but integrate into the sublimated ethos of a society another ideological ingredient—a most hard-won open-mindedness that is both respectful to and protective of "big Others", who might be diametrically different in every possible respect. In this sense, postsecularism will help commit a society to a great "anti-cause" whose sub-causes should include anti-fundamentalism, anti-assimilationism and anti-terrorism. It could be seen that fundamentalism is the very starting point off which its followers set out to their ultimate goal—assimilationism, and to achieve the goal, some blood-spilt terrorism must be practiced in order to wipe all dissenters off the surface of the earth. No matter what relationship is functioning between these three "-ism" s, what lies at the common bedrock of them three is for sure exclusivism and its resultant intolerance, which is exactly what a postsecularized society strives to root out. Inclusivism, whose scope of influence has been expanded by postsecularism, will diffuse across the globe an atmosphere of tolerance that is to cool down the blood-thirsty fervor of all forms of exclusivism and so, pacify the world. In a nutshell, reverential tolerance of Others, both small and big, is what postsecularism's second-tier ethicization is meant to fulfill, whose success is both reliant on and more glorious than the first-tier ethicization of individual followers.

In all probabilities, no one who works in the field of contemporary American fictional writing should have acquired a profounder understanding of postsecularism's multiple-tier ethicizing function than Don DeLillo does. DeLillo represents it both completely and artistically in his plot designs and character portrayals throughout his half-a-century writing career in the hope that American reading public could be thus prodded into drafting in full sincerity a blueprint for re-launching their spiritual pursuit. In *White Noise*, Jack Gladney frames up a plan to murder Mink, the Dylar salesman who cuckolds him, and executes it well until the last moment when Jack stops short all his killing acts and goes as far as to save Mink's life. Besides, Eric Packer, the 28-year-old billionaire in *Cosmopolis*, surrenders his control of the pistol—the deadly weapon with which his ex-employer Benno Levin can kill him for revenge—to his murderer and has himself killed at last. These two characters' seemingly whimsical suppression of their murderous impulses when, as a matter of fact, they are at advantage can function most soundly in exemplifying the first-tier ethicization of postsecularism. Their last-moment voluntary abandon of a murderous use of weapon evidences their strongest possible determination to struggle free off logos's stringent restrictions and entrust the decisive power of the spiritual with all that is going to occur. This anti-rationalism determination cannot but be so utterly illustrative of their sincerest affirmation of the spiritual as an ultimate source of all earthly meanings, which never fails to teach them to reverence in full piety the divine will incarnated in every being by not encroaching upon their inborn right of existence. The final decisions the two characters make in *White Noise* and *Cosmopolis*, especially the latter one that costs Eric Packer's young life, are indeed convincing, though extremist, cases in which a postsecular belief executes its first-tier ethicization.

Sister Alma Edgar, the main character in the Epilogue of *Underworld*, performs her duty of demonstrating, to DeLillo's readers, how to postsecularize one's treatment of his "small Others". As Cold War Mentality melts away in her heart at the right moment when Sister Edgar witnesses in person the projection upon a Bronx-based billboard of Esmeralda's spirit, she comes to grip her long lost faith in the spiritual and has herself so much ethicized as to overcome her serious mysophobia right away on the spot. Her warm and unreserved embrace of her fellow spectator-believers can exhibit her thoroughgoing affirmation of the value of a human life, sanctified by the spiritual and shared by all the beings that walk or creep on the earth; and mutual affirmation of each other's life-value, in her regard, should serve as the very basis to build a new American society characterized by mutual respect, unity and harmony. DeLillo's personal endeavor to postsecularize America's relations with "big Others" has been made in the terrorism-related novel *Falling Man*. Don DeLillo fulfills his mission of assisting postsecularism in finishing its second-tier ethicization in *Falling Man* by explaining further both its possible means and effects. Lianne Glenn, a DeLillo-like dedicator to language, after being traumatized by 9/11, starts a writing workshop, into which, she enrolls only Alzheimer's patients as her pupils. In such a writing group, which operates, in fact, as a postsecular community, Lianne manages to consolidate her faith in the spiritual that she has just regained from her in-person observation of Falling Man's performance, and disseminates her hard-won bliss among her aged students. After one seminar after another, she and all her students come to a consensus that their full recovery from traumas cannot be achieved without their forgiveness or acknowledgement that humanity, whose sanctity is decreed by the spiritual, is shared by all humans, regardless of nation, race and religious belief. This consensus is, for certain, the one that Don DeLillo expects in earnest, since at the depth of his heart, the novelist admits too that though those terrorists who are held accountable for the 9/11 attack must be condemned and punished with no respite, other Muslims who are truly virtuous believers in non-fundamentalist and benevolent tenets of the religion deserve to be treated in the way postsecularism deals with "big Others". Only by refraining from misdirecting revengeful anger against all Muslims, most of whom have not been stained with innocent blood, and further on, getting along with them in a mutually tolerant, respectful and beneficial way can postsecularism's second-tier ethicization accomplish its ultimate goal—peace, the word Don DeLillo presents in an independent paragraph to end his 827-page *Underworld*.

It is also in the Epilogue of *Underworld* where Don DeLillo stresses, time and again, with some plots he works out with much discretion, his non-committal attitude towards postsecularism that might be undeservedly exalted as an elixir to cure the human life of all its problems, once and for all. The two plots that DeLillo depicts after Sister Edgar and Sister Gracie witness together the projection of Esmeralda's face upon the billboard are worth closer investigations since these two are so deconstructive as to enfeeble secular spirituality—the cornerstone of the theoretical edifice of postsecularism and so shake the edifice in its entirety. Having observed at close quarters "Esmeralda's face" on the billboard, Sister Gracie slights "the incarnation" of the murdered girl's spirit by offering a purely reasonable and therefore totally spirituality-unrelated explanation: "It's just the undersheet. A technical flaw that causes the image underneath, the image from the papered-over ad to show through the current ad. When sufficient light shines on the current ad, it causes the image beneath to show through." (822) Sister Gracie's unconscious reiteration helps downgrade a postsecular faith in secular spirituality to be nothing more than "a consciousness revolution" (Habermas, 2008: 20) as Jurgen Habermas has defined it, which is at most one of mankind's epistemological modes and no better than any of the others. DeLillo's deliberate presentation of Gracie's reiterated explanation when the book is drawing very close to its finish line is to restate, with fullest self-assurance, the non-essential essence of postsecularism—a thoroughgoing deconstructionist stance that allows even reason—its exact obverse—to deconstruct itself. No proof is stronger in evidencing postsecularism's deconstructionist nature than its innate predilection towards self-deconstruction, from which derives its uncompromised resolution to emancipate the human mind from all grand narratives. Don DeLillo carries on Sister Gracie's persistent effort to deconstruct secular spirituality by sealing the fate for the billboard upon which Esmeralda's spirit is once projected: "The next evening the sign is blank. What a hole it makes in space. People come and don't know what to say or think, where to look or what to believe. The sign is a white sheet with two lonely words, *Space Available*, followed by a phone number in tasteful type." (824) As is suggested by "Space Available", the postsecular mode of faith does not operate with even the slightest intention of predominating the human epistemology or banishing reason from it in an unrelenting way. On the contrary, postsecularism and all other perceptive modes should humble down themselves and work in conceited efforts to keep the "Space" of the human epistemology in an everlasting state of "Availability", or a state that can be modified or renovated whenever need be. Both the two plots presented at the close of DeLillo's most voluminous book originate from the novelist's firmest belief that any new mode of faith, with postsecularism included, can be so easily reduced to another variant of fundamentalism and thus become subservient to logos again if no sufficient "Space" is left vacant, and more importantly, such a "vacancy", deconstructionist and constructionist in the meantime, is what can secure the success of the multiple-tier ethicization that the postsecular faith is born to fulfill.

Don DeLillo's non-committal or ambiguous stance that persists throughout his writing career helps him safeguard "Space Available" as a most treasurable quality of both postsecularism and postsecular writing of fiction. By so doing, DeLillo can save his readership from hastening to accept him as a problem solver, which is testified to by Kathryn Ludwig as she argues when commenting on *Underworld*: "DeLillo is by no means ready to offer a spiritual solution to the world's problems. Like so many other postsecular works, DeLillo's novel supports 'play' and open-ended readings over the affirmation of any existing discourse or the formulation of any new master discourses." (Ludwig, 2009: 89) DeLillo's cautious detachment from any unconditional commitment to postsecularism, according to Kathryn Ludwig, should be read as his unshakable determination to protect its "open-endedness" from sliding off to the well-disguised traps set by either "existing discourse" or "master discourses". So, there is no more accurate a summary of what DeLillo has achieved in his decades of postsecular practice of fictional writing than Ludwig's conclusive statement in her Ph. D. book that "it (DeLillo's fictitious world) is one in which secularist despair and religious hope coincide" (Ludwig, 2010: 71). What DeLillo does in his open and ambivalent endings is to remind his readers that "religious hope" that postsecularism should have re-ignited in its believers' hearts needs to be tampered a little by "secularist despair" that is produced by DeLillo's insistent refusal to confirm his characters' final redemption, or else, "hope" is most likely to be heated up and become a fundamentalist and fiery thirst for blood. There is no wonder that Martin Buber, when asked about his warm advocacy of the deconstructionist nature of postsecularism-like "new religions", should announce with unreserved resoluteness that "we would not exchange our dizzy insecurity and our poverty for your security and abundance" (Buber, 1970: 41). Martin Buber's high-sounding statement is the best recapitulation of all the musings that Don DeLillo, as an American postmodern writer and critic, has been doing throughout his career about what a postsecular faith is and how it could work in the present conditions.

Bibliography

ASAD T, 1997. Europe against Islam: Islam in Europe [J]. The Muslim world, 87(2): 183 – 195.

ASAD T, 2003. Formations of the secular: Christianity, Islam, Modernity [M]. Stanford: Stanford University Press.

ATCHLEY J H, 2010. Attention, affirmation, and the spiritual law of gravity [J]. The pluralist, Fall, 5(3): 63 – 72.

BARKER C, 2002. Making sense of cultural studies: central problems and critical debates[M]. Thousand Oaks: Sage Publications.

BARRETT L, 2001/2002. How the dead speak to the living: intertextuality and the postmodern sublime in *White noise*[M]. Journal of modern literature, 25(2): 97 – 113.

BARRON J, 2003. DeLillo bashful? Not this time[N]. Chicago sun-times, 03 – 23(1).

BAUDRILLARD J, 1983. The ecstasy of communication[G]//FOSTER H. The anti-aesthetic: essays on postmodern culture. Port Townsend: Bay Press.

BELL D, 1973. The coming of post-industrial society[M]. New York: Basic Books.

BELL D, 1976. The cultural contradictions of capitalism[M]. New York:

Basic Books.

BENJAMIN W, 1969. The work of art in the age of mechanical reproduction [G]//Illuminations: essays and reflections. Trans. Harry Zohn. New York: Shocken.

BORN D, 1999. Sacred noise in Don DeLillo's fiction [J]. Literature & theology, 13(3): 211 - 221.

BOSWORTH D, 1983. The fiction of Don DeLillo[J]. Boston review, April: 29 - 30.

BOXALL P, 2006. Don DeLillo: the possibility of fiction[M]. London and New York: Routledge.

BRAECKMAN A, 2009. Habermas and Gauchet on religion in postsecular society: a critical assessment [J]. Continental philosophy review, 42: 279 - 296.

BRYANT P, 1987. Discussing the untellable: Don DeLillo's *The names*[J]. Critique, 29(1): 16 - 29.

BUBER M, 1967. Prophesy, apocalyptic and historical hour[G]//GLATZER N. On Judaism. New York: Schocken Books.

BUBER M, 1970. I and thou[M]. Trans. Walter Kaufmann. New York: Touchstone-Simon and Schuster.

BUBER M, 2000. On the Bible [M]. Ed. Nahum Glatzer. New York: Syracuse University Press.

BURKE E, 1958. A philosophical enquiry into the origin of our ideas of the sublime and beautiful[M]. Ed. James Boulton. London: Routledge.

CAPUTO J, 2002a. Looking the impossible in the eye: Kierkegaard, Derrida, and the repetition of religion[J]. Kierkegaard studies yearbook, (1): 1 - 25.

CAPUTO J, 2002b. Richard Kearney's enthusiasm: a philosophical exploration on *The God who may be*[J]. Modern theology, 18(1): 87 - 94.

CAPUTO J, 2006. Before creation: Derrida's memory of God [J]. Mosaic (Winnipeg), 39(3): 91 - 102.

CAPUTO J, 2007. What would Jesus deconstruct? The good news of postmodernity for the church[M]. Grand Rapids: Baker Academic.

CASANOVA J, 1994. Public religions in the modern world[M]. Chicago: The University of Chicago Press.

CHAMPLIN C, 1984. The heart is a lonely craftsman[N]. Los Angeles times, 07-29(7).

CHANDLER A, 2009. "An unsettling, alternative self": Benno Levin, Emmanuel Levinas, and Don DeLillo's *Cosmopolis*[J]. Critique: studies in contemporary fiction, 50(3): 241-260.

CHEN J S, 2010. Political engagement in contemporary American historigraphic metafiction[D]. Shanghai: Shanghai Foreign Studies University.

CHEN J S, 2014. The poetics of terror in Don DeLillo's short stories[J]. Foreign literature, (3): 3-11, 157.

CIVELLO P, 1994. American literary naturalism and its twentieth-century transformations: Frank Norris, Ernest Hemingway, and Don DeLillo[M]. Athens: Georgia University Press.

CONNIFF B, 2013. DeLillo's ignatian moment: religious longing and theological encounter in *Falling man*[J]. Christianity and literature, 63(1): 47-73.

CONNOLLY W, 1999. Why I am not a secularist[M]. Minneapolis: University of Minnesota Press.

CONNOLLY W, 2009. The human predicament[J]. Social research, 76(4): 1121-1140.

CONNOLLY W, 2011. Some theses on secularism[J]. Cultural anthropology, 26(4): 648-656.

CONTE J M, 2008. Conclusions: writing amid the ruins: 9/11 and *Cosmopolis*[G]//DUVALL J N. The Cambridge companion to Don DeLillo. Cambridge and New York: Cambridge University Press.

COWART D, 2003. Don DeLillo: the physics of language[M]. Athens: Georgia University Press.

DECURTIS A, 1991a. "An outsider in this society": an interview with Don DeLillo [G]//LENTRICCHIA F. Introducing Don DeLillo. Durham: Duke University Press.

DECURTIS A, 1991b. The product: Bucky Wunderlick, rock n' roll, and Don DeLillo's *Great Jones Street* [G]//LENTRICCHIA F. Introducing Don DeLillo. Durham: Duke University Press.

DELILLO D, 1973. Great Jones Street [M]. Boston: Houghton Mifflin.

DELILLO D, 1982. The names [M]. New York: Alfred A. Knopf.

DELILLO D, 1985. White noise [M]. New York: Viking.

DELILLO D, 1986. End zone [M]. New York: Penguin Books.

DELILLO D, 1988. Libra [M]. New York: Viking.

DELILLO D, 1989. Americana [M]. New York: Penguin Books.

DELILLO D, 1993. Don DeLillo: the art of fiction CXXXV: interview conducted by Adam Begley [J]. Paris review, 35(128): 274 – 306.

DELILLO D, 1997a. The power of history [J]. The New York times magazine, 09 – 07: 60 – 63.

DELILLO D, 1997b. Underworld [M]. New York: Scribner.

DELILLO D, 2001a. The body artist [M]. New York: Scribner.

DELILLO D, 2001b. In the ruins of the future [J]. Harper's, December: 33 – 40.

DELILLO D, 2003. Cosmopolis [M]. New York: Scribner.

DELILLO D, 2007. Falling man [M]. New York: Scribner.

DELILLO D, 2010. Point omega [M]. New York: Scribner.

DEPIETRO T, 2005. Conversations with Don DeLillo [M]. Jackson: University of Mississippi Press.

DERRIDA J, 1978. Writing and difference [M]. Trans. Alan Bass. Chicago: The University of Chicago Press.

DERRIDA J, 1981. Positions [M]. Trans. Alan Bass. Chicago: The University of Chicago Press.

DERRIDA J, 1982. Margins of philosophy [M]. Trans. Alan Bass. Chicago: The University of Chicago Press.

DEWEY J, 2006. Beyond grief and nothing: a reading of Don DeLillo [M]. Columbia: South Carolina University Press.

DOUGLAS C, 2002. Don DeLillo [G]//BERTENS H and NATOLI J.

Postmodernism: the key figures. Malden: Blackwell.

DUVALL J N, 2002. Don DeLillo's *Underworld:* a reader's guide[M]. New York and London: Continuum.

DUVALL J N, 2008. Introduction: the power of history and the persistence of mystery[G]//DUVALL J N. The Cambridge companion to Don DeLillo. Cambridge and New York: Cambridge University Press.

ECHLIN K, 2005. Baseball and the Cold War [G]//DEPIETRO T. Conversations with Don DeLillo. Jackson: Mississippi University Press.

EMERSON R W, 1983. Spiritual laws[G]//PORTE J. Essays and lectures. New York: Library of America.

ERMARTH E D, 2000. Beyond "the subject": individuality in the discursive condition[J]. New literary history, 31(3): 405 - 419.

FAIGLEY L, 1992. Fragments of rationality: postmodernity and the subject of composition[M]. Pittsburgh: University of Pittsburgh Press.

FAN X M, 2014. A new historicist study on DeLillo's fiction[D]. Xiamen: Xiamen University.

FANG C, 2003. Postmodern fiction's inheritance and formulation of naturalism: Don DeLillo's *White noise*[J]. Contemporary foreign literature, (4): 93 - 99.

FELLUGA D, 2012. Modules on Fredric Jameson: on late capitalism[EB/OL]//Introductory guide to critical theory. (04 - 27)[2016 - 05 - 23]. http://wwwclapurdueedu/english/theory/marxism/modules/jamesonlatecapitalism. html.

FRIEDMAN M, 1988. Martin Buber's life and work: later years, 1945—1865 [M]. Detroit: Wayne State University Press.

FROW J, 1991. The last things before the last [G]//LENTRICCHIA F. Introducing Don DeLillo. Durham and London: Duke University Press.

FRYE N, 1990. Anatomy of criticism[M]. Princeton: Princeton University Press.

GIAIMO P, 2011. Appreciating Don DeLillo: the moral force of a writer's work[M]. Prager: Santa Barbara.

GIOIA T, 2012. *Point omega* by Don DeLillo[EB/OL]. Great books guide. (04-06)[2016-05-28]. http://www.greatbooksguide.com/point_omega.html.

GIRARD R, 1972. Violence and the sacred[M]. Trans. Patrick Gregory. Baltimore: Johns Hopkins University Press.

GOLDSTEIN W, 1988. Don DeLillo[J]. Publishers weekly, 234(8): 55.

GORDON P, 2008. The place of the sacred in the absence of God: Charles Taylor's *A secular age*[J]. Journal of the history of ideas, 69(4): 647-673.

GOTZ I L, 2001. Spirituality and the body[J]. Religious education, 96: 1-19.

HABERMAS J, 2002. Religion and rationality: essays on reason, God, and modernity[M]. Cambridge: MIT Press.

HABERMAS J, 2003. The future of human nature[M]. Cambridge, the UK: Polity Press.

HABERMAS J, 2008. Notes on post-secular society[J]. New perspectives quarterly, 25(4): 17-29.

HARRIS P A, 2010. Spiritual politics after Deleuze: introduction[J]. Substance, 39(1): 3-7.

HEIDEGGER M, 1971. Poetry, language, thought[M]. Trans. Albert Hofstadter. New York: Harper and Row.

HEIDEGGER M, 1977. The age of the world picture[G]//The question concerning technology, and other essays. Trans. William Lovitt. New York: Harper & Row.

HILL P C, PARGAMENT K, HOOD JR R W, et al, 2000. Conceptualizing religion and spirituality: points of commonality, points of departure[J]. Journal for the theory of social behavior, 30: 51-77.

HUNGERFORD A, 2006. Don DeLillo's Latin mass[J]. Contemporary literature, 47(3): 343-380.

JAMESON F, 1992. Postmodernism and consumer society[G]//BROOKER P. Modernism/Postmodernism. London and New York: Longman.

JAMESON F, 2005. Postmodernism, or the cultural logic of late capitalism [M]. Durham: Duke University Press.

JOHNSON D, 1977. Beyond radical chic[N]. New York times book review, 01-16(13).

JOHNSTON J, 1989. Generic discontinuities in the novels of Don DeLillo[J]. Critique, 30: 262.

JOHNSTON J, 1994. Superlinear fiction or historical diagram?: Don DeLillo's *Libra*[J]. Modern fiction studies, 40(2): 319-342.

KANT I, 1952. Critique of judgment[M]. Trans. James Creed Meredith. Oxford: Clarendon.

KAVADLO J, 2004. Don DeLillo: balance at the edge of belief[M]. New York: Peter Lang Publishing, Inc.

KANTROWITZ B, PATRICIA K, 1994. In search of the sacred [J]. Newsweek, 124(22): 52-56.

KEESEY D, 1993. Don DeLillo[M]. New York: Twayne.

KELLER C, 2003. The face of the deep: a theology of becoming[M]. New York: Routledge.

KELLNER D, 2002. Jean Baudrillard[G]//BERTENS H and NATOLI J. Postmodernism: the key figures. Malden and Oxford: Blackwell Publishers.

LAIST R, 2008. Oedison Rex: the art of media metaphor in Don DeLillo's *Americana*[J]. Modern language studies, 37(2): 50-63.

LECLAIR T, 1987a. Deconstructing the logos: Don DeLillo's *End zone*[J]. Modern fiction studies, 33(1): 105-123.

LECLAIR T, 1987b. In the loop: Don DeLillo and the systems novel[M]. Chicago: Illinois University Press.

LECLAIR T, MCCAFFERY L, 1983. Anything can happen: interviews with contemporary American novelists [G]. Urbana: University of Illinois Press.

LENTRICCHIA F, 1991a. *Libra* as postmodern critique[G]//LENTRICCHIA F. Introducing Don DeLillo. Durham and London: Duke University Press.

LENTRICCHIA F, 1991b. New essays on *White noise*[G]. Cambridge: Cambridge University Press.

LEVINAS E, 1969. Totality and infinity: an essay in exteriority[M]. Trans. Alphonso Lingis. Pittsburgh: Duquesne University Press.

LEWIS P, 1985. John le Carre[M]. New York: Frederick Ungar.

LI G Z, 2003. The tendency of violence in names and naming: DeLillo's *The names*[J]. Journal of PLA University of Foreign Languages, (2): 100-103.

LI N, 2014. On *Cosmopolis*: machine and death[J]. Foreign literature, (2): 82-89, 159.

LI X L, 2012. The pathogenic mechanism of terrorism in Don DeLillo's novels [D]. Shanghai: Shanghai Foreign Studies University.

LIU T S, 1993. "The Cold War", "Containment" and the Atlantic Alliance: a selective reading of American strategic policies during 1945-1950[M]. Shanghai: Fudan University Press.

LONGMUIR A, 2007. Performing the body in Don DeLillo's *The body artist* [J]. Modern fiction studies, 53(3): 541.

LUDWIG K, 2009. Don DeLillo's "Underworld" and the postsecular in contemporary fiction[J]. Religion & literature, 41(3): 82-91.

LUDWIG K, 2010. Postsecularism and literature: prophetic and apocalyptic readings in Don DeLillo, E. L. Doctorow and Toni Morrison[D]. West Lafayette: Purdue University.

LUKACS G, 1995. Aesthetic culture[G]//KADARKAY A. The Lukacs reader. Oxford: Blackwell.

LUTER M, 2012. Resisting the devouring neon: hysterical crowds and self-abnegating art in Don DeLillo's *Great Jones Street*[J]. Critique: studies in contemporary fiction, 53: 16-29.

LYOTARD J-F, 1979. The postmodern condition: a report on knowledge[M]. Trans. Geoff Bennington and Brian Massumi. Manchester: Manchester University Press.

MA Q Y, 2009. "Who will die first?": an analysis of the fear of death of Jack couple in *White noise*[J]. Journal of Jimei University (Philosophy and Social Sciences), 12(2): 92 -97.

MACZYNSKA M, 2009. Toward a postsecular literary criticism: examining ritual gestures in Zadie Smith's *Autograph man*[J]. Religion & literature, 41(3): 73 -82.

MALTBY P, 1996. The romantic metaphysics of Don DeLillo [J]. Contemporary literature, 37(2): 258 -277.

MATUSTIK M B, 2008. Radical evil and the scarcity of hope: postsecular meditations[M]. Bloomington: Indiana University Press.

MCAULIFFE J, 2005. Interview with Don DeLillo [G]//DEPIETRO T. Conversations with Don DeLillo. Jackson: Mississippi University Press.

MCCLURE J A, 1995. Postmodern/Post-secular: contemporary fiction and spirituality[J]. Modern fiction studies, 41: 141 -163.

MCCLURE J A, 2007. Partial faiths: postsecular fiction in the age of Pynchon and Morrison[M]. Athens: Georgia University Press.

MORLEY C, 2009. The quest for epic in contemporary American fiction[M]. New York: Routledge.

MOSCO T, 2000. Empire of conspiracy: the culture of paranoia in postwar America[M]. Ithaca: Cornell University Press.

NADEAU R, 1981. Readings from the new book on nature: physics and metaphysics in the modern novel[M]. Amherst: Massachusetts University Press.

NICOL B, 2009. The Cambridge introduction to postmodern fiction [M]. Cambridge: Cambridge University Press.

O'DONNELL P, 1994. Engendering paranoia in contemporary narrative[G]// PEASE D E. National identities and post-Americanist narratives. Durham: Duke University Press.

O'DONNELL P, 2000. Latent destinies: cultural paranoia and contemporary U. S. narrative[M]. Durham: Duke University Press.

O'HARA J D, 1977. Two mandarin stylists[J]. Nation, 225(8): 250 -252.

OLSTER S, 2011. Don DeLillo: *Mao* Ⅱ, *Under world*, *Falling man*[M].

New York: Continuum.

ORIAD M, 1978. Don DeLillo's search for Walden Pond [M]. Critique: studies in modern fiction, 20(1): 4-24.

ORSI R, 2010. The Madonna of 115th Street: faith and community in Italian Harlem, 1880—1950[M]. New Haven: Yale University Press.

OSTEEN M, 2000a. American magic and dread: Don DeLillo's dialogue with culture[M]. Philadelphia: University of Pennsylvania Press.

OSTEEN M, 2000b. Marketing obsession: the fascinations of *Running dog* [G]//RUPPERSBURG H and ENGLES T. Critical essays on Don DeLillo. New York: G. K. Hall & Co.

PACKER M J, 2005. "At the dead center of things" in Don DeLillo's *White noise*: mimesis, violence, and religious awe[J]. Modern fiction studies, 51(3): 648-666.

PASSARO V, 1991. Dangerous Don DeLillo [J]. The New York times magazine, 05-19: 38.

朴玉, 2011. 从德里罗《坠落的人》看美国后"9·11"文学中的创伤书写[J]. 当代外国文学, 2: 59-65.

PIAO Y, 2011. Trauma of "9/11" fiction and Don DeLillo's *Falling man*[J]. Contemporary foreign literature, (2): 59-65.

REMNICK D, 2005. Exile on Main Street: Don DeLillo's undisclosed *Underworld* [G]//DEPIETRO T. Conversations with Don DeLillo. Jackson: Mississippi University Press.

RETTBERG S, 1999. American simulacra: Don DeLillo's fiction in light of postmodernism[J]. Undercurrent, 7: 1.

ROBSON L, 2010. The latest phase in his dying[J]. New statesman, 139 (4991): 50-51.

SANDS D, 2008. Thinking through differance: Derrida, Zizek and religious engagement[J]. Textual practice, 22(3): 529-546.

SCHNECK P, SCHWEIGHAUSER P, 2010. Terrorism, media, and the ethics of fiction: transatlantic perspectives on Don DeLillo[M]. New York and London: Continuum.

SCHUSTER M, 2008. Don DeLillo, Jean Baudrillard, and the consumer conundrum[M]. Youngstown and New York: Cambria Press.

SHELDRAKE P, 2007. A brief history of spirituality[M]. Hoboken: Wiley-Blackwell.

SHONKWILER A, 2010. Don DeLillo's financial sublime[J]. Contemporary literature, 51(2): 246 -282.

SIMMONS P E, 1997. Deep surfaces: mass culture and history in postmodern American fiction[M]. Athens: Georgia University Press.

SUZUKI D T, 1994. Essays in Zen Buddhism[G]. New York: Grove Press.

TABBI J, 1995. Postmodern sublime: technology and American writing from mailer to cyberpunk[M]. Ithaca: Cornell University Press.

TAYLOR C, 2007. A secular age[M]. Cambridge: Belknap Press of Harvard University Press.

TAYLOR M, 1991. The politics of theory [J]. Journal of the American Academy of Religion, 59(1): 1 -37.

TAYLOR M, 2013. Rewriting the real: in conversation with William Gaddis, Richard Powers, Mark Danielewski, and Don DeLillo[M]. New York: Columbia University Press.

THATAMANIL J, 2009. The immanent divine[M]. Minneapolis: Fortress Press.

TILLICH P, 1951. Systematic theology[M]. Chicago: University of Chicago Press.

TILLICH P, 1962. Spiritual presence[J]. Pastoral psychology, 13(7): 25 - 30.

TILLICH P, 1963. What is basic in human nature[J]. Pastoral psychology, 14 (1): 13 -20.

TOIT C W du, 2006. Secular spirituality versus secular dualism: towards postsecular holism as model for a natural theology[J]. HTS theological studies, 62(4): 1251 -1268.

TRACY D, 1981. The analogical imagination: Christian theology and the culture of puralism[M]. New York: Crossroad.

VATTIMO G, ZABALA S, 2002. "Weak thought" and the reduction of violence: a dialogue with Gianni Vattimo[J]. Common knowledge, 8(3): 452-463.

WAAIJMAN K, 2002. Spirituality: forms, foundations, methods [M]. Brussels: Peeters Publishers.

WARD G, 2006. The future of religion[J]. Journal of the American Academy of Religion, 74(1): 179-186.

WARD G, 2010. How literature resists secularity[J]. Literature & theology, 24(1): 73-88.

WEIL S, 1951. Reflections on the right use of school studies with a view to the love of God[G]//Waiting for God. London: Routledge and Kegan Paul.

WEINSTEIN A, 1993. Nobody's home: speech, self, and place in American fiction from Hawthorne to DeLillo[M]. New York: Oxford University Press.

WILCOX L, 1991. Baudrillard, DeLillo's *White noise* and the end of heroic narrative[J]. Contemporary literature, 32(3): 346-365.

WILLMAN S, 1998. Traversing the fantasies of the JFK assassination: conspiracy and contingency in Don DeLillo's *Libra*[J]. Contemporary literature, 39(3): 405-433.

WINQUIST C, 1994. Theology: unsettled and unsettling[J]. Journal of the American Academy of Religion, 62(4): 1023-1035.

WOOD G S, 1982. Conspiracy and the paranoid style: causality and deceit in the eighteenth century[J]. William and Mary quarterly, 39: 401-441.

YEHNERT C A, 2001. "Like some endless sky waking inside": subjectivity in Don DeLillo[J]. Critique: studies in contemporary fiction, 42(4): 357-366.

ZHANG J S, 2012. American national trauma in Don DeLillo's 9/11 novels [J]. Contemporary foreign literature, (3): 77-85.

ZHANG R H, 2013. Pleasure and anxiety: a study on the media culture in Don DeLillo's novels[D]. Beijing: Minzu University of China.

ZHANG Y P, 2009. The quandaries of the postmodern characters in *White noise*

[J]. The world literature criticism, (1): 167 - 169.

ZHOU M, 2009. The American "under" world during the Cold War Era: a cultural reading of DeLillo's *Underworld*[J]. Foreign literature, (2): 18 - 25, 126.

ZHOU M, 2010. An interpretation of DeLillo's *Americana*[J]. Journal of Graduate School of Chinese Academy of Social Sciences, (6): 112 - 118.

ZHU M, 2010. *Underworld* and the ecological injustice of a post-Cold War America[J]. Foreign literature review, (1): 165 - 174.

ZHU R H, 2013. Technology and subjectivity in Don DeLillo's fiction[J]. Contemporary foreign languages studies, (4): 51 - 55.

ZHU X F, 2005. The ecological consciousness in *White noise*[J]. Foreign literature studies, (5): 109 - 114, 174.

Epilogue

The completion of a project as colossal as a book would have been unthinkable if I have not been blessed with a lot of unselfish and enlightening help from all who care about me and the book. First and foremost, my heartfelt thanks go to Prof. Jin Hengshan at the Department of English at East China Normal University for his painstaking tutorship, insightful guidance and unfailing encouragement. Under his persistent encouragement and guidance, I never even thought of abandoning my project and the book at last comes to its present form.

Prof. Edward Whitley and Prof. Mary Foltz, two faculty members of the English Department at Lehigh University, also very well deserve to have my gratitude. Their hospitable reception made me feel much less lonely during my one-year stay in Bethlehem, U. S. and all the suggestions they offered me in our routine meetings were thought-provoking and conducive to the final establishment of postsecularism as the theoretical framework for the book.

This book has also been made possible by my constant engagement in academic exchanges and conversations with my colleagues in recent years, whose profound knowledge and brilliant wisdom have never failed to inspire in me new plans to execute and new goals to pursue in my studies on American culture and literature. My heartfelt thankfulness goes to Prof. Liu Qin, Prof. Hang Gelin, Prof. Ni Jincheng, Prof. Gao Wencheng, Prof. Liu Man, and Dr. Ma Bailiang.

Last but not the least, I wish to extend my special gratitude to the Chinese

Ministry of Education and College of Foreign Languages of University of Shanghai for Science and Technology for their generous sponsorship of the publication of this book.

"Gratitude" is not a word that is of any help in saying how great my thanks to my parents are for their unconditional love and support. I also owe many thanks to my wife and daughter for granting me their unselfish understanding and support when I was preoccupied with my writing.